RUNNING IN
A TRENCHCOAT

CHRIS JAMES

To my parents, Debbie and Mike James

Each of whom gave me the gift of a life-long love of words and thoughts.

Tobi. Sunday. Night

A slit cracked down the centre of the hardened skin. A thin black limb emerged through it. A second joined it and the tear grew wider. The cocoon collapsed in on itself as its prisoner struggled free.

Tobi watched the tiny motions of the chrysalis rocking back and forth with fascination. It had been a while since he had stared so intently at something that wasn't his daughter. Lily's butterfly farm was to the right of the sink. She had made it from simple things; an upside-down plastic pint cup, a piece of gauze, and a rubber band. She placed it out of direct sunlight. Very important, dad. They can't take too much heat, you see? It needs to be just right.

Yes, my love. Quite right.

A month ago, Tobi watched as Lily tried to suppress her excitement at finding two caterpillars writhing in the earth of a flowerpot beneath the kitchen window. They had been barely a day old. She shared the same passion that he had at that age; the love of running her fingers through dirt, searching. She was more careful than he had been, though. It took him a lot longer to learn that level of patience.

Together, they built the simple farm for the newborn pair. She assumed responsibility from the start; fresh leaves twice a day and cleaning and replacing the gauze at the bottom that caught their shit. Or 'frass', as Tobi was told to call it, which he did. He'd nodded under instruction. Caring for these living things was a serious business. She nursed them under her father's curious eye.

After a month, the pair made their way to the top of the upturned cup and attached themselves to its flat surface. Lily raced through the house to find him. She watched with her small eyes as they shed their skin and encased themselves within it over the following days. Each chrysalis turned from white to black as the fullness of a butterfly developed.

She looked at nothing else besides that plastic dome that weekend. And now, late on an uneventful Sunday night, and well past her bedtime, one of the hard cases was rocking back and forth with life. The other remained still. Tobi might yet be able to capture the moment she had been desperately waiting for. He reached for his smartphone.

But then he heard his brother's voice.

Tobi walked around the kitchen counter and into an open plan lounge with a large TV at the far end. He settled into the armchair closest to it and nudged the volume up. He took in the scene that appeared before him.

His brother's hands rested on the armrests of a tasteful leather chair. He sat to the left of the shot. To the right, the show's presenter was elevated at a table on a stage. The stillness of Yorick's hands contrasted to the fidgeting of the host's, which bounced up and down as if controlled by invisible strings. The man waving his fingers was dressed in a sharp suit and tie with a checkered shirt. The frames of his glasses were thick and piercing; much like his voice. The audience nodded and laughed with the host in a hollow tone, seeing the world through his lens of scepticism.

Tobi watched as the interview played out. It was an exchange that didn't feature winners or losers, just an infuriating stalemate. His brother's suit jacket was unbuttoned, his shirt open at the collar. He looked assured. Comfortable with his place in the world.

"What do you want me to do? It wasn't my fault." Those were the last words the host had allowed Yorick to say. Not words associated with an honest, salt-of-the-earth kind of guy. Not ones that dripped of naked menace. Something in the middle. The sort of grey area where Yorick had spent most of his adult life, Tobi thought to himself.

As the show closed out, Tobi's hand rested on a sidetable. It was made from a restored piece of wood with an irregular pattern and looked like it held stories of its own woven into its fibres. As he listened to Yorick talking, his fingers yearned to twitch, fiddle and toy with a knot on the table beneath his wedding-ring finger. His brother's closing words caused a tension to rise inside him. It was hot and uncomfortable. A small but strong power that his younger brother had always had over him. He fought it back down his throat, ignoring the allure of the knot at rest under his fingertip. The camera panned towards the host, who signed off weakly.

The screen flashed to black and Tobi's lips parted, revealing a sliver of his pink tongue trapped between his teeth. His incisors pressed into the soft flesh until a flash of pain brought the taste of blood to his lips.

He dug his fingers into the table, allowing himself a stroke of its singular smoothed bump as he rose to his feet. "He'll never change, will he?" he heard himself mutter as the closing credits scrolled across the screen.

4

He moved to the kitchen to finish the washing up. The remnants of a homemade sourdough loaf had been left to dry on the counter, and Tobi worked away at the little pieces, freeing them from the marble surface beneath. The soft tugging and pulling of the dried dough allowed him to work loose his tensions. But he couldn't shift Yorick from his mind.

And then his phone sprang to life.

An image of his brother, with a neutral expression, stared back at him from behind the screen. Letters spelled out his name and were held in a constant white against a black background; Y-o-r-i-c-k. Below them, two circles spun and alternated in size. One was green, the other red. Tobi's thumb hovered in the middle of the shapes, an inch above the device's surface.

He tried to remember the last time his brother had called him. It must have been almost a year ago, in April, that much he knew for certain. That was the one time of the year they were guaranteed to talk. It wasn't the reason that his finger hovered in-between and above the green and red circles, though.

His thumb lowered towards the glass and paused for one last beat. It dropped to the surface and the green circle grew larger and larger. He slid it upwards to the edge of the screen and waited for Yorick to speak.

"Tobs - did you watch that? Load of biased, liberal crap," he said, spitting the words into the phone.

Tobi looked to the ceiling and let the diatribe continue uninterrupted. He had heard it all too many times before. The white of the paint above him transformed into a canvas as scenes from their past danced across it.

He saw a book of raffle tickets being fanned in front of his face. At twelve years old, Yorick auctioned off a cinema date with Justine. The Justine. She was the most popular girl in the grade above Yorick and his peers at their school in east London. But she was at a neighbouring all-girls school. Friends and enemies of Yorick, and those who didn't even know him, snapped up the tickets without hesitation or question. Yorick had never spoken to Justine. However, through their father, he had discovered that she and her family were due to move to another city at the end of the school term. The last day came and, in an elaborate ceremony on the main football field, Yorick drew the lucky winner.

Niall, a quiet but confident boy, had stepped forward. A few days later, when the time arrived to confirm the arrangements of the summer holiday date, Yorick called Niall to break the unfortunate and sudden news - Justine was no longer available. He promised him a full refund for the price of his ticket, however. And then he had asked Tobi to come with him when he went to hand it over. In case of any trouble. Which there hadn't been. That time. It was the only refund he handed out, of course. When school resumed after the summer, the rest of the boys had forgotten all about the raffle. And Yorick was using the proceeds from it to fund his next dubious venture.

Tobi wondered to himself what his younger sibling was about to get them into this time. His eyes flicked back to the TV, an image of the bespectacled host appearing in his mind. "He asked about China. Anything I need to worry about?" Tobi said, at last.

A pause hung in the air, before his brother spoke. "Unlikely. But it's worth us getting our stories straight. Just in case, you know?"

As their conversation played out, the battle for life continued in the plastic dome. The first of the two butterflies had scraped, scratched and clawed its way out of its self-made encasing. Perched on the remnants of its shell, it would stay there for a few hours and wait for its wings to dry. Wings that would continue to develop over the course of the night until they were mature enough to attempt flight the next day. If someone let them free.

The other chrysalis remained still, undisturbed by the movement of its fellow inmate.

Away from the kitchen sink, Tobi lost himself in his brother's perceived injustices - his back turned away from his daughter's little world.

Tobi. Monday. Morning.

The underground train screeched to a halt. The doors sprung open, and he was off; one foot slapping the ground in front of the other, running as though his life depended on it. Maybe it did.

Tobi glimpsed the man; a dark blue woollen hat set atop a stubbled face and wrapped in an old, padded trenchcoat. The coat was black on the top and blue on the bottom, with a tear that ran from below the right shoulder at a downward angle for a couple of inches. It was a precise cut, as if made by something clean and sharp. Tiny tufts of stuffing spilled from the slash as he ran.

Tobi's gaze moved down the front of his own outfit. His spring coat hugged his waist. It was perfectly tailored to his unchanging midriff. Tailing off beyond the neat edges of his coat were a pair of tan brogues, polished to a modest sheen. They had never seen a day's scampering in their short-lived life. Tobi knew they never would. He was one of the lucky ones, these days.

The tube doors chimed, signalling their imminent closing, and jolted him back into the present. He stepped off the carriage and felt a brush on the back of his coat as the door ratcheted into place. The man with the torn trenchcoat drifted further from Tobi's mind with each step he took towards the exit of Green Park station.

He liked using public transport.

"Thank god we don't have to touch the stuff anymore, eh Tobs?" His younger brother's voice rang in his head from one of their annual catch ups.

Yorick had spent most of his adult life getting himself as far away from the average man as possible. As soon as he had made a name for himself in one of London's impressive venture capital firms, he had constructed a variety of walls against his past life.

In response, Tobi had nodded and smiled, with a lop-sided grin. It was easier that way. They both had the means never to set foot in an underground station or on a bus ever again. But watching people as they went about their lives fascinated him. The hiss of music being played through cheap headphones gave him the chance to decide if the tune matched the listener. Usually it did, but he had witnessed enough grannies with a taste for punk metal to remind him that London held little regard for stereotypes. When he felt the familiar sticky crunch of the remains of a spilt cup of coffee, he didn't feel the heat of disgust or annoyance, but pictured a whimsical encounter between two strangers that resulted in the accident.

"Tobi don't start with another coffee story again. They're like holiday romances; they're only cute and enchanting to you because they happen so rarely. Everyday love, and the tube, is nothing like that." That was Clara's voice floating through his mind. His executive assistant. Who did everything for him. Her tone was full of a rich indignation that her upbringing didn't warrant.

She was right, of course. She always was. Her phrases toyed with his subconscious in moments across the day. The world of hissing earphones and tacky coffee was only ever a visitor's destination for someone like Tobi. She saw it as her duty to remind him of that. And he was grateful for it.

He emerged from the underground and sought his preferred exit. It was the only one with a ramped pathway. He let his legs stretch as he made his way up the rise. At the end of it lay a corner of Green Park, quiet and enchanting. The sun's glow crested the line of buildings in the distance.

The neat green space lay in the middle of central London and was the capital's smallest royal park, covering just shy of twenty hectares. Tobi suspected that was why it was his favourite; it was compact enough to feel like a piece of something bigger, but not overbearing. Its mowed lawns, curated shrubs and manicured trees worked together to sell the park to him as his personal oasis amongst the surrounding financial plains of London's banking districts. He lived in this world now, but he didn't come from it.

At the entrance to the park, he found a coffee stand that was setting up, not yet open for business. But open for Tobi. He greeted the vendor with a nod and a smile, handed over a five-pound note, and received a cup of hot chocolate in exchange. No words were said, but an amiability between the pair rose into the April air along with the steam from the warm drink.

Flat green fields lay beyond the stall, but rather than pressing forward, Tobi retraced his footsteps. He strode beyond the underground exit, to where a magazine seller had been in place since well before first light.

The Big Issue publication had long been an institution in London and other major cities. It aimed to give the homeless from across the globe a chance to make a decent living by selling a journalist-based supplement. The sellers kept half of the cover price while the rest went to the editors, writers and producers of the magazine itself. The current street price was £2.50.

He placed his right hand on the shoulder of the seller and offered the sweet beverage with his left. A grateful hand accepted the drink and the woman's weathered face cracked a broad smile at Tobi; another silent morning exchange. Tobi refused her offer of a magazine, as always; he didn't need one. Being at the heart of London's money flow meant he knew the stories.

He turned on his heels and made his way back past the coffee stand, its register now lit up. His rituals completed, he broached the plains of the park. The dew on the ground mulched beneath his shoes as he made his way across a corner it. His walk took him four minutes, to the second. Almost every day.

But the conversation with his brother rolled over in his mind, refusing to be budged. His wandering thoughts transmitted through his body and his predictable, straight path veered to the right at the first junction he came across. He let his feet carry him down the detour. The unfamiliar feel of cement beneath him brought his mind to focus. He followed the foreign path for a further hundred yards before another junction presented itself, this time veering back to the left. The conversation with Yorick hadn't been a long one and by the time he reached the intersection, he had replayed it in full. He took the left turn and brought his gaze back up in front of him, up from the trail where he had lost himself.

Yorick had begged him to make the Chinese introductions all those years ago. Tobi had hesitated. Once you started on that road, it was hard to turn back. It was why Tobi had never ventured down it. But Yorick had insisted. Tobi couldn't have known how deep his brother would travel. But he should have guessed.

He resumed his usual gait and exited through a black iron gate. He turned right into a quiet street that greeted him with gutters of scattered leaves. He made his way to a set of stone steps. For his last morning custom, he glanced up to the words high above him on a vast expanse of glass walls; 'West & West'.

He checked his watch, nodded to himself, and bounded up the staircase two steps at a time. He pressed the palms of his hands onto each half of the double glass doors and felt them spring open under his force. He made his way up two flights and into his first order of business of the day.

For now, Yorick, and China, would have to wait.

Yorick. Thursday. Morning.

A young flight attendant bent down to retrieve a fallen tumbler. Rays of sunshine broke through the clouds and cast a shadow over her taut skirt. The hem rode up a couple of inches as she crouched. A crystal glass lay next to a cuff-linked sleeve. Pressed crisp, white and clean just a few hours before, it was now dishevelled and stained. The dirtied strip of material ran along the sunbeam on her knee.

"Morning, Kate".

If she saw him in the street, in an expensive suit, striding with purpose and power, she'd think he was attractive. She could admit that. His bald head was shaved and spoke to a man of detail. He had a strong, well-proportioned build. She remembered how he had strained to duck his head when he had entered the 8-seater cabin for the first time. He was slumped in his seat, but no position could hide that he was a man of stature.

But when she felt the unwelcome hand on her bent leg; she knew the game. She had known it from the moment he stepped on with his five collared colleagues. She knew that, like the times before, she was likely to be reminded of who paid her bills. And what that might be mistaken to mean.

"Morning, Yorick—what will it be this morning?" she said in a hushed tone as she rose up, looking down at him.

"Some of that famous coffee of yours."

Even for a man used to heavy celebrations, last night stood out. Yorick looked around the cabin and saw a familiar scene; collapsed younger colleagues in various states of disorder and undress. Craig had got rid of his shoes, at least. He had fared better than the other three.

The youth of today, Yorick mused to himself. Sometimes he wandered if the good whisky was wasted on them, but when it came in such abundance, it was hard to argue that it was wasted on anyone.

The whisky, champagne, cognac and whatever else they'd drunk, snorted or inhaled last night was well deserved. Sunday night's television ordeal and his phone call to his brother had been pushed comfortably to the back of his mind. But as morning broke, thousands of feet in the air, the thoughts came creeping back.

He had called Tobi on his way home from the studio after the interview. His older brother had sounded weary when he'd spoken. The conversation had only lasted the short drive home from the studio, on the banks of the Thames, to his apartment in Canary Wharf. He had told his private driver to wait while he ran up; he wouldn't be long. Just needed to throw two clean shirts, a second suit, two pairs of shoes, underwear and socks for two days into a bag.

The driver was new to Yorick's beat, and he had mentioned to him that the change-around needed to be swift if they were to make his plane's departure time. Yorick packed his things in no great hurry. And then stopped as he made his way through the large open-plan kitchen. He dropped his soft leather bag to the tiles and reached a bottle of expensive brandy and a glass and poured himself a healthy measure. He took a moment to savour the mix of sweet and wooden flavours that came up to him and then took three slow sips before placing the glass back on the surface, watching it ratchet back and forth. It was then that he grabbed his bag and made his way down from the 32nd floor and out to the street below. As he settled into the back seat, he forced out a pocket of air from his lungs. The smell of the liquor flooded the car. It hung for a full second before Yorick barked a short "Let's go". And off they had sped into the night towards Luton Airport.

Forty-five minutes later, they had arrived at one of the three FBO areas of Luton Airport, the fixed-base operators, where private jets could take off and land with much greater freedom than commercial liners. It was an expedited process for him at border control, meaning that less than half an hour after arriving, he and his three colleagues were in the air and headed east. Gone were the early hours of Monday, the interview behind him as they sped away in darkness over a sleeping London.

Now it was late Wednesday night, their latest business in China complete, and their plane was returning while London slept once more.

If it had been down to him, Yorick would have travelled alone. The sight of the underpopulated districts of Guizhou from the air brought him a calm that he struggled to find on his other travels. Or in London. He kept promising to himself that he would return for a trip that wasn't to do with work. But that was one lie he could admit to himself; he didn't do personal travel.

He pushed the minor grievance aside and reminded himself that his three junior associates had their uses. They could handle the paperwork. He hated dealing with the local Chinese software engineers to iron out the technical specifications. Yorick would rather use that time to cement his relationship with his partner, Huang.

Huang was one of the few people in the world who could meet Yorick eye to eye. His Asian counterpart's shoulders were broader and more rounded. His shiny, black and immaculately combed hair was the distinguishing factor between the pair. Huang had transitioned from a fortuitous acquaintance to the most powerful partner on his client list in five short years. Over that time, they had signed a series of lucrative contracts. Yorick was the financial dealer in London and Huang was the man in the shadows of the far east. Yorick had never worked in such close quarters with someone; a true yin to his yang. Together, they pulled on invisible strings that set a series of actions into motion. Black ink flowed from their pens onto their contracts, and an endless stream of cash was released in its place.

Their most recent agreement was signed the previous Friday, and somehow, between then and Sunday night, the story had leaked. After the television interview, he had needed Huang to apply some pressure to seal it. And he'd agreed. It had made his trip more tense than it needed to be, but no less successful.

The movement of two shapely calves caught his attention as Kate returned. She placed a steaming cup of coffee down in front of him. Ethiopian, he guessed, and as soon as she took a step away, the smell filled his nostrils. It was strong and full of aromas. He'd been right, she'd remembered. She always did.

He reached for the cup and felt his fingers shake at their tips. He dropped them to the small table and steadied himself. He tried again, but only rattled the cup on the saucer. Kate turned back to him at the sound.

"Everything alright, Yorick? She asked, a trace of concern in her voice.

He grabbed the hot cup with his entire palm. "Just a little rough from a big night," he said, raising an eyebrow. "You've saved another life, Kate, you know that right?"

"All part of an honest night's work, Yorick. Buckle up, we've got a little turbulence headed our way."

He felt for the metal clip of his seatbelt as he looked up and asked,

"Where are we?"

She cleared up the rest of the night's wreckage that lay in front of him, which meant gathering up assorted miniature bottles; no one had bothered with any food. She answered him before moving back to the galley with a standard black trash bag. "We're passing over the east of the Netherlands."

He clipped the belt into place and kicked out at the leg across the aisle from him, rousing a young ginger-haired man, Tom, from his drunken slumber. He motioned for him to clip his unfurled seatbelt as he threw a one-word, Dutch response towards Kate's retreating figure, "Dankje."

He took a sip of coffee. The taste was more bitter than the sweet smell that had greeted him. He put the hot cup down and glanced out of the nearest window. His eyes battled with the early rising sun. The clouds lay thick below them, but he could guess that they'd soon be passing over Den Bosch, in the southern regions of the Netherlands.

Memories of his early childhood from the area were fleeting, but a few distinct details had survived. The blue door of his father's family business. The yellow of the tulip fields that lay beyond their small, simple back yard. The orange of his mother's favourite ribbon that she'd fix to her hair for those early Christmases.

He shook his head to clear it and pulled his thoughts back to the day ahead of him. They would land in under an hour, due in at 06h30. He would head straight to the office for the full run-down of last night's events with the gossip mongers of the office. Then he would need to attend to the morning's events with the senior partners. He'd make his excuses after a late lunch. No one would question him after the deal he'd just signed.

Finally, he checked his diary and saw confirmation of the doctor's appointment scheduled for the afternoon. He finished drinking his coffee, gripping the cup once again.

And then he would head to east London for the evening. He pulled out his iPad to check the details. Thursday, The Waldorf, Plaistow. 19h30.

He would need to be careful what he said to Tobi about China.

Tobi. Thursday. Afternoon.

Tobi met his reflection in the large glass windows. Deep and blue, he held himself in a gaze that rolled out over the lawns of Green Park. Behind him were twenty other eyes, boring into his styled mess of hair. He could feel each one of them. He soaked up one last glance at his patch of park.

As an intern, he would take his foil-wrapped sandwiches, cheese and pickle, down to the tree-lined pathways and find a bench. It hadn't mattered if it was a sunny day or not. It just needed to be dry, so it didn't make his bread soggy. He would sit with no distractions, taking slow mouthful after slow mouthful. After a quarter of an hour, he would make his way back along the path, nudging leaves with the toes of his shoes, until he reached the same gate he still passed through every morning. He would pause for a moment and look across the road at the foreboding glass doors of West & West. It hadn't been the heart of venture capital in London in those days of cheese and pickles. Back then, everyone beyond the glass threshold had lived and ground away in the uncertainty of whether they would make it big. No one knew for sure.

But today there was no doubt. If you were a company with a big idea, but no money—you came to West & West. They were the dream-weavers. He'd often heard it said that the idea was king. But in this world, an idea was just a hole in the ground. And without the bottomless pockets of his firm stepping in to fill it at the right time, that's all it would ever remain. Few in the game knew those moments better than Tobi. He didn't just spot them; he crafted them for all to admire and acknowledge. As he had done for years with the group behind him. They had all grown close. More than just business associates. True partners. Friends.

In his right hand, he held a trusty companion. A stress ball with a baseball decal. And a faded New York Yankees logo. His lucky charm. He had picked it up on his first visit to The Big Apple from a roadside seller. It reminded him of the insatiable appetite for success that he linked to that city. He tossed it against the window before catching it with the same hand with a satisfying thud. He repeated the trick, this time shifting the angle of release to send his charm rebounding across to his left hand; thunk.

He turned to meet his expectant audience. "Morning, friends - great day, right?"

He faced a crowd of young entrepreneurs. They were mostly Dutch. Their idea had first breathed life in the Netherlands but, since moving their operations to London to expand, they had developed a cosmopolitan and global mix. From a garage in the plain southern district of Tilburg, they had nursed their idea for five years; a revolutionary security system for Dutch banks. Over that time, they had flown the coop from a single-storey garage across the channel into one of the many looming towers at the heart of London's growing technology district. Two and a half years ago, they had approached Tobi and his team for funding. He had taken an instant liking to the group. They were driven and sensible enough to realise that they required expertise beyond their current standing. Yet they maintained enough of the naivety of youth that he felt was necessary for impossible ideas to break through entrenched mindsets.

"It is. And we hope it's about to get better, Tobi," said the leader of their pack, Dirk. He had a powerful jaw that wrapped around a relaxed smile and a defined hairline that spoke of good breeding. Impeccably well-dressed, these days. He tugged at a gold cufflink that had wandered away from the centre of his left sleeve. Then, he pushed into the back of the ergonomically designed chair, all the while never taking his eyes off the fake ball in Tobi's left hand. But all Tobi could think of as he watched on was how young he looked as he spoke.

Tobi had known from the start that he wanted to invest in them and hadn't hesitated in stumping up the twenty million Euros they needed to move to their next phase of growth. The money was mainly for software engineers; hard talents to keep pace with a ferocious workload as they gained more and more banks as clients. They were running out of physical server space and needed new data warehouses to store, process, and manage the vast amounts of information they were generating. They were facing the typical growth problems of the modern era of entrepreneurs.

Messrs West & West hadn't batted an eyelid over the amount. Tobi had long since earned their trust. He had kept a keen eye on the developments of his Dutch protégés, taking every opportunity to head out to their home base. It was less than an hour's drive from Tobi's childhood home in Den Bosch.

They had grown quickly. They had impressed him. Through his connections in the banking industry, he had arranged the crucial networks they needed to secure their proof of concept. And from there they'd run with things, which was the dream of every angel investor. He had waved a guiding hand over proceedings when he felt it necessary, but this group of talented young upstarts knew what they wanted and how to get there. Tobi saw his job, his proper work, as getting them to where they didn't need him anymore.

"You've made me so proud over the past few years, all of you." The ability to speak with a smile that exuded genuine sincerity is rare, and Tobi possessed it. When you add to that the most charming of lisps, you understood how Tobi was as successful as he was. Not an overt speech impediment. But the subtlest hint of a tongue that gets too excited and wants to get in on a small piece of the action. It wasn't a conscious action, but Tobi knew the charming effect it had on others.

He clenched the ball in his right hand as he spoke. "Such growth, such success." He could sense them hanging on to each word. "Especially you, Dirk. We go back, what, five years?"

"Five significant years," agreed a man who would have been attractive if he hadn't been so earnest. "Tobi, the matter at hand, please," Dirk pressed on.

Tobi knew the moment had arrived. His mind wandered to his precious daughter. She had her mother's soft features and her father's hard stare, even at her tender age. On the day she was born, Tobi had felt a spark within him, which he'd only read about in books. The only time he'd come close to that was the feeling he felt in this room, at this moment. Today, this group of young dreamers from across the channel were his children. And Tobi, just like with his daughter, loved giving them good news. The smile broke from him once more. He couldn't resist any longer. "I've got some excellent news for you all."

Clara found Tobi in the same position that he'd been in an hour before, facing towards his park. He turned to her as she entered the room.

He had known to hire her from the second he'd seen her. There had been a steel to her emerald eyes that told him he could trust her. She had what it took to get a messy job done. And she was yet to fail him over the past decade.

"Another satisfied customer?" She knew how to break the ice.

Tobi met her eyes with his. "They all end up satisfied, Clara. They just don't realise how long it takes. The folly of youth?"

"The folly of ignorance, if you ask me. I've sent the papers across—I wouldn't be surprised if we receive some tulips tomorrow."

He offered a sly wink, covering up eyes that had glossed over. Clara knew his tells. Like how he preferred to make light about anything related to where he grew up. "Just glad we got them the deal that they deserved. Let's hope they don't spend the whole windfall at once. Like I would have done."

"You did them proud, Tobi. And, speaking of extravagance, you're due at The Dorchester for your early dinner with Sarah in twenty minutes. I'll call you a cab?" Nothing about her tone was any different from any of the hundreds of conversations he had with her every week. But when a sentence of hers mentioned his wife, it sounded different. Or maybe it sounded the same. But it echoed within him. And that unsettled him.

"No, the weather looks like it'll hold. I'll take a stroll. You head off—go enjoy an early evening with meathead Joe."

"Pretty sure they don't let meatheads operate on hearts, Tobi. And you know his name is Fred. Meathead Fred was sitting there, right in front of you."

"It's been a long day. Get out of here." Clara turned, bending at the knees, causing her skirt to tighten across her hips, and opened his office door. He had one last question before she left. "Did you confirm tonight with Yorick?"

"Yes, Tobi—seven-thirty, The Waldorf, just like every year. He said he might be late as he had an appointment before." Clara called the words out over a thinly covered, slim shoulder as she made her way through the doorway.

Tobi turned back towards the window, catching himself in a smile that had lingered for longer than it should have. Looking out over the park, he planned the route across it that would lead him to his wife. His anchor.

His thoughts were interrupted by a different reflection in the window. Staring back at him were Dirk's excited and grateful eyes. Tobi's smile grew wider as he turned to head off into the April afternoon.

Tobi. Thursday. Early Evening.

Tobi chased the remnants of the rib-eye steak around his plate with his fork. If his father had been there, he would have scolded him for his poor table manners. Now, like then, he wasn't sure what to say. His distracted thoughts were playing out through his hands.

"It's not that I'm not happy for you, Tobi," said Sarah. She leaned in towards him and reached out with her arm, bringing his fork's adventures to a halt. "I just don't know when we're ever going to see you with yet another full time client to look after. We barely see you as it is."

He left her hand resting on his as he composed his thoughts. The excitement of a fresh new deal being signed, the start of something new and bold on the horizon, had ebbed away over a glass of wine and two steaks. "This is the one, love. Just this push and they'll have to make me partner. And then I'll have all the time I need to spend with you and Lily."

She drew her hand back across the table and folded her arms in her lap. Her plate, still packed with food, lay cold in front of her. He looked up at her, expecting to see anger or disappointment. But all she offered was frustration.

"It's always just one more deal, Tobi. How many times do we have to have this fight?"

"I know, but-" he reached for the fork again but caught himself before continuing. "I can't just walk away from them. They're young and naïve - without me, it'd all fall apart. They need me."

As quickly as it had arrived, the frustration drained from her face like a piece of material crumpling to the floor. In its place sat resignation as she stood from the table. She leaned towards him and whispered hotly into his ear, "We need you, Tobi! This is the last time. I won't keep putting Lily and I through this. We deserve more." She snatched her jacket and strode past him, leaving him alone with his thoughts and half eaten steak.

Yorick. Thursday. Afternoon.

"I just don't fancy a sport that lacks any give-and-take, you know? If you can even call it a sport," said Ben, a 20-something year old and self-confessed digital guru. A floppy clump of hair that draped over the rest of his shaved hairline transfixed Yorick. The strand was vacuous, much like the statement.

Horse-racing was more than just a sport to Yorick. It took him back to the feel of metal rails needling into his forearms. He could smell the churned grass. And the air of equine muscularity that came with it. He could feel the long pink betting slips curled between his hands. Yorick did his homework. and he got to know the trainers. When a breakout horse came across the paddocks, he worked every angle and network he could to understand what made each animal tick. He leaned on owners to get the information he needed. And then the gates would open. Beast against beast, with men bumbling along, trying to hold on. It was those moments that had brought Yorick back time and time again. Before he had met Huang. Before he was released from the spell.

He had never considered himself to be a creature of habit. He and his brother had moved around too often during their childhoods to establish any routines. But for a time, he found himself in that same trap, every Friday in June, for a period that ran for twelve years. It was an equine lure that had ensnared many over the years. Its monster fed on victims of boredom, desperation, or simple addiction. Yorick had spent enough time around a spread of punters to see the differences that drove them there. He'd also told himself that he was above all that. He wasn't like them. He didn't do it for the money or excitement; he had enough of both. And he knew there were far more thrilling things to be addicted to. But when he looked down at those pink betting slips, a hungry smile would creep across his lips. The markings he made on those papers drew a clear but secret story. They represented the chance for him to pit his wits against the odds of fate. That was how the tracks held him.

Yorick knew the history of the give-and-take well. One of his father's lectures still rang in his ears. He was sitting across from him at a white Formica table. It was in those early, hard London days. "An exchange of ideas," his father would proclaim in a neutral tone, before referring to its origins in horse-racing. The give-and-take plate was used to balance out the odds. Horses that exceeded a standard height carried more weight, and those which fell short of it, less.

Ben had used the phrase to mean lucky. But in Yorick's world, the concept of give-and-take had nothing to do with luck. It had everything to do with tilting the odds in your favour.

"I just can't get past the animal rights side of it," said Yorick. His eyes gleamed with a practised sincerity. His weight shifted to spread it across both feet while he waited for his shot to find its mark. "Beautiful creatures like that should run free."

"Exactly. Not many people from your era get it like you do, Yorick." Ben meant this as a compliment.

"We'll add the battle for animal rights to the growing list of evils that our app will solve. But for now, let's get this deal done. You can use my pen to sign."

Ben furrowed his brow, while opening his mouth in the shape of an 'o'. But before a sound could escape, he caught himself and spread his lips in a smile, revealing a line of tiny teeth. "That Dutch humour of yours, mate. Still can't read it."

Yorick spread his lips but bore no teeth, concealing the hunger that lay within him.

He had just agreed to take a majority share in a breakthrough digital signature app that Ben and his band of misfits had developed. They were an all-male cast with an assortment of ambiguous facial hair. Their app would allow for greater security to anyone needing to sign Level A Privacy documents such as mortgages, business contracts, wills. Biometric access had replaced the concept of ink drying on contracts. Instead, digital vaults had replaced them in the ever-growing fight against data breaches. This was the future. This was the new age of personal responsibility. Or so Yorick had willed the public to believe on Sunday night from an interviewee's chair. It was safe for everyone to trust, he'd promised. Just like the banks themselves.

He had secured large, profitable agreements with three of the leading high street lenders to trial Ben's software as soon as it was ready. And if ever there was a well-trodden path to entrepreneurial success, it was in the business of getting people to move money and move it faster than ever before. Taking minuscule but very real slices of a huge pie added up. London had taught him that. Not lessons from across a chipped Formica table. Rome wasn't built in a day, father; it was built through the exploitation of countless tiny human efforts.

Yorick had spent years building business cases of promising start-ups. He could trace and plot the money trail that led to big fat black lines being cleared. Ben would most likely be looking to retire within five years. He would buy himself a comfortable house in a comfortable area like Guildford. And a Porsche Boxster. He would feel he'd made it, that he had enough to invest and live off. His neighbour next door would wonder if Ben should take his not-yet-30-year-old-self back to work to trade that Boxster in for a proper Porsche. And life would go on.

But that wasn't Yorick's burning desire. He didn't care about the cars. He cared about what lay beneath all those signatures within the app. For each one held personal insights into millions of people's habits. What they bought, how they spent their money, how they were planning for their lives beyond the grave. That was Yorick's lifeblood. Those infinite lines of data were his currency.

Ben had been talking as Yorick's mind had wandered, but it didn't appear that anything he'd said needed a response. He nudged the pen in Ben's hand as a final prompt.

"It's a great deal, Yorick. I don't know how you do it, but this is better than we could have dreamed. It's going to make a big difference on our margins."

What Ben had just signed was an extension to keep storing his app's data in China, in one of Huang's data warehouses. The extension meant that it would include all future app updates and client permissions in the warehouse deals. Huang and his partners had been well ahead of the technology start-up curve, building facilities since the mid-2000s. Now, they offered fields of them, housed in optimal conditions and ready to accept the ever-growing needs of excitable minds all over the business hubs of Singapore, Berlin, London, New York and San Francisco. While they had found little success in the other western cities, London had been open for business. In particular, Huang's relationship with Yorick and his connections in the start-up world had proved crucial to keeping their momentum going. They hadn't looked back since their first meeting a decade ago. It was Tobi who had vouched for his brother when Huang's associates had come calling. They hadn't even met Yorick, but they'd heard about him. Since then, they had added app upon app, building out their capabilities and facilities as they did so. And as they grew, they passed their profits back to Yorick as exclusive deals he could offer to people like Ben. Unbeatable deals. It kept the tall Dutchman at the top of his game. It kept the money flowing. It kept the warehouses teeming with data. It kept everyone happy. And wealthy. Their carefully crafted and energetic circle turned with ever increasing speed, with Yorick and Huang in the middle.

"It's what I do for my best people, Ben," said Yorick, sliding the pen into his jacket pocket. "I grease the wheels; you keep them turning."

"Treee-mendous, Yorey," said Ben, adding an unnecessary stress on the first syllable. "That's the last step we needed ahead of the sale." He was referring to the deal that Yorick had been working on for the past two months to take the company public. The IPO was ready to go, but the supplier agreements needed to be inked before they could formalise the float. "You'll be at the celebration tomorrow, right?"

"Hundred percent," he replied with an orchestrated wink. "Might even have a guest of honour for you, too."

"Always full of surprises, Yorick - love it!" Ben said while punching him lightly on the shoulder. If he had expected Yorick to absorb the blow in good humour, he was wrong. He lowered his hand to his side.

Yorick hated surprises. So when his phone started ringing, his doctor's number flashing at him, he turned away from Ben without hesitation, looking for somewhere private.

"Mr. Van den Berg? Did you hear what I just said?" The doctor's words were steady. The absence of emotion in her voice was intentional. She recognised the silence on the other end of the line and let it linger.

When Yorick spoke, his tone matched hers. "Yes, doc. And you're sure?"

"As far as we can be. We believe the diagnosis is correct based on your symptoms; the issues with poor motor function, the lapses in memory," she continued to match the rhythm of his speech. Her words flowed over him like a cool breeze as his mind flicked back to fumbling with his coffee that morning. "The MRI all but confirms it with the early signs of brain damage in the areas we would expect to see it. But," she paused and took a brief intake of breath, "I must say that without access to genetic testing from your parents, we can't yet confirm it. But we're confident enough to recommend a course of treatment."

His voice broke rank and rose an octave as he responded. "Treatment? You just told me it was incurable? That hereditary diseases like this are terminal."

She paused for a beat to let his rise of emotion dissipate. "That doesn't mean we can't recommend ways to manage it, Mr. Van den Berg. Symptoms can take years, decades, to increase in severity if we implement certain lifestyle changes. It's best that you come in as soon as you can so we can talk about your options."

Yorick's back pressed against the brick wall of a seldom used stairwell. The warehouse that housed Ben's startup was always too cold, and Yorick felt the chill of the surface through his jacket. He glanced up at the circular set of stairs, winding their way up and away from him and pressed away from the wall, dropping his gaze to the cement floor, willing the dizzying feeling in his stomach to disappear. He pulled his watch in front of his face. He was going to be late to meet Tobi. "Call my office. My assistant will set up a time. I have to go."

Tobi. Thursday. Night.

Tobi glanced down at his watch. 19h29. He shifted his focus to the cold, frosted pint of lager sitting opposite him at the table. The condensation beaded down it. He looked at his own beverage, fixating on the thin layer of foam resting on his pint of ale. He wondered how long he would be waiting this time. It wasn't a worry laced with irritation. His feet remained still and he didn't feel the need to tap away at the edge of the rusted table runner, as he might have done in years gone by. He simply wondered, and realised he spent a lot of time doing that with Yorick.

Light from the fading sun crept through the window behind him. It cast across shuffling elderly feet to his right. They told the room that they were comfortable with their pace and couldn't be damned to quicken it up, thank you very much. A man in his 80s had taken to the small stage. His name was Alan, but 'Frank' was how he was known around Plaistow, a sleepy hollow of east London. He had brilliant white hair, plastered with a generous helping of brill cream, and it sat atop a man of below average height. He approached the microphone stand and took a second to adjust his tie. A sensible, perfectly executed Windsor knot that needed no adjusting was fiddled with for a second. Once to the right, once to the left, and back to its original position; not a fibre out of place. It was a well-practised routine that made Tobi smile.

"Good evening, ladies and gentlemen, and thank you for joining us this evening. You're in for a special one tonight," Alan announced and extended his right arm across the room, accompanied by a wink. The gathered crowd of perhaps ten or twelve pairs of hands offered determined applause back towards him. This pleased Alan, and a shaky left hand grasped the handle of a microphone that was worn smooth from numerous hands over many years. From his position, Tobi saw the strain of the old man's knuckles against the hard plastic. Except it wasn't Alan, anymore. 'Frank' was in the room. And he was ready to entertain.

And now, the end is near.
And so, I face the final curtain.

The first bars of one of Tobi's favourite Sinatra songs, *My Way*, rolled off the crooner's tongue and filled the air of The Waldorf. Tobi itched to reach for his ale, but tradition was tradition. Even if it led to ale that had been left to sit for too long.

He pressed back into his chair, resulting in a satisfying creak under his slight build, and took in the other patrons. At an immediate guess, he ventured he brought the average age down by at least a couple of decades. No mean feat for a man nearing forty. But as a gentle wave of grey hair bobbed back and forth along his vision, he realised there was nothing old in the crowd's fervour. They fixed their eyes on 'Frank' with a treasured intensity. Memories flickered throughout the room: last dances with lovers, furtive glances of strangers in cities across the world, harder yet simpler times and all that they brought with them. Above all, a sense of being lost in the moment. Tobi envied them.

His thoughts went no further as a movement out of the left corner of his eye arrested his attention.

No one entered a room quite like his brother. It wasn't through any grand gesture or deliberate movement. It came through Yorick being Yorick. All 6'11" of him. Hard not to make an entrance. But it wasn't his height that most people noticed first. It was his gleaming dome of a head. Tobi supposed there must have been a time when his younger brother had hair, but he couldn't remember one. Such had been the lasting impact of this clean scalp. Even childhood images were now imprinted with this version of him.

Whilst an intimidating sight for many, and Tobi didn't doubt that his brother used that to his advantage, Yorick's appearance invited warmer memories in his own mind. Skeletor, the villain from an 80s kids cartoon show, "He-Man and the Masters of the Universe". Cloaked in a dark cotton shroud, the skeletal villain was a walking contradiction, as his bulging muscles proved. His chief enjoyment was to rain misery on those around him. He and Yorick spent hours watching the show, memorising and re-enacting scenes of their favourite episodes. But as memories of the title character faded over the years, Skeletor made frequent appearances. He wondered when a reference would be made tonight to his unusual yet trusty steed—a purple panther. It was a running gag of their strained relationship.

He watched his brother take in his surroundings. They knew the game and every year, each played it out to the beat of their own drum. A few moments to relive personal reflections, each taking from The Waldorf's questionable atmosphere what they needed. Before they found each other.

Yorick. Thursday. Night.

It was a quiet street. One trying its best to go about its business unnoticed. But its ordered appearance kept popping its head up over the wall to draw attention to itself. It was a street that wasn't used to the sort of shoes making their way down it. They clacked with long strokes. Their owner wasn't in a rush. He made his way through falling shadows and enjoyed creating the only noise on an otherwise silent stretch of road. Click-clack. Click-clack. Click. They stopped. A white sleeve reached out into the air, the shine of a chrome watch poking out from beneath. 19h45. He knew he could expect a pint of lager to be waiting for him at their table, tucked at the back of the room. Yorick's hand grasped the brass handle. A sharp twist downward and the door sprung open. The same entrance their father had stepped through many times in the past.

A familiar scene greeted Yorick. To the left, a clutch of tables that, in other parts of London, would have been curated from chic haberdashery stores. But that wasn't the case in The Waldorf. Time had worked its magic. Each chair was a different height, acting as levellers over the years. One was his favourite; it had a classic, latticed wooden back, drawing its downward facing rods together at the base of its seat. Just like the ones he had grown up playing, sitting and leaning on. He noticed a large occupant perched in it tonight and wondered how long his old faithful companion would hold out.

He cast his eyes ahead towards the bar in front of him. Three ale pumps stared back at him. They were serious items with wooden handles that said out loud that beverages of stature lay beneath. Next to them, a lonely metal lager tap adorned with a garish blue haze. When their father had trodden on the floor's uneven tiles, taps like that hadn't existed. Above the pumps lay coasters from across the British Isles. A scattering of royal busts, woodland creatures and crafted puns leered out from behind simplistic designs. They were a hat tip to all those who passed beneath them; they represented a slice of home within these four walls. If such a place fell within the English home counties.

Yorick drew in the mismatched chairs, the smell of bitter ales being poured and the coasters of yesteryear. They reminded him of simpler times. They reminded him why he had left.

He turned to take in the right side of the room. As he did so, the noise of the elderly man singing hit his ears. He'd been aware of the music from the moment he'd walked in, but like an overbearing child demanding attention, he pushed it to the back of his mind as he soaked up his surroundings. The man behind the microphone had a pleasant voice. He was dressed in his Sunday best. A Sunday from the 70s, it seemed. The would-be crooner rolled out the last chords of a favourite in The Waldorf:

'The record shows
'I took the blows
'But I did it my way.

A grin formed on Yorick's lips and he tracked his gaze further right, to the only table on that side of the room. A table where two pints of beer sat, untouched. And where behind one of them lay another smile. One with a similar pursed look to it. It was a lopsided smile that hid a glimmer of the teeth behind it.

Yorick stepped towards the table. Click-pause-clack. "Hallo, little panther."

Brothers. Thursday. Night.

"You know I hate that," Tobi said.

He offered his glass across the table towards his brother. Yorick responded, bringing them together with a loud chink. "Proost". Their toast coincided with 'Frank's' final chords. He shuffled off stage, signalling the scheduled interlude.

"So, how was China?" said Tobi.

"Good. Busy. You know how it is, in and out, blurs on either side. But useful for me." Yorick drained a long swig. Tobi brought his own glass up again and overcompensated with his next sip, leaving himself with a bigger swallow than he'd intended.

He cleared his throat and picked up their conversation. "You still need my help, then?"

Another swig from Yorick. The level of his beer sank quickly. Tobi sighed to himself, knowing that this pace spelt disaster for him if he were to match his younger brother's thirst. He took another sip, digging deep into the lower reaches of the glass vessel

"Nah, I've got someone looking into that. Clearing it up in the background. But-" he rested his glass on the table, allowing Tobi to drain another few centimetres from his own. "If you could have a quiet word with Kim, that'd be... appreciated." His glass was back in his hand, but hovered above the table, as if waiting for his older brother's permission.

Kim was a long-time friend of Tobi's. They had begun their careers together at West & West as interns. Intensely bright, caustically funny and ramrod pretty, her light had shone much brighter than his in those early days.

But she had only lasted eighteen months within those walls. The end games weren't for her. She and Tobi had dealt with little of the actual money making at that stage. But her natural sharpness had cut through the fog and allowed her to see the path ahead. It wasn't one she wanted to tread.

So, she had got out and started up her own public relations firm, using the small but persuasive black book she'd compiled during her time at the firm. Fourteen years later, she had the ears and texting fingers of the most influential members of Westminster at her beck and call. She'd sweep a problem like Yorick's away while picking up her first coffee of the day.

"I owe her so many already, Yorick," Tobi started, his glass held in the air to match his brother's. "What's one more to add to the list?" he said with a gentle lisp before flooding his mouth with ale. Yorick slammed his empty glass to the table and stood. A compact figure shuffled towards the stage behind the wide frame of his brother. "But don't drag me into China, Yorick. You know I don't work that patch."

Yorick drew himself to his full height. He attracted the eyes of the room as he did so. He turned to walk towards the bar and called out over his shoulder as he did so, "Dankje". Thanks. The rest of the bar's inhabitants relaxed and looked towards the stage once more.

Tobi raised his eyebrows to no one and stared down at the remnants of his ale. The sounds of a guitar and harmonica doing battle carried over to their table, followed by a melodious female voice as Tobi saw off the rest of his drink.

'There must be some way out of here,
'Said the Joker to the Thief.

His brother's looming figure seemed to swallow up the rest of the lyrics. Two firm thunks on the table brought Tobi back to what this night was about. They brought their drinks together once more, but with a new toast. "Rust en vrede". Rest in peace. Together, their eyes tracked to the wall behind and above Tobi's head. They came to rest on a narrow wooden shelf.

Time had caused the front edge of the shelf to warp, giving it an uneven and wavy appearance. But it was sturdier than it looked and easily held the weight of a small box. It was of a simple design; dark mahogany in colour and featuring a gold clasp on its front. The clasp itself clung to the wood despite the small signs of rust that appeared around the edges. There was a matching set on the back, but no one ever saw those. They had long since become decorative, used just once. If you looked under the shelf, you would find two screws burrowed into the wood. They bored up through the inch-thick surface and into two opposite corners of the box, holding it in place. On top was a plain, square gold plate with engraved details:

Pieter van den Berg
1957 - 2005
Father to the village

It was the name the brothers shared, van den Berg. The brothers hadn't been able to agree on a resting place for their father's ashes. It had been a protracted death following a long battle and after discussions with those in the Plaistow community they had been swayed to choose his favourite pub. Tobi had broken first, and then Yorick had agreed.

Pieter had been an immigrant, not uncommon in the area. But an immigrant from Europe was. It wasn't a rags to riches story, but after building a successful toy company from the ground up, he had been quick to ensure the spoils of his work extended to the surrounding community. Whether that meant employing those who had fallen on hard times, or who needed a helping hand to get started. Or giving out free toys to children whose parents were working two jobs. He was a giver to the Plaistow village. At the expense of his sons, at least in their eyes.

'The village' referred to the small area that surrounded the north-east corner of Plaistow Park in the borough of Newham, five miles east of the city of London. The relative recency of the neighbourhood and the melting pots of cultures had drawn crowds of immigrants in the 80s and 90s. Families from South Asia and Afro-Caribbean heritages soon filled the streets, shops, and small homes.

Yorick's eyes moved back to his glass, where his fingers were fidgeting with its rim. "He was lucky he never lost his sharpness. Mind or body. Until the very end, I guess," he said, speaking down into his drink.

Tobi watched his younger brother with a furrowed brow. Yorick never spoke about their father beyond what was necessary. "You're right. He was frail when his time came, but who isn't with cancer. But he had a good run. We can be grateful for that, at least."

His brother's head faced downwards, and Tobi's eyes moved to his hands. His knuckles were almost white, gripping his pint glass with such force that he thought it was sure to break.

Gabbi. Thursday. Night.

The smashing of a pint glass has a specific pitch to it. Sufficient weight to be noticed, but not enough to stop conversation. But it carries a distinct sound in a damp basement of a pub. When the cause of the sound is a drunk accountant - and one quarter of an audience - everyone notices it. Especially the comedian on the stage.

Gabbi wasn't bothered by the drunken acts of the incoherent. She was used to dealing with them. But they were harder to ignore when they left you standing on a stage, alone, running through a comedy set that's become as stale as the remnants of the beer seeping across the floor towards you.

"Karen? I'm going to call you Karen. Yes, I know that's not your real name. Keep up with social discourse at all? Of course, you don't," Gabbi said and paused, one of her hands trapped in mid-air, fingers pointed to the sky. And then she dropped it. "Fuck it, I'm done."

She exited stage left and went up the stairs at the back of the room. On her way to the bar, she paused at the signed photograph of Andi Osho, Plaistow's biggest celebrity. And one tendril of true comedic significance in The Rams & Lion. Andi had made it from Plaistow Park to the Hammersmith Apollo. With a touch of the picture, Gabbi could remind herself that the journey was possible, without having to take the bus. Her left hand edged its way towards the frame but hung halfway as the first bars of a Van Morrison song floated towards her down the staircase.

When it's not always raining,
There'll be days like this.
When there's no one complaining,
There'll be days like this.
When everything falls into place,
Like the flick of a switch.
Well my mama told me,
There'll be days like this.

Perfect, Gabbi thought, and forced herself into a chuckle as she emerged from the top of the rickety staircase. She looked across the bar towards the jukebox in a corner of the pub. Her small smile flooded into a grin at the sight of the music machine's faithful companion-Rikki.

How do you describe someone like Rikki? Well, in Gabbi's world you don't. Can't. She looked sixtyish, although no one knew for sure. Her short legs were offset by a tall torso and her face was lined with thin trails. You couldn't describe how she dealt with Karen either. Or whatever her name was. Rikki's had a unique style as a bouncer. After little commotion, The Rams & Lion's protector returned to the sanctuary of the bar, closing the door behind her, leaving the drunk Karen stranded outside.

The pub had seen its best days in the 80s, and even those all too briefly. It wasn't a place you expected to house as many suits as it did. But it was close enough to the city centre and the right side of 'up-and-coming' to attract clutches of young bankers, lawyers and assorted money movers who had spare cash and few responsibilities. A modern high-rise building had sprung up one street over, towering over the small park in front of it. It was complete with a spinning studio and a Little Waitrose at the bottom. It wouldn't be long before other streets followed, like so many boroughs across east London.

Rikki settled onto a seat at the bar next to Gabbi. They sat as two outcasts bobbing along on a river of pencil skirts and tailored jackets. Any other night in any other city and you'd be forgiven for thinking that a dialogue might strike up between this pair, surrounded by this crowd. But this wasn't any old pub, in any old city on any old night. This was Gabbi's place.

It had belonged to her gentle-hearted foster father, an icon of the local community. But it was now hers. She and Rikki kept it going in his memory. Not for the money. That would have been nice, but it wasn't true. Tailored sleeves lost their length when it came to finding tips in deep pockets. On the surface, and to each other, they kept it going for the fanciful idea that it would launch Gabbi's comedic career. But in reality, they did it because it kept them together. They sat in silence amid the murmur of the crowd. The muddle of a London night flowed around them as they sipped on tumblers that mirrored each other; remnants of a double whiskey on the rocks. It was hard enough trying to make it as a comedian without having to talk about it. And that was her first set of the night.

The other staff member of the pub, Brian, made his way to them, noticing the ice cubes chinking against the bottoms of their glasses. "Afraid that's the last of the Balvenie," he said with a sympathetic smile. He'd brought with him a bottle of Jura and offered it towards the pair. Rikki tipped her glass in his direction and he sloshed in a healthy dash. Gabbi held hers to her chest and smiled at him as he sprang back to where he'd come from.

She swirled the ice cubes, finished the remaining sip and said, "Have you spoken to him, yet?"

Rikki's accent was difficult to place; a hint of gruffness served as the perfect foil to a mix of origins. But it was gruff. And she spoke with a stilted rhythm. "Sure did. First thing when he came in at lunch. Like ripping a bandaid."

"Nothing gets to him," Gabbi added, throwing a glance at the salt-and-pepper hair of the man who had just served them. In his early fifties and stooped, he was now serving a brusque lad three decades his junior with his never-ending enthusiasm and politeness. The two women brushed their feelings of guilt into the carpet beneath their stools. Gabbi pressed on, "How did he take it?"

"With a smile. Of course," said Rikki, letting her gaze pause on Brian as she continued to survey the wider interior scene.

A sadness ate away at Gabbi. At 24, she should have been the one fearing the loss of a bit-part bar tending job at a pub overextending itself, not a man old enough to be her father. That Brian had taken it so well and stayed to serve his shift, while exuding his natural warmth at this stage of the night, only drove the pain home further.

A new silence descended on the pair, but one that brought comfort to neither. Rikki reached over and placed her hand on top of Gabbi's, breaking the spell. "Had no choice, child. Needs must. We had to let him go." She patted her once more before taking her tumbler back in both hands, feeling the coolness of the melting ice against her calloused palms. The glass shook in her grasp until she clamped it back down onto the surface.

Gabbi stood, made her way around the far edge of the bar, emptied her ice into the sink and gave the tumbler a rinse. She added water from the tap and slurped a couple of thirsty sips to clear her mind. She had a second set to get through, and it needed to go better than the first.

Brothers. Thursday. Later that night.

Yorick and Tobi surveyed the street from the steps of The Waldorf. It was Yorick who lurched into the next plan of action. "We can't spend our entire night rehashing the old days," he said, his Dutch roots having taken hold in his speech. "Let's find a miserable stranger to laugh at instead." He stepped forward from the steps and stumbled. Tobi reacted and grabbed him by the shoulders, steadying Yorick long enough for him to find his feet.

"You alright? We only had three pints," he said, his arm stretched across his younger brother's shoulder like a loyal resting hound. Yorick shrugged out of his grasp and straightened up.

"Damn cobblestones on this street. Need fixing. Like everything else around here."

Tobi sighed and changed the topic. "What did you mean about laughing at miserable strangers?"

"There." Tobi traced the end of his brother's extended finger to a dimmed sign across the road, three doors further down. Propped up next to the door was a rickety blackboard that read 'Open-mic Comedy'. Above the entrance was a dated-looking piece of signage that featured a mix of symbols. In its centre was a Greek cross with four equally sized corners. Each had a concentric circle that wound inward. Framing the shape was the head of a lion, but no mane. A lioness. The image danced and swirled in Tobi's eyes as he looked at it. He couldn't make anything of it, but the odd name stood out to him, 'The Rams & Lion'.

"Alright, I'll bite," said Tobi with a sharp intake of the fresh night air. "But there better not be jokes about children and toys."

It was Tobi who first pressed forward into the well-trodden carpet. If he were a betting man, he'd have placed a confident wedge on seeing the traditional night-crawlers of east London dotted across the bar. That bet wouldn't have paid off as he looked at several well-dressed young businessmen and women scattered from seat to seat.

Tobi went into autopilot. He navigated his way to the bar and took a moment to register his surroundings. After a brief wait he turned, two whisky tumblers in his hand, and saw that Yorick was nowhere to be found. "Standard," he murmured to himself.

And then came the laugh, that unmistakable noise. Loud, and from below.

"Downstairs. That's where that brother-in-arms of yours is. Comedy." Tobi turned at the gruff voice and looked down at a much older woman. He took in her small tufts of spiked red hair and the lined skin of her face. She carried herself with tales of ageing and a permanence that dared you to trifle with her. Tobi didn't. She inspected him with unblinking eyes, as if trying to work out what he was thinking. He shifted his weight, nodded in her direction and made his way to the staircase.

The steps creaked and moaned beneath him as he descended into the basement. At the bottom, the lights blurred together, and Tobi identified a small stage. He struggled to make out its occupant through the burning bulbs above her. He leaned his elbow against the edge of a chair in the back row, one of just five, and Yorick sidled along.

Tobi had been a member of an improv group of comedians through his university days. The business of being funny for money was tough. He knew it was no mean feat to make a successful career of it. He knew what it took to make it. Fight. Large mouthfuls of your own pride. Not for the faint-hearted or those after a simple life.

But this girl carried a fresh air. She was young. Her face was a portrait of unblemished, light brown skin that was framed by strands of curled auburn hair that clung to her jawline. She dragged and leaned the clunky microphone stand this way and that as she worked her way through a well-practised patter.

For the first time that night, Yorick focused on something in front of him. Tobi drifted off, turning over the night's conversations in his mind. Just as he thought he had made sense of some of Yorick's actions, he felt his body rocked by the force of his brother's convulsions alongside him. A pleasant metronome of drifting thoughts and jarring reversions settled in as the minutes ebbed away.

"So, I called her Karen and ended it there. Not my finest effort, but there you go. Another reason I hate accountants. No offence," she said, rocking the microphone back to its original place. "Thank you, enjoy your night upstairs."

Tobi had missed the closing joke's set up, so the payoff had meant little to him. He shook himself back into the room as the small crowd laughed and clapped, some more than others. He was aware of the comedian's body moving past him and up the stairs at a determined pace.

Yorick was up and pushing past him. "She seems fun," he said and before he knew it, Tobi was twenty-one again, following another one of his brother's impulses as he flounced away with a bounce and a charm.

Tobi emerged at the top of the basement staircase and picked out his brother from the crowd. He was standing next to the small, fierce woman with the red tufts of hair. She was between him and the comedian. The small huddle was clustered in the furthest corner of the bar, next to the main entrance. A tinny jukebox sat nearby, wheedling out the last chords of a song Tobi struggled to remember. The old woman was closest to it, perched on a barstool over a glass of whiskey. Yorick leered over her in what Tobi assumed was his attempt at a convivial stance.

Tobi drank in the scene ahead of him. Blurred movements of couples and friends swapping jokes and flirtations. Drinks being poured and sloshed back. And then his eyes found the artwork on the walls. He scanned the pieces, which ranged in colour and intensity. But all were vivid, and of flowers set in wild scenes. Familiar, but not like the countryside of England as he knew it. He held himself for a moment and then pressed forward. But time had played a trick on him, as no sooner had he ventured ahead, than he was bumping into his brother's right shoulder as he swooped past him onto a nearby table.

"She's different," said Yorick, banging his fist on the table as he settled into a tired chair. Tobi took his place next to him, steadying himself as he took his seat. He said nothing. Yorick had been frenzied all night, and he had no idea where this conversation might lead. "Sort of girl papa would have liked, no?"

Tobi's gaze snapped to his brother's hands, that twitched with a nervous energy he didn't recognise. He replied, "Doesn't look like a pushover, I'll tell you that much."

The distinct clanging of an old brass bell above the bar rang out across the room, piercing Tobi's ears.

"Last rounds!" bellowed the old woman in an accent that left Tobi confused. She met his eyes as if issuing the order to the pair.

Tobi turned away from her gaze and towards his brother. "Finish your drink, Skeletor. I've got a big day tomorrow."

Yorick. Friday. Morning.

Yorick was no stranger to the unpredictable arcs of champagne corks. What was new to him was seeing them held firmly in place by well moisturised palms. There was no uncertainty about their final destinations. Within these walls, they only ever found their way into the correctly coloured recycling bins.

"Orange juice topper?" asked the newly minted millionaire, Ben. The sale of his digital signature app had closed without a hitch. Ben, along with seventeen colleagues below the age of thirty, had just become very wealthy, very quickly.

The crew varied in their degree of motley-ness. Whilst some hailed from north of London and the esteemed, traditional colleges of Oxford and Cambridge, others had dropped out at various stages of school, having chosen to embrace the speculative journey of the backyard entrepreneur. Yorick couldn't help but compare the group's path to money to his own. There was a complexity of differences; they had shunned the route of slow, methodical progression backed by a well-established graduate's degree. But the similarities were there, too. For all of their contrasting backgrounds, their adherence to social norms shone through as brightly as any corporate office. Yorick took in the exposed brick walls and warehouse-styled ceiling and then turned sharply back to Ben.

"Of course. It's only 10 in the morning," he replied.

Ben sloshed orange juice into the glass of reassuringly expensive champagne.

"It's satisfying to deliver something that's going to make the world a better place, you know? People out there are just going to feel so much safer. And safety's important to everyone today," said Ben, with a furrowing of his brow. Yorick was halfway through his glass before he reminded himself that he needed to slow down. He wasn't with his people.

"I have someone I need you to meet, Ben. With everything over the line, it's time we think about the next phase."

Ben laughed out loud and said, "Do you ever let yourself celebrate?"

"No rest for the wicked," said Yorick, tipping his glass towards the youthful face. He added, "These are your celebrations, Ben. I'm still working." Another smile, this time with a flash of his teeth. He glanced down at his phone and said, "He's just arrived. I'll let him up." He turned on his heel, downing the rest of his drink in one gulp as he did so.

He returned from the lobby of the co-working office space with a man of equal height and stature. His partner had a broad head, heavily starched shirt collar, and flat shoulders. He had no discernible neck.

"Ben, this is Huang Hao. Huang, Ben. It's time you two met," said Yorick, motioning with his right arm towards his Chinese partner.

The Asian man held a neutral pose with both arms by his side as he soaked up the awkward display that unfolded in front of him.

Ben first brought his hands together and paused, as if he'd lost himself halfway through a clap, then dropped them. He settled on holding them palms up and extended towards the newcomer.

"You can call me 'H'," said Huang, as he placed his right hand on top of Ben's and turned it upwards while gripping it in a friendly handshake. "It's a pleasure to meet you. Yorick has told me many great things about your company. And congratulations on today's success."

"Thank you, Hua- 'H'. It's great to meet you, too," said a wild-eyed Ben. "Thanks so much for making the trip."

Huang smiled to himself, and then to the others. "Of course. I foresee us doing a lot more business together."

Yorick took a small step forward as he wedged his body between the pair. "Huang has an entire section of his data warehouses set aside for FORT-ify," he said, gesturing to the room at large with a topped up champagne flute.

"But all that can wait, at least until next week," Huang added in response. He patted Ben on his left shoulder. "Now is the time for you to enjoy your party."

Not sure what to do next, Ben nodded twice, opened his mouth as if to add something, but thought better of it and settled for a raised set of eyebrows and a cautionary smile towards Yorick. "Sounds great."

Yorick revelled in introducing Huang to others. His towering height and stocky stature, neatly clipped but unusually short fringe, and mixed accent caught everybody off guard. There was too much to take in at once, which meant most took in as little as possible. One piece at a time, Yorick watched as they tried to add it all up, but failed to solve the equation.

Small huddles of curious minds had formed within the office and were glancing towards them. Yorick noticed one group of three software engineers plucking up the courage to make their way over. He nudged Huang's elbow. "Ready to move on?"

"More than," Huang replied, rolling away from the crowd and towards the lifts. Yorick followed him, pressing the button three or four times in quick succession. The ping of the doors sounded, and they stepped in together. He waited for them to close and watched the shuffle of junior engineers turn on their heels and lose themselves back into the crowd.

The lift descended a floor in silence before Huang broke it. "So, Yorick. Are you ready to take this to the next level?"

Yorick. Friday. Midday.

The unlikely pair sat alongside each other, hips and shoulders forward, but eyes locked together. Huang to Yorick's left. They were in a bar that held a dankness in the air. But it chose to cloak rather than oppress its occupants. The small bar was empty but for the two of them. It was midday, but it only opened at two. Unless you were Yorick. Someone always opened the door when they saw his frame approaching down the alley. Today they had seen two, matching each other stride for stride and taking up most of the space between the flanking walls.

Yorick tipped a short crystal glass towards his long-time business associate. The clear liquid inside sloshed towards Huang as he did so, and he replied in turn. A crisp clink rang out. Upon hearing it, the barman took his cue and made his way to the back room where some kind of inventory, cleaning or sorting duties awaited. It didn't matter, so long as he found something to occupy himself.

The gin was tart and smooth, with a flavour that was difficult to pinpoint. The warmth of the juniper flowed through, but the mystique of lemongrass both bolstered and softened the alcohol. It was not something you'd find in any other bar in the UK. Yet. It represented just one of the many business interests that Huang had his fingers in. Like most of the projects he and Yorick had worked on over the years, there was a clash of British and Chinese culture. Unique to Yorick and Huang.

Huang held a tight grin as he spoke. "I'd like to toast to our next step."

Yorick took a long sip. He rolled the gin around his tongue, allowing the liquid to touch each part, and savoured the mix of flavours. His associate took a series of three small sips before placing his glass squarely on the coaster in front of him.

"You are coming to visit the site soon then, yes?" said Huang.

"My flight's tomorrow morning. Are you staying in London tonight? I can arrange a Friday night on the town for us?"

Both had now settled into their preferred positions; eyes forward, aligned with their shoulders and hips. "No, I leave this afternoon. My bosses messaged. Duty calls." Their stares drifted into the middle distance, which contained bottles from around the world. The mix of colours and shapes melded into one amorphous mass.

"Every time I think I work hard, you put me to shame," Yorick said as he drained the rest of his drink and tapped the glass three times on the wooden surface of the bar. The barman appeared as the third clunk rang out. He topped up Yorick's glass and added ice to Huang's. Yorick lifted the fingers of his right hand from the bar's surface and the young man left the bottle before he moved out of sight.

"Mr. Mao is looking forward to meeting you. It's been a long time coming," said Huang with a slight nod. He prodded a single protruding ice block, forcing it to settle down in and amongst its compatriots.

"It's only been seven years," Yorick said, struggling to hide the touch of bitterness he felt inside. He added, more lightly, "He might as well be a father figure to me, so I'll be on best behaviour, don't worry."

"You've achieved much for us in that time."

"You've paid me back many times over already," said Yorick and turned back towards Huang. Maybe it was the lemongrass that opened the floodgates of memories for Yorick. They were gates that caved in at a nudge and were always ajar when the two got together.

There was a time when Yorick's love for horses had extended far beyond the month of June. He had seen those blades of grass change colour through sun, rain, sleet and snow and back again, many times over. The one constant in that kaleidoscope of colour was a litter of discarded pink betting slips.

The love affair had started off as short and merry. It had been a corporate function, hosted by his firm for 'a bit of fun'; a rare break from the labours of the office. The proximity to those powerful beasts had stirred something in Yorick. Man-made machines, cars or planes, had never spoken to him in the same way. But it wasn't the power within the natural flesh which had its grip on him. It was the churning of the grass. The graceful yet violent act of hooves that pressed, sank, twisted and lifted, releasing with them a mix of overturned grass, soil and debris. Followed by a near replica next to it, yet different. Like snowflakes, Yorick had often thought. And then two more in quick succession. Rat-a-tat-a-tat-a-tat. Rhythmic and purposeful. Chasing fate down.

His appetite was ignited that bland June afternoon, while surrounded by suits that had different names sewn into their inside pockets but were all the same style and cut. He had escaped to relive those feelings whenever he could in the weeks and months that had followed. The slips that fell by his feet had become longer and the piles larger.

It was the following Autumn that Huang had found him. Yorick had been pleading with the cashier to extend his credit line. Just one more time. He could pay by Friday once his next deal came in.

No dice.

Until a looming stranger with a broad forehead and high cheekbones had stepped to Yorick's side. He had drawn up alongside him, imposed his presence, and asked how much the debt was. He didn't flinch at the six-figure sum, and handed over a black bank card with no fuss. Yorick had lost his words, and let it happen.

"Let me buy you a drink, Mr. Van den Berg. I have a proposition to discuss with you." It was the first time Yorick had experienced the bewitching effect of his accent.

Huang was the most upfront person Yorick had ever met. "Data, Yorick. May I call you Yorick? Data - that's what I'm buying from you." That was when he learnt about the warehouses. He had not yet been to China. But it now felt like a second, maybe first, home. Huang never mentioned how he found Yorick by the tracks that day. Yorick never asked. It was their unspoken agreement, reinforced in silence time and time again over dried ink and empty tumblers. But both knew it couldn't have happened without Tobi's connections.

The memories were a painful reminder of the only time that weakness had taken hold of Yorick. He'd lost control, and the experience had strengthened his resolve to never let it happen again. But now he fought to keep a solid grip with his left hand on his glass. His fingers itched with the involuntary spasms the doctor said would become more frequent. He wondered how much time he had left to hunt down fate. To pay Huang back and assume control back once more.

The remaining ice blocks bumped against each other at the bottom of Huang's glass. They had become smaller versions of themselves, giving up their identity to the lemongrass liquid.

"We look forward to receiving you. Dress warmly, Yorick, you know how cold it can get there even at this time of year."

Huang slunk from his chair and made a swift exit up the steep, unstable staircase. Yorick reached for the bottle of gin, took it by the neck, and lifted it to his nose. He savoured the smells as they made their way up the thin funnel and filled his nostrils.

Yorick. Friday. Afternoon.

Yorick barely noticed as his assistant, Craig, left his office. The space was glass-walled with spectacular views out over the reaching buildings of London's finance district. Muted colours from the carpet and sparse furnishings surrounded him. The only item of genuine interest was a large TV screen which ran the latest news, along with a financial information ticker along the bottom. The red bar announced that the PM was due to address the public.

Craig confirmed his itinerary; a flight to China the next morning, returning a day later. He used to work an extra day into his schedule to allow him to adjust to the jet lag. But these days he simply made notes of the dates and confirmed the departure time. His eyebrows raised when Yorick said that he would travel alone.

The warm gin had settled in Yorick's stomach and his thoughts went over what needed to be done that evening. He would head home, throw a suit in a bag, and one of many pre-packaged frozen meals into the microwave. That was it. He'd have time to head out for a drink.

The ringing of his phone annoyed him. He'd asked Craig to divert all calls that Friday afternoon, but knew he couldn't handle the simplest of tasks. He snatched at the handset on his desk and barked his name into it.

"Yorick, it's Sam," said a voice that oozed with refined breeding. "How are you doing? Feeling ok?"

Yorick adjusted his position, straightening up his back at the voice of his firm's senior partner. Everything about this was odd. Sam never called on a Friday; everyone knew he regarded it as the start of his weekend. And he never asked him how he was feeling.

"Never better, Sam. I presume you've heard the good news of the FORT-ify deal being completed?" said Yorick as he adopted a more neutral tone.

"Yes, yes, I had heard of that. Splendid stuff, Yorick. Another fine feather in your impressive cap," Sam replied, with a pause. His voice sounded soft and distracted to Yorick. Conversations about his making partner had intensified in the preceding months. Yorick had been making his case for years, and the numbers backed it up. But achieving that final milestone at a sought after company like his went beyond the numbers. Every detail of your life was scrutinised and examined. The risks of failure were too high to take a chance. Clients were tetchy and the slightest hint of impropriety or weakness would mean they'd take their millions of pounds elsewhere. Yorick tensed as Sam breathed, and then spoke again,."You see, Yorick, we've been made aware of your, well, your conversation with Doctor Feinstein."

There it was. Every industry has its price to pay, many more than others. For some it's money, other's time, or a lack of either. Sometimes it's putting yourself in the way of physical harm. For Yorick, it was privacy. Nothing was off limits with what the firm was allowed, or able, to know out about you. That had been made clear from the start. He knew the rules. But the invasion still felt personal. And abusive.

Yorick swallowed hard at the shock of the words. The reality of his diagnosis hadn't yet sunk in, but somehow, with the mentioning of his doctor, it became impossible to deny.

Huntington's Disease. He had heard of it from a film, or a distant work associate. He couldn't remember. But never enough to know the horrific nature of its power. As a neurodegenerative disease, it paraded the haunting ability to strip you of your physical and mental capacity until it left you as nothing but a burden to those around you. Useless. Until it put you out of your misery. Maybe he'd have another twenty years, Feinstein had said; if he adopted the recommendations that she needed to detail at their next appointment. The one he was yet to schedule.

He gathered himself enough to speak. "Well, it hasn't yet been conclusively diagnosed, Sam. They'd need genetic testing for that. Which won't be possible for me. But regardless, Dr. Feinstein is putting together a treatment plan and the symptoms are barely registering. We got it early. I'll be fine."

Further silence crawled to him through the line, and then another deep breath from Sam. "I hear that you're off to China first thing tomorrow. Do you not think that perhaps a rest might be in order? You know, while we figure out what all this might mean, Yorick?"

He snapped forward and crouched himself over the handset. "I'm fine, Sam. Consider it nothing more than a minor bump in the road. And that road has been paved with plenty of good fortune for both of us. No reason to doubt that it won't continue into the future."

"Yorick, this is -..." Sam's voice caught itself mid-sentence and Yorick heard a sharp intake of air. "Alright, Yorick. We can do it your way, for now. But we need to talk about this. We're worried about you."

You're worried about my ability to handle my business, Yorick thought to himself. This had nothing to do with him, and he wasn't going to let Sam use it against him. "Once I'm back from China, I think you'll find that I'm very much on top of things. Now is not the time to worry, Sam."

After they'd hung up, Yorick's attention switched to the big TV in front of him. The Prime Minister had shuffled out to the podium in front of Number 10's famed black door. It was a simple plinth with a microphone on a tall stand alongside. The PM was dressed in a dark suit, which at first glance appeared an austere black. But as the camera panned in more closely, and when the light caught the drizzle in the air, it revealed the true colour beneath. Yorick could see the dark blue. The colour of the man's tie was a lighter, but still serious, shade of blue, and it sat on a starched white shirt. The Prime Minister had finished making a series of opening remarks and was moving to the main topic.

"I stand before you today to notify you of a national security cyber breach that occurred in the early hours of this morning." Data breaches had become common practice in the news media in recent years. It seemed like most weeks contained confirmation that another large global company was compromised and thousands, or millions, of private data accounts had spilled out into the wider world. There was a flurry of activity when they happened in the early 2010s. News outlets would make a hoo-hah about what this might mean for individuals, promote the importance of updating your security software and issue some platitudes about password safety. But now it was reported as though a rainstorm had been spotted coming in from the east. It might be prudent to arm yourself with something sensible, but if you found yourself caught in it, you could grin and bear it until it passed.

The man in the blue tie gripped the podium in front of him, baring his white knuckles to the journalists.

"This breach concerns the accounts of many Britons, but we, at this time, are unsure of the exact number." Sam's words ebbed away as Yorick watched the weathered face talking about something he knew too little about. "We have identified that the NHS was the focus of the attack." The UK's National Health Service was a common topic of debate tossed about in the House of Commons. It was batted this way and that before settling back into

46

its starting point. Rarely did it command a tight grip from one side, whatever the comments being made about it. The PM clenched his right fist as he continued the address.

"This attack may have created significant concerns for individuals across the British Isles." Yorick clenched his lips together in a tight smile over these words. "We ask you all to remain vigilant as we work through the situation." And that was it. He moved onto the next topic concerning an update on trade negotiations with Australia.

Yorick relaxed back into his chair. The chances of getting the public at large to take heed of digital security warnings were as likely as someone standing behind that podium in sandals, swimming shorts and a sleeveless shirt. "If only you knew," he thought to himself, as he prepared his agenda for his meeting with Huang.

Tobi. Friday. Afternoon.

Tobi pressed the red circle on his smartphone. The call disconnected, and it left him staring into his wife's eyes, peeking out from behind a myriad of icons. She was rushing home from a yoga session to get supper on the go. Just another afternoon. Tobi was looking forward to opening something red and reliable and settling onto the couch with his small family to push the past few hours behind him.

And then a set of small feet, perched on fashionable heels, came tapping to his ears. Clara had perfected the art of knocking with one hand whilst opening his door with the other. It was a balance of decorum and efficiency.

In her left hand, she brandished a digital tablet. On it was a news article, zoomed in on a tacky headline.

"PILL-LORRIED!!! Pharmaceutical app entrepreneur caught playing doctor and nurse on company property!" blared a font that no tactful delivery could conceal. And to her credit, Clara didn't try to.

"It's Simon," she said. Except she didn't. She zoomed out with a quick pinch of her thumb and index finger. It left Tobi staring at the contorted shape of Simon Pentworth, caught in a compromising situation. With a young female employee - who was neither his wife nor a trained nurse. He was one of West & West's biggest and most well-known clients.

"Right," said Tobi, as he leaned back into his chair. He didn't take his eyes off the image. It had been lifted from social media by a miserable sub-editor who hadn't the inclination nor decency to find an approved version first. They could remove an online article and replace it with a more suitable one. But not before bursts of hungry clicks had poured in. Tobi's face didn't show any signs of shock at the news. Clara saw the wheels turning behind his steel-blue eyes.

She read from the opening lines of the article. "Simon Pentworth, one of Britain's most recognisable, and wealthy, entrepreneurs in recent years, has extended his company's capabilities to include many new delivery services, as our pictures exclusively reveal." Her mind was three or four sentences ahead, which meant her narration was devoid of any emotion. The craven words didn't warrant it.

"People can be their own worst enemies, can't they, Tobi?" she said as she placed the tablet down squarely in front of him and took a seat opposite.

It wasn't a grand office by any means; Tobi had designed it that way. As successful as he had become, he had kept an eye for casual elegance that pleased Clara. Others in this industry were addicted to displaying superiority through minimalism, which led to gauche interiors blasted with identical statement pieces. But Tobi had resisted. Tastefully chosen knick-knacks adorned the surfaces. Each one contained its own story, and Tobi revelled in boring her with their fascinating histories. He delved into an item's provenance, offering opinions on the political environments from which it had been extracted. Maybe she'd feigned the boredom in bouts of friendly jesting. She enjoyed listening to the stories he told.

"They certainly can, Clara," Tobi replied, his thoughts wandering out of the window beyond her.

Mikey and his crew had done their job. They'd taken the pictures Tobi knew wouldn't be hard to source. Simon's fall from grace was an annoyance that would leave the broader investment community flustered. "What would it mean for the leadership team of the rampant enterprise?" they would ask as one. But, as was standard with all of his business interests, Tobi had installed himself on its board as a condition of its sale two years ago. Alongside the twenty percent of the proceeds that he had banked for the firm.

Six years previously, Simon, had sat in the chair Clara was in and asked for Tobi's trust. He had been a dry, staid man, working within the stagnant industry of pharmaceuticals. But he'd possessed foresight into the digital world that was about to revolutionise his industry.

He had created an app to allow pharmaceutical sales reps across the United Kingdom to short-circuit a small path in the regulatory rigmarole of the industry. Small was enough in an ocean awash with prescription money. It hadn't taken them long to shift gears and head overseas with their ambitions. So many new and important drugs, destined for markets where they were desperately needed, died a smothering death amongst the ever-shifting sands of regulation. In Tobi's eyes, this app was more than just an investment. It was going to improve people's lives.

Creating an online, globally distributed market of approved medications meant Simon could get drugs to markets quicker and more efficiently than anyone else. The drugs they were approved to handle were limited but important; beta blockers for coronary artery disease, low level steroid treatments for anti-inflammatory and allergy use, along with a handful of less known daily and chronic ailment treatments. Their solution layered sophisticated data algorithms on top of customer data to predict where medication was most likely to be needed ahead of time. This proved vital in central Africa and Southeast Asia, where they had struggled to access what had become standard treatments in the west. It was the sort of thinking Tobi admired, and made a mission to become financially and personally tied to. Simon had named it HEAL-y as a placeholder, but it had stuck.

They had formed a tight and formidable working relationship. Simon brought his industry knowledge and connections, while Tobi used his innate charm to knit together a web of players within the sector. It meant many late nights together. They had shared countless dinners at each other's houses. Tobi had put Simon's children to bed, reading to them while their father worked to design the new medical ecosystem that they would grow up in. Tobi, through West & West, first provided money, but gave so much more. He was baked into the fabric of the idea.

He had steered the business more actively than most of his interests. He attended every board meeting; he exercised his voting rights. He believed in the company because he believed in Simon's cause.

But, over time, that belief eroded.

Simon was not an attractive man. He wore glasses with thin frames that gave him a squirrel-like appearance. He had an unkempt goatee beard and failed to tidy the rest of his stubble. Insignificant details in most men, but ones that meant something when a rampant, scurrying self-interest took hold of Simon.

Simon had been harbouring a touch-paper greed that lurked beneath the surface, out of Tobi's sight, for years. But once ignited, it showed no way of extinguishing itself - at the expense of millions of innocent people. That was where Tobi drew the line.

"How soon do we leave it before calling the lawyers?" said Clara.

Tobi toyed with his soft toy baseball. "Tomorrow. Today, I need the full report from Mikey and the crew," he replied while reaching for the tablet. There was one image of the illicit truck. It was shot from behind and out of focus. But it was clear enough for Tobi to recognise Simon's face and the number plate of the vehicle; GN14 RUD. The same licence plate that Mikey had shown him on a separate image just seven days before. That had been a very different photograph. One of many. All of those had been razor sharp in their clarity. Taken by a high-end camera from multiple angles. By one of Mikey's crew.

Tobi had hoped that Simon could prove to him that his burning greed could die off. He had turned over millions of pounds a year from a business Tobi could be proud of. They were making lives better for people and impoverished cultures, while helping themselves to grow wealthier. Win-win, right? Capitalism at its finest. But three months ago, Simon had called Tobi with an idea. It wasn't an original idea. It was one that had existed since the dawn of the new digital age. An age now owned and dominated by the big social media platforms. Simon had veered off script and held his own conversations with founders of the leading social networks. They wanted his business - it held a lifeblood of personal data into what ailed millions of people across the globe.

HEAL-y customers were often desperate people looking to break individual cycles of pain, struggle or monotony. The HEAL-y system housed the data of what doses they required, when and in what quantities. There were thousands of companies Tobi knew couldn't wait to get their hands on their unique dataset. But he recognised these people had trusted this breakthrough technology to keep their inner most secrets, vulnerabilities and fears secure. Companies would pay vast sums of money to understand those fears because it would allow them to advertise to them. Nothing sells like fake promises designed to target fear and insecurity. But selling those secrets on a data's black market wasn't how Tobi wanted to make money. That wasn't how West & West did it. When Simon slipped into that dark world below, Tobi knew it would drive him to action to protect their reputation.

He had tried to talk Simon out of it. He had asked how he would feel if it were his own daughter, and her personal experiences as a young, vulnerable teenager, at risk of being shared across the internet with faceless corporations. Her intimate details in danger of being breached and spilt across public forums. His attempts to appeal to common and relatable sensibilities had fallen on Simon's unwilling ears.

They had been together when the initial purchase offer had come through. The offer was legal on the surface, but laced with tacit acknowledgements of what would happen in the background. Illegal data manipulations buried within reams of terms and conditions. They had opened the document on Tobi's computer screen. As they scrolled through the initial pages, Tobi could sense Simon's fingers kneading into his own knees with an increasing pace. The kneading gave way to a light and rhythmic tapping. And then their eyes arrived at the killer line in the document. It had a figure at the end.

The figure looked ridiculous in its composition of innocuous shapes; simple circles that were elongated at either end. They were all together and lined up. On their own, each seemed harmless. But grouped in the way they were, they transformed Simon. They formed a large number. His fingers had stopped tapping at the sight of them.

Those simple, oval shapes held a collective power that was too strong for a soul like Simon's. Tobi tried to point to the truth behind the agreement, and what accepting that figure would mean in the long run. They could find a new investor, maybe less lucrative, but without the tacit acknowledgements sewn into the seams. But Tobi knew that he'd lost him.

Tobi had tried to trick himself that he could avoid telling Mikey to gather his camera. Not to make his way to the outskirts of Lancashire. Not to go to HEAL-y's industrial warehouse site. Where he knew Simon arranged for clandestine meetups with impressionable female employees in the name of career progression.

But he hadn't been able to sidestep the inevitable. Simon's greed and complicity to exploit had proved too great.

For all of his recent and grave foibles, Simon still had an admirable trait that reminded Tobi of his gentler times. For all his riches, his working-class roots shone through in one small indulgence. Simon liked to get behind the wheel of one of their fleet vehicles and make the brief journey from their warehouse outside Preston and drive south to Liverpool. There, he would find the primary port from which their pharmaceuticals could be distributed to their global markets.

Mikey had been informed that a figure with thin-framed glasses and a poorly maintained goatee would emerge from within the walls of the grey warehouse. A man who had built a business that had aimed to help people towards better health.

Simon, who moved with a limp of the left hip, still loved the idea of driving his own products across the country. He was a self-made man and connecting rubber to tar re-established his own connections to the island he'd grown up all over. Connections that he had long since lost in his daily routines. A loss that had made him more susceptible to the lure of those simple, oval figures. A loss that had made Tobi's call to Mikey an inevitability. But Mikey and his team didn't need to know all that. In fact, they made it their business to know as little as possible. The details they dealt in were different. They involved top end cameras and selective surveillance positions. Mikey's team operated with their usual efficiency. And then the waiting had begun.

In the early hours of that Friday morning in April, they set the scene. It was the time of day Simon felt it could be just him and the road, free of the distractions of what his life had become. It was a frosty morning; Mikey had seen the mists of steam coming from the overweight man's mouth as he clambered into the truck. And then, a young blonde woman, no older than a university graduate, made her way towards and into the van. Some relied on coffee for early morning road trips, Simon relied on other stimulants to get his blood flowing.

In Tobi's world, decisions have consequences. And Simon's decisions and habits meant that the reins of his company were about to be in the hands of the man who had helped him to build it. The man whose signature was alongside his own at the bottom of the paperwork they had signed together at shared dinner tables. The man who had always prided himself on turning his back on rampant greed— Tobi.

Tobi needed to convene an urgent board meeting to vote on Simon's future as CEO of the company he had founded. But he already knew the outcome; the board wouldn't stand for this level of scandal. Tobi's fingers worked over the tablet and scheduled a call with West & Wests' lawyers as Clara watched on from the chair opposite him.

Yorick. Friday. Night.

"Double whisky?" said a voice Yorick recognised. It was a hazy recollection, but one he had hoped to hear again. He lifted his eyes from the surface of the bar. The frizzled hair that he'd previously seen tied up behind a microphone was hanging loose. Each looped strand found its way down to her shoulders as though it had all the time in the world to get there. Its colour matched the bar.

"Please," replied Yorick. She turned to grab the nearest bottle from the shelf behind her, an open denim jacket catching the cask ale pumps in front of her as she did so. Yorick didn't think to check the bottle she'd reached for and waited while she poured a couple of large splashes on top of two fresh blocks of ice.

"The last time I saw you, you were on stage. And then in front of the bar, not behind it," he said as she moved away to grab the bank card machine. Yorick reached inside his left jacket pocket and pulled out a twenty-pound note.

She returned with the device and saw the note on the counter. She took it and turned back to the till, calling over her shoulder as she did. "Drunk, vomiting accountants don't pay the rent bills as easily as pouring tumblers of whiskey." She came back with a five-pound note and a single heavy coin, which she placed down in front of Yorick. He seemed not to notice. She had remembered that night, too. "Don't forget your change." She moved back down the bar to another customer a few feet to Yorick's left.

The Rams & Lion wasn't close to any of Yorick's sparsely decorated flats, at least in London terms. He most frequently slept at his property in Canary Wharf. It was an area that breathed in the energy of strident suits during the day, only to exhale them in stuttered gasps over deserted streets once night fell. It was four miles from where he sat, a significant detour by taxi. He had remembered requesting the Waldorf to the driver as he got in. But that wasn't where he had got out.

He felt the press of a forearm leaning onto his right hand.

"Just trying to squeeze in," said a female face he had seen a thousand times around the area he lived. During the day.

She was attractive. Prominent cheek bones, one higher than the other, created a balanced imperfection. Her styled eyebrows were cocked to exaggerate the effect. Purposefully done. Yorick dropped his arm to the top of his knee in response and reached for his tumbler at the same time. He tapped it on the bar and lifted it to his lips, catching her eye but saying nothing. His gaze settled back into his glass, onto the ice cubes as they drifted in a counter clockwise direction. He followed them for one ponderous revolution. Their direction of travel led his eyes further along the bar, back to where the girl with the electric hair was measuring out a measure of white wine. The glass caught the soft light from above and threw it across the room for a fraction of a second. Yorick took a long swift draw of the tumbler, placed it back down on the top of the five-pound note and spun from his seat.

The door of the pub banged shut behind him with a thud as he stepped outside. "What am I doing here?" he asked himself. He scanned the quiet street for any sign of a taxi. Nothing. He reached for his phone, but as he did, he heard the door swing open. This time with a subtle creak. His hand paused in the pocket of his trousers, his fingers wrapped around the edges of his smartphone.

"Got a light?" she asked. He looked up into the comedian's smiling face. His fingers shifted from his phone and slipped to the bottom of his pocket, where he found a cheap plastic lighter, almost full of its fluid. He offered it to her. His right thumb jerked with the wheel mechanism as he jostled it into action. A spark caught and spirited away from them before a flame sprang up in its place and licked the end of her cigarette. She took a couple of short puffs and pulled back into the cover of the doorway.

Yorick went to return the lighter to his pocket, but she caught the corner of his jacket with her hand, something folded between her index and middle finger.

"I need a new lighter and doesn't look like you use that one much. I'll take it for a fiver." And with one motion, she pressed the folded bill into the palm of his hand while she removed the lighter. He felt a dampness from the bottom corner of the bill. He smiled as he placed the change that he'd left under the whiskey tumbler into his pocket, back into the depths of where the lighter had lain.

"What makes you think I don't use it much?"

"You're not a smoker. It's a prop, yeah?"

"Prop?"

"For moments like these. Strangers asking you for something in a moment of need." She exhaled with her lips pressed together, and pointed to the side, forcing the smoke away from them.

"You seem to have me locked into some kind of box," said Yorick, folding his arms behind him and pressing them into the wall.

"I wouldn't take it personally. Lighter, expensive car key, business card; I'm used to seeing the trinkets of my crowd here." The words left her mouth with an edge to them, biting into the fumes that rolled from her lips.

Yorick paused - had she caught him staring? - and then began, "What's your --," but before he could get the sentence out, a moaning of the door interrupted them.

"Oi, Gabbi Gabs, you're on," said a gravelly voice from inside. The door had opened just wide enough to allow the words to escape, directed at her ears. She scraped the cigarette against the face brick wall beside her and dropped it into a small metallic bin screwed to the door frame.

"Thanks for the light," she called behind her as she disappeared back into the clutches of the dark pub.

Yorick navigated his way back to the pub's basement. He once again chose a seat near the back. It was nestled against a red curtain that was pulled across the room, dividing it in two. As he sat, his head brushed against the wrinkled surface and it gave way against his touch. Emptiness lay behind it. He glanced down behind him and saw the legs of a row of empty chairs poking out from underneath the bottom of the draped red sea.

The crowd around him was different. He felt it in the air. But couldn't identify why. Scattered across the five rows in front of him were an array of heads. One balding; cut close like his, but lacking his precision. There was a burst of flowing red hair. In and among, a couple of shortish cropped blonde styles and a smattering of brunette do's of varied lengths. A mix of men and women. But none seated together; all dotted neatly apart from each other. It was an unusual arrangement of strangers. His focus shifted to the microphone and the small, square black stage. It was no more than two metres by two metres in total. Tonight a single, not particularly bright, stationary spotlight shone down into the middle. Yorick rested his hands on his knees.

"Alright?" she called out to the crowd. "It's me Gabbi. By name and trade, as Rikki always says," she began, nodding to the bottom of the staircase. The elderly woman was perched with a foot on the first step. She jerked her head to the ceiling, snatched a fast look at Yorick and made her way upstairs.

Yorick monitored the comedian's movements over the next fifteen minutes as she melded together sex, religion, economics and experiences of casual racism under a cloak of dark humour. Her movements were small but distinctive. A raised and retreated hand, a kicked-out foot, a brief fluffing of her hair out and to the side. She painted all these images while sat perched on a tall chair this time, drawing Yorick's eyes towards the mic and the light that spread onto it. Yorick broke out in a series of small laughs that were aware of the strange surroundings but furtive enough to spring forth and break cover from one joke to the next. Not his usual dominant outburst. An odd murmur of appreciation rippled across the rows in front of him, but in a tired fashion. As though crawling onto a couch after a long day of work.

And then he was clapping. He had taken his initial cadence from the assembled rows in front of him, but, unsatisfied, had sped up to overtake them.

There was no need this time for Rikki to return and clear up the mess of the room. Gabbi muttered a quick "cheers" and something about the usual bar specials being available before returning the mic to its resting place and heading up the tired stairs in the corner. As Yorick stood to follow her, his attention was caught by the balding man as he stood and shuffled forward to the stage. He placed the high stool to the side, grasped the mic with a loose fist and audibly sighed, "Alright, all" into it. No question mark. Yorick took the gap of the silence that followed to bound up the staircase before the newcomer began talking.

He made his way to the far corner, the one with the jukebox. It wasn't a busy Friday night in the pub. He found her huddled over the well-used machine, running her finger up and down the lists dotted across the front in handwritten block capitals.

Her finger paused as he got within an arm's length of her. "Now you know it's Gabbi. And I'm afraid I'm off the clock for tonight, but Rikki will serve you."

Yorick couldn't see her face. Her finger remained paused in its pursuit. "Why did I feel like I was the only person in the audience downstairs?" said Yorick, stopped in his tracks.

Gabbi's finger resumed its journey through the songs, hovering every other second. It stopped for the last time, and she pressed a button. The first beating bars of Toto's "Africa" sounded across the dampened speakers of the bar as Gabbi turned to face him.

"Well, in a way you were. Everyone else was a struggling comedian, some more than others. Just like me."

"An audience full of colleagues?" he offered with a weak smile.

"Pretty much. It's our own little fucked up version of an office, I guess. The equivalent of throwing corporate shit at the wall to see what sticks. While those around you simultaneously try to shit on those ideas. Just a lot of shit in the end, really."

Yorick pulled at the lapel of his collar. "It's a relief to hear that these things aren't mandatory to have the chance to experience that."

In return, Gabbi thumbed her shoulder, running it along a long line of threads that had gathered around a tear too irregular to be there by design. "Doesn't pay a-ma-zingly if you're considering a career change."

A movement above the jukebox caught Yorick's attention and his eyes were drawn to it. There he found a large, faux-brass framed mirror, cracked in the bottom corner. In the centre of it, he saw the same old woman shifting the high stools into place along the bar. Her movements were slow, but precise. Further beyond her, the crowd were gathering their assorted belongings of suit jackets and thin scarves, along with laptop cases. Closing time was nearing. The dying chords of the song floated out over their heads from the speakers above the mirror. The jukebox clicked. Gabbi bent down beside it and flicked a switch on the wall, killing the lights. Yorick glanced down at his shoes but in doing so, slowly rotated his left wrist enough to reveal his watch face. Six hours until his flight was due to take off.

When she spoke, she took him by surprise. "There's an Afro-Caribbean late-night food shop a couple of doors down. Rikki and I know it well," she nodded over Yorick's shoulder to the hunched but otherwise strong looking figure. "I'm not in the habit of inviting strangers in suits to eat late night chicken but, and don't take this the wrong way, you look fucking awful. And like you could use it."

He flicked back to the mirror. She wasn't wrong. He wouldn't describe the reflection as unfamiliar.

She brushed past his shoulder, made her way behind the bar and bent down, emerging with what Yorick thought was a blanket, but as she trussed and thrust it around her shoulders, he realised it was an impossibly large scarf. He turned around. And was confronted by Rikki. She placed the last of the line of stools neatly against the foot rail. It pressed against Yorick's shin.

"You go on, child. I'm full up tonight," she said, the words directed towards Yorick but with enough force to deflect off of the mirror behind him and back to Gabbi. Yorick felt her eyes settle on his forehead for a count of two, above the lines of his eyebrows. He towered over the woman as she sized him up. Her hands were laid to rest, dead still on top of the stool in a vice-like grip, as she held her stare. Her fingers looked strong. Yorick attempted to meet her gaze, but she was fixated elsewhere, looking through and beyond him to a different place. Or time. Tiny grey flecks within her green eyes reflected the light of the bar at Yorick. For a moment, he felt lost. Gabbi was right. He must be tired.

The chicken leg and thigh were still sizzling when they hit the cardboard plate beneath. The blackened skin spat and hissed at Yorick alongside a selection of cut cucumber, tomato and onion that had been pulled from a fridge. A massive hand gestured with an upward palm along the raised counter towards a selection of sauces that lay at the end. A toothy smile encouraged Yorick to take his pick. He was terrified enough of the chicken. He didn't trust food that bit back. But the aura of the friendly man implied that 'no sauce' wasn't an option. He chose the one that looked the most like dairy, a pinkish cream colour, sprinkled it gingerly across the joined chicken piece and stepped away to the single table in the shop. Gabbi was tearing the leg from the thigh by the time he settled into his seat, her fingers covered with the blackened stains of the skin. He began to do the same and found his eye wandering across the contrast of the three skins: chicken, hers and his. He picked up the leg, too, feeling the heat of the inner bone and gristle scratching at his fingertips. The smells steamed into his face. Tangy lemon, a rasping spice that he couldn't place, and the promise of succulent meaty aromas. His hunger overcame him and he gripped the fleshiest meat of the leg between his front teeth and wrestled it away from his face. Juices splatted the corners of his mouth.

Gabbi stopped and paused. Her eyes met his. She wore a plain expression across her face. Yorick first felt the force as his vision began to blur. Gabbi melted into a shapeless almond pool as he felt the power of the searing heat fill his mouth. A stifled shock ran through his mind. His ringing ears blocked out all other sounds. The rest of the chicken clattered to his plate as his fingers scrambled towards the bottle of water that Gabbi had bought. He gulped down two mouthfuls while he felt his brain sizzle. Like a struck pothole, as quickly as the heat had arrived, it disappeared into the night.

Gabbi's laugh was in full force. "Why did you pick Charlie's hottest sauce?" she squeaked in-between a flurry of snorts.

"It had a dairy-like look to it - I assumed it was the safest!" Yorick retorted. His shaved head flushed red; he was sure the heat from the spices was trying to escape through it. As salty tears rolled down his face, they pooled in the corners of his mouth where a small smile had started to form.

"You got to read the label, man," said a voice with heavy nasal tones behind him. They were words that brimmed with friendly and clipped endings. Yorick spun around and took in the full view of the four red X's staring back at him from the offending bottle. He flashed an awkward grin at Charlie and spun back to see his plate being lifted away from him and replaced by Gabbi's. Her chicken was stained a fiery red.

"Take this on, He-Man," she said as she slid it across the cheap plastic.

The red version was far friendlier and lacked the excitement of his. But it was delicious.

"Thanks," Yorick said as he smiled and prodded what remained of the chicken leg towards Gabbi.

"That first bite was worth the admission fee alone. So why is dairy such a trusted friend of yours?"

"You don't grow up in the Netherlands and not eat a lot of cheese. A lifetime's worth for most. I'm always drawn back to it, I guess," he said with a shrug.

The chicken pieces had been demolished; the evidence lay scattered across their plates. They mirrored each other's movements as they pushed, scraped, and gathered the remaining meat and skin scraps with their fingers and brought them to their lips in tiny mouthfuls. Across the scene, they traded small talk back and forth.

Where was she from? Zimbabwean descent. But east London was her home.

Where in the Netherlands? Small town, Den Bosch. Don't worry, few have heard of it.

Who was the guy you were with that night? My brother.

"I wonder if that's what I saw in you two. Comrades stumbling around our pub isn't an uncommon sight. But there was something different about the pair of you."

Yorick held her gaze for a moment. He was the one used to doing the sizing up. He tensed at the thought of being the prey in the headlights. "How so?"

She looked to the ceiling, searching for words, and then said, "In my experience, drunken friends have a forgetfulness about them. Especially those in suits. Their nights are about distributing power around them. Sometimes that can be hearty laughs to ring around attention. Often, it's as simple as just occupying space in such a way that others choose to steer clear of. But your brother was different when he was with you. He held his distance but kept you close at the same time."

"He's always been overprotective. Even though he only comes up to here," Yorick said and lifted a flat palm to in line with his shoulders.

"Protection's not just physical. I've done a fair bit of it in my time. When you come from an African background, you see the signs." Her hands rose to the air as she gesticulated with purpose. "It's a glance and an aura. You let those around you feel your presence from afar."

"The old woman from the pub used more than an aura that first night we spent in the pub," said Yorick with a smile.

"Well, protection from danger and protection from life's idiots are different things. Thankfully, Rikki is all-weather purposed."

Yorick sensed movement behind him and risked a backwards glance. He saw Charlie's hand as he reached up behind him and retrieved his array of sauces. He moved around the counter with broom in hand and started sweeping up the temporary artefacts of another night of choices in London. They took their cue and gathered their coats. Yorick glanced out over Gabbi's head to the street that had become slick with a steady rain. He realised that he was the only one who had put on his jacket and he flashed a confused look around the room.

"I live close," said Gabbi. Her eyebrows flicked upwards towards the ceiling.

"And it's late, Ms. Gabbi," chimed Charlie from the doorway, pronouncing none of the t's. He stood with his foot wedged against the door, holding it ajar. Yorick met the man's soft eyes, framed in dreadlocks that were clipped neatly to the side of his head.

"Thanks for the chicken. And a break from the suits. You were right. I needed that," he called back, turning to the table next to the counter that now stood empty.

"I do some protecting of my own where I can," Gabbi said as a flash of denim swinging through the door signalled her exit.

Yorick glanced down at his watch. Four hours until take off. He tipped his head to Charlie and stepped out into the night. The word 'protection' ambled across his mind, behind eyelids that grew heavy at last.

Yorick. Saturday. Morning.

The buzz and hum of Luton Airport's small collection of runways was dulled on this stretch of tarmac. Yorick's strides ate up the hundred-yard walk to the plane. He cruised up the staircase and into the familiar cabin of the chartered jet.

"Morning, Mr. Van den Berg. Coffee will be with you right away," said a voice that he didn't recognise. He paused on his way to his seat and looked back towards the cockpit. He saw a petite blonde girl no older than twenty-five.

"Where's Kate?" he fired in her direction. He was running on thirty minutes of sleep, snatched from the large leather couch in his living room.

"Kate is no longer with us, sir. My name is Hazel, and I'll be providing you with anything you need for our trip to Guizhou today," said the fresh face. She brushed his shoulder and placed a fresh cup of coffee down at his seat.

In the space of a few minutes, the main doors were closed, latches clicked into place, and items stowed into the galley in front of Yorick. The flurry of activity died, and he noticed the presence of Hazel.

"Whenever you're ready, Mr. Van den Berg, and we'll get the wheels rolling," she said while her eyes moved across his face and down to the coffee in front of him. The wisps of steam had lost their enthusiasm and made their way from his cup in scattered directions. He wrapped his right hand around it. In two swift gulps, he felt the rush of the hot liquid chasing down the back of his throat. The burn settled at the top of his chest and seeped downwards.

He glanced up and backwards towards Hazel, who stood with her left hip cocked higher than her right, and she stepped forward to clear away the still-hot cup. His eyes scanned across the five seats in the cabin. All empty.

He was travelling alone at last.

Twelve hours later, the jet touched down at Guiyang International airport in the province of Guizhou. Yorick was back in the heart of China's burgeoning data centre.

He tried to snatch more sleep in the air, but turbulence had rocked and rolled each time he dropped off. He was irritable. He grumbled past Hazel as he left the plane and was whisked into a large, air-conditioned black sedan. As the wheels rolled across the smooth road, just a decade old, Yorick felt settled at last. They steered away from the airport and, instead of taking the usual highway east towards Qiannan, the driver navigated through a network of exchanges and headed north.

East of the airport lay a suite of corporate offices where local proprietors headed up large technology start-ups, all trying to forge their way through teeming amounts of data. Squadrons of ambitious, smart young men and women were flocking to the region to tackle these massive stores head on. In past eras, hard-working parents would have sent these brains to universities to get medical, legal or engineering degrees. Some still did, of course. But growing numbers were chasing coding and artificial intelligence ambitions up, down and across the country. The Guizhou region hemmed and hawed with the new possibilities that data interrogation brought with it.

The soft vibrations of the rubber on the undulating surface sent Yorick back in time.

His first client, fifteen years ago, had been a large Chinese consortium. He remembered standing at a table and waiting. His firm had briefed him on the decorum of Chinese business interactions. But he had done his own, more personalised research. A small team of men had entered a large conference room in Guizhou. Yorick and a senior colleague had been waiting for twenty minutes. They had arrived early. As their counterparts entered, Yorick's partner clasped his hands together in front of his hips and pointed his fingers towards the leader of the advancing pack. As his colleague's hips hinged forward, Yorick felt himself overwhelmed by the need to cease all movement. His sudden, arrested stance hung in the air alongside the bobbed grey head of his colleague, who bolted back upright as if controlled by a spring. Their main client extended his hand towards Yorick, who grasped it while meeting him eye to eye. From that point on, Yorick had revelled in doing business with this group of men.

He'd never seen this team sweat. Not once in their time across the seasons; through the stifling humidity of the summer or the biting cold of the winter, not a bead had sprung forth. Yorick had matched them over the years. He prided himself on it. He knew how much sweat others hid beneath strands of hair.

Two hours later and the car climbed into the mountain district of Zunyi. Condensation formed on the windscreen and the clouds that had been hanging low in the air grew heavier.

They hadn't ascended for long when the looming mountains in front of them broke free of their jagged edges. In their place rose the uniformity of long, grey and straight-edged buildings. There were many, all with mirrored surfaces that reflected the surrounding peaks. The walls of the closest building grew higher and higher until the car pulled to a stop in front of a set of doors.

"Mr. Yorick, welcome," said a quiet but commanding voice. The owner of it met Yorick eye-to-eye and led him through the doors. His handler for the day.

Once inside, the path to find Huang was long and complicated. The building's rectangular exterior gave way to a myriad of twisting corridors within. After a long combination of left and right turns, they arrived at a large office with its door closed. Yorick's aide knocked, waited and then opened it, stepping aside for the Dutchman to enter.

On their approach from the road, Yorick had estimated the size of the building to be eight football pitches laid out in an array of rectangles that made up one singular large square. The building was the height of a double storey building but had only one ceiling throughout. It towered above them in an unyielding metal hue.

Huang was sitting behind a desk that was pushed back to the far end of the office. A large painting above his head drew Yorick's eyes towards it. He saw what looked like a solitary Chinese sage emerging from tree lined mountains, taking a step towards a misty pathway that lay before him. There were no discernible features beyond the first feet of the path, which itself disappeared as if into thin air. The image unsettled him and he dropped his eyes away from it.

A few feet in front of where Huang was sitting lay a large square desk. On it were four pieces of paper. They covered the size of two average doors laid down next to each other. A series of precise lines traversed the papers, intersected at intervals by a vast number of geometric symbols. Equidistant triangles, perfect circles and hexagons dotted the measured terrain of lines. In the top right corner of each page were Chinese symbols that Yorick couldn't decipher, but next to them was a series of numbers.

1 / 8, Zunyi Location Λ.

Eight buildings identical in layout to this, he assumed. Similar double-door sized pieces of paper sat on other tables in the surrounding buildings. They, too, would be covered with lines and their own unique combinations of triangles, circles and hexagons.

Huang called out from behind his desk, his voice muffled as it made its way across towards Yorick. "What do you think?"

He didn't know what to think. He knew their relationship had been building towards this moment. But he swallowed as he confronted the shapes before him. His tongue pushed up against the ridges of his mouth. Huang's eyes were on the square desk in the middle, his hands spread out towards it as if controlled by a puppeteer from the ceiling.

Yorick took a measured breath, buying himself a second to think, and then said, "I can guess the circles but talk me through the triangles and hexagons." Huang sprang up and grabbed his jacket, shouldering into it in one movement. He did up the sole button and made his way across to the table with its paper doorways.

"Yes, most of the circles are the projects we've been working on with you," Huang began.

"Мoзt?"

Huang brought his hands in front of him in a peaceful movement. "We're working with several partners across territories, Yorick." He placed his hands down flat on the table. "The others represent our interests in the US, although not as many as we might have hoped, and a fair few through Africa, too. Particularly Southern Africa along the east coast, where we've been able to make significant inroads in the past decade. They all represent sizable and malleable trade routes for us."

As Huang explained, Yorick smoothed the front of his pressed jacket. "Right, of course." He scanned the expanse of paper and did a quick approximation of the number of circles: twenty. Based on Huang's explanation, he hoped he could account for at least half of those. And then he remembered the title at the top of the pieces of paper; 1 / 8.

Huang continued and Yorick picked up the trail, "... with each hexagon hoping to be completed in the next six to twelve months."

He gathered the hexagons represented the future expansion plans for more established corporate companies. So far, they had dealt solely in the start-up scene, but Huang had never hesitated to clarify that their ambitions extended into the world of public companies to bolster their data supplies. Another scan of the assembled papers, but this time it was quicker; there were only 10 hexagons in total. 1 / 8.

"And the triangles?"

His associate of almost a decade straightened up and moved to the opposite side of the square from Yorick. As he moved, he trailed his hand across the lines that connected the shapes. "Let's start with these. Each represents the work of those based back in Guizhou, in the offices and factories in Qiannan that you know so well. They are the lifeblood of the system."

"The algorithms that the teams have been producing?"

Huang hesitated for the briefest of moments. "Yes. Indeed."

"So the algorithms are designed for each of the circles, the deals we've struck, to talk to each other," Yorick said while pausing with a hand in the air, hoping to buy time as his eyes raced from line to circle to line and back to circle. It hadn't been obvious from the start, but the number of triangles was overwhelming. There were too many to count, and they existed in a dizzying array of sizes and shades of grey. Lines upon lines passed through a circle and on the other side, a triangle, before splitting off into more lines, only for the process to repeat itself. "I understand the lines, the algorithms," said Yorick, questioning himself how much he did. But onward he pressed, "So now tell me about the triangles."

"Yorick. I haven't been authorised to provide you with that level of information at this stage."

Over all their years of knowing each other, Yorick had constantly wondered where Huang sat on the food chain. He was enigmatic in his secrecy. He'd hoped this trip might provide clarity. "So, when do I get approval?"

Huang had made his way back to his desk but refused to sit. He offered his hand towards Yorick and invited him to take the chair opposite. "It is the hexagons, the big fish corporations, we need to discuss today. They are where we need to focus. Triangles do not currently concern us."

"Spare me the geometry lesson, Huang. We can talk phase two when you've explained phase one to me." He turned to the door and found it filled with a familiar shape. The shape of the man who met his gaze eye to eye.

Yorick sensed that the etiquette of the conversation had turned to unchartered waters for him. Huang removed his jacket slowly, draping it on the back of his chair. He lowered into his seat and smoothed his tie. Satisfied, he said, "You are not yet at that stage of our path together, Yorick. What separates our culture from yours is the ability to embrace the unknowns of the journey with dignity. And venture together without knowing, but trusting in the way itself."

Yorick gritted his teeth in a flash of emotion. "Forgive me, Huang, but I'm going to need something more concrete than a promise of a journey. I'm about to gift wrap and hand to you the data of millions of private citizens in one of the wealthiest economies in the West. But I need a show of faith from you."

Huang studied him. Yorick's attempts to restrain the frustrated energy within were failing; it seeped from every pore across the desk. But he would hear him out. What he was offering was worth it. "What did you have in mind, Yorick? You seem to have come here with a plan."

Yorick dropped himself into the chair opposite Huang. As he did so, he felt the burden of the past weeks and months collapse into him. An involuntary spasm of his right leg, causing it to straighten in front of him, reminded him of why he was here today. Dr. Feinstein's words rocketed through his brain once more; *We cannot say when, but there will be cognitive impairment in time, Yorick. The physical tremors are the first signs of the neurological damage. But you need to tell me if you feel that you're struggling to concentrate, or have difficulty focusing as it might be a sign that the disease is progressing more quickly.*

Circles. Hexagons. Triangles. Yorick willed himself to fix Huang with a confident stare.

"My firm is the best at what is does in London. You know how powerful it is, it's why you came to me. And that power has only grown, because of my work. Our relationship. But I can only take us so far as a junior partner." Yorick gripped the armrests of the chair as the words fell from his mouth with no emotion.

"Go on, Yorick. What is it you need from me?"

"It's what I can give you, Huang. If you buy us out, and install me as CEO, there's no limit to what we can achieve. We'd have influence across all the sectors that control decisions across the UK; business, healthcare, government - you name it. We can control it all."

The top of Huang's head pressed against the headrest of his chair. A single wisp of hair was standing upright, pointing to the picture of the sage in the forest above him. Yorick's focus broke for a second as he started at the path before the mystical man in the painting. It no longer unnerved him.

He looked back at Huang, who was watching him with a thin smile. "And what will become of Sam, your mentor? He won't go quietly."

Yorick paused for a beat. Memories of his formative years flicked before him, but it was Sam's voice on the phone from the previous day that held firm. "Do what needs to be done. This is my time."

Tobi. Tuesday. Morning.

Clara knew they should have driven. She glanced down at her watch; 09.32. Ninety seconds until the train doors closed. Two minutes until departure. She refused to look along the platform to see if he was running the length of it. Life stopped imitating the movies after the umpteenth viewing. And for someone who kept his affairs in order, Tobi's inability to be on time for public transport was the one thing Clara allowed herself to get annoyed about.

In response, she pulled out an antique makeup mirror from her purse. It was round with brass edges and a faded turquoise material inlay. Within the blue was an embroidered image of Canterbury cathedral. Her grandmother had made it, passed to her mother and then to her. Her predecessors had always taken pride in their appearances. "It's what keeps us out of the gutter and away from the kitchen." Her mother's words rang in her ears. She'd ensured her life had contained little of either. But that had nothing to do with her looks and everything to do with rejecting that notion. There were now less than sixty seconds until the doors closed. No frantic footsteps, yet.

The mirror opened with a sharp click as she began a leisurely inspection. She arched her eyebrows. They were thick and dark and contained a wildness that needed only a hint of taming to fall back in line. She ran the middle finger of her left hand across the top of each, smoothing away non-existent miscreants. Her lips mirrored her eyebrows, differing only in colour. Packed with moisture, a sombre shade of red held them back. A swift dab of her naked left index finger to the corner of her mouth satisfied her tinkering. She snapped the mirror's hinge. It was a failed attempt to mask the clattering of the train doors closing on Tobi's forearm.

"Godammit, I'm here, I'm here!" Tobi's flushed face followed his arm into the carriage. "Damn things never run on time."

She knew it was futile arguing over things that would never change.

"Coffee's on the way, and your eggs. Oh, and don't forget to brush off your sleeve."

"Thanks," he said with his tongue caught between his teeth. He ran his hand along his arm, loosening the specs of dust deposited there from the door, and settled into the seat opposite her. His feet brushed her black-stockinged legs as he shuffled into place. "Did I choose the right tie?"

A small lie. Sarah had chosen the tie. It was a dark purple with a single small black and white penguin on the bottom right of the main tongue. The colour was muted but different enough to be noticed. The penguin was an homage to Simon's love of the beaches of Southern Africa - his favourite holiday destination. It all came together well.

"Sarah has excelled herself once again," Clara said while tucking away her pocket mirror. Tobi's wife paid close attention to the details. What you might expect from a dutiful spouse, she'd credit her with that.

The arrangements were made swiftly following the news of Simon's indiscretions. The front pages of the newspapers died down in a day. Just like they always did. The news of another member of the *nouveau riche* getting caught up in extra martial activities had long since lost its ability to shock. But the front pages weren't what Tobi, Clara, and West & West were worried about. Over the three days since the news broke, they had scanned the financial section of London's most prominent news sources, digital and physical. Tobi's public response and statement had hit the right notes. After an initial wobble, the markets had accepted his installation as interim head of the new pharmaceutical juggernaut, following Simon's resignation in disgrace.

The train jolted and veered as it wormed its way out of King's Cross station and headed north. It traversed the tracks before settling on its accepted path and into its rhythm up to Leicester.

"Coffee with milk 'n sugar?" said an eager server, rolling the 'r' with a West Country lilt. Clara offered a polite smile to the grey-haired man, who paused before placing it down in front of her. "The hard stuff must be for you then, sir," he said placed a steaming hot cup of black coffee in front of Tobi. "And the eggs, soft".

"Perfect, thanks," said Tobi, his tongue trapped once more. They waited for him to shuffle down the carriage. Tobi peered over his shoulder, checking that any other passenger requests wouldn't stall him. He scanned the other end of the carriage, but Clara stopped him.

"We're alone, don't worry," said Clara. She doubted Tobi ever wondered how they always had an empty carriage to themselves. Of all the trains that ran across the UK on any day, the chances of them happening upon a completely empty one were next to none. But for it to happen each time on one of these trips? Impossible. He'd never mentioned it. All she could be sure of was that the partners of West & West seldom asked questions when Clara put together their travel arrangements.

Tobi's focus switched back to their table as he dived into his eggs. Between mouthfuls, he ran through conversations with their lawyers from the preceding days.

Due to the public nature of the incident, the board had gotten twitchy feet over Simon's position as CEO. As the prepared to go public the following year, a scandal was the last thing they needed. Their lawyers had advocated for his immediate removal and a replacement sought. In the interim, they had signed over interim control of the company to the person listed on the founding agreement, Tobias van den Berg.

"There was one other thing that they mentioned", said Tobi, as he placed the small metal knife and fork either side of the last mouthful of egg. "They brought up NanoTech."

"We knew we had to expect that," said Clara. Her lips tightened.

A silence descended on the table. Scandal had plagued West & West in the past and hung above them once more. The carriage shook from left to right while cloaking them in darkness as they passed through a tunnel. The light and smooth passage returned just as quickly as it had disappeared.

Simon wasn't the only ambitious, young business leader that had fallen foul of temptation while under Tobi's watchful eye.

Rubin Thomas had latched onto the nanotechnology scene early. He had been an avid computer-game fan in the early 80s, much like Tobi. His fandom had started with the small scrolling creatures of Space Invaders; little green, irregularly shaped 8-Bit images that twitched across black and green screens. That first enthusiasm had morphed into adventurous first-person shoot-'em-up games, like Wolfenstein and Doom, hunting haunting creatures through abandoned locations. As they got older, the characters he and Rubin were drawn to weren't fighting aliens any more, but rather dysfunctional systems. By then, Rubin was turning his passion into his work. He was a natural coder and one of the early minds to predict the growth in motherboards. Or rather, the shrinking of them. As they got smaller and smaller over the coming years, Rubin's appetite for testing technology advancements had grown unabated. His passion was in squeezing more and more out of what technology could achieve as it shrank in size. He had been one of the first to set up a nanotechnology firm before the rest of the world even had a name for it; he'd just needed them to catchup.

"Explain it to me like I'm a 5-year-old," Tobi remembered saying to Rubin and his team at their first meeting over a decade ago. He had been Tobi's second client, and the excitement and passion he had brought to the project had dragged everyone along for the ride. The early days were exciting and full of possibilities. But as the years rolled on, his inability to remain satisfied with evolutions in computing technology exploded beyond the realms of the everyday world.

They'd set up their factory on the outskirts of London's major motorway, the M25, in the sleepy commuter town of Slough. But Rubin's eyes became fixated on sights beyond that circular stretch of asphalt. Over time, he took more trips, further afield, claiming them as research endeavours.

"There's no sensible reason for him to be in Azerbaijan." Clara had only been days into the job, but it was the first time she'd made Tobi sit up and take notice. As it transpired, she'd been looking into Rubin from the get go and had discovered that he'd been meeting with an assortment of characters on a spate of unscheduled trips across the globe.

Rubin had an infectious personality, she'd admitted, and it attracted all types. But it also meant that he rarely stopped to check and reference those who entered his circle of influence. That circle spun out into a web and Rubin was left in the middle. He'd found himself staring out at a set of military strategists based in Eastern Europe. He'd been approached, wined and tempted by local flavours of every choice until he was happy to accept their crisp, too clean cash in exchange for military-grade weapons technology. Nanotechnology was simply the next step for the people he had met in what would form the basis of a new breed of warfare in the age to come. For some people, there will never be enough, Tobi remembered thinking at the time; be it money, power, influence.

Once Tobi learned of these developments, he took a particular interest in another hobby of Rubin's - poker. Tobi always tried to be helpful. So much so that he didn't hesitate to introduce Rubin to a close friend of his who could get him into the hottest game going in London. This connection was a genuine salt of the earth type of guy. That side of him shone through in the regularity of his name. Mikey.

Tobi had known Rubin well enough, worked with him in close enough quarters, to understand the addictiveness of his personality. It was the driving force behind his success, perhaps honed in those early days of basic video games. But he knew the allure of gambling would hold a powerful grip over him. And it hadn't taken long for Rubin to overextend himself when surrounded by true sharks of the game.

Word got back to Tobi, through Mikey, that his business partner was making all the wrong enemies in all the wrong places in London's gambling scene. He was wracking up debts, and late on payments, and making outrageous promises that he had no hope of keeping. He needed to be bailed out, for his own good. And removed from the temptation of London. He didn't have the strength to deal with it all. Tobi knew that was true from the moment he found out about the weapons contracts in Eastern Europe. If only Rubin had been strong enough to resist temptation, then Tobi wouldn't have had to get Mikey involved.

It hadn't been hard for Mikey to gather all the evidence - video, financial and anecdotal - that Tobi needed to confront Rubin. His long-time partner crumbled in the face of it. But Tobi offered him a way out, buying him out of his portion of the business in exchange for him removing himself from the company. And London. He'd accepted.

From there, Tobi had moved to cut all ties with the company's contact in the murkier reaches of Europe, to right its path once more.

"And? What did they say about NanoTech?" Clara had removed a small black notepad from her bag and sat poised with a compact ballpoint pen as she spoke.

"They expressed their concern at how disconcerting it must be for two scandals to occur under our watch. 'Unfortunate', was the word they used." Tobi pushed the plate to the edge of their small shared table. "And then asked how I was coping with such an expanded portfolio beneath my control."

Clara nodded and said, "And? How are you coping, Tobi?"

His eyes flicked to the window beside them, letting the green fields filled with grazing sheep wash over him for a moment. He turned to her. "Don't worry. I remembered the script. I walked them through the separate companies we have set up to dissolve the original organisations into. They agreed that new management for HEAL-y seemed the best start for all concerned. On an interim basis, of course. Before we find a suitable, permanent replacement."

The train bounced along the tracks. It was the only sound that filled the carriage for a long tick of time. Clara broke the silence. "You know what I'm going to say, Tobi. You're taking on too much. You have to let go of something."

He looked from the window to her. He felt himself searching her face for an answer. But he didn't know the question he needed to ask.

The train resumed its rhythm along the tracks, rolling onwards as it swayed and rocked.

Tobi. Tuesday. Noon.

Clara and Tobi boarded the train in Leicester for the return leg of their journey. Clara pressed ahead and sat at the middle table of the carriage. It was once again clear, like the rest. Tobi removed his jacket and dropped it onto the seat across the aisle from him. He folded his tie on top of it and remained standing. The train jerked as it pulled away from the station. Tobi rode the sudden movement without losing balance. He began a rhythmic pacing of four steps forward and four back.

"This feels different," he said.

The encounter with Simon's wife, Jennifer, had caught him off-guard. He hadn't expected it to be her that opened the door when their taxi pulled up at Simon's sprawling home in the secluded suburb of Rothley, north of the city centre. But in hindsight, it made sense. He hadn't been there for days, perhaps longer.

She had opened the door, a large wooden thing, to its full width, and stood alongside it in a firm stance with her hands bunched together. Her flowing, curly red hair and emerald eyes issued a challenge to them; she wouldn't be the one to break the silence.

Tobi greeted her, and asked how she and the kids were doing. She invited them in, while keeping her answers short and to the point. She stressed the importance of routine, and that she was thankful that they were at their school's lodgings. She gave away nothing as to her true feelings. They stood in a huddle in the middle of a large atrium. The light thrown down from the ceiling played with the sparse decorations of the space, casting shadows and blurs all about them. Jennifer was standing in the middle of a ray of sunlight, its beams illuminating a trail of fine dust in the air as it lit up her hair. The small talk subsided, and she would not bring up her husband.

The grandness of Simon's home stood in stark contrast to both his and Tobi's upbringings. It filled the space around them with a sullen irony. They had both come from humble backgrounds. He remembered them sharing the stories of their single-parent households. Tobi had his father, while Simon had relied on his mother. But it was the work ethics of their parents that had united them.

Tobi's father, Pieter, had struggled for years as a middling east London bookkeeper to make a life for his boys. But any time that he had to spare, he would tinker at creating the perfect child's toy. It was his deluded dream that if he could just perfect that toy, that riches would follow. The world would never run out of one thing; children needing to play. It meant that his own children saw precious little chance to play with their own father. But he did it, thought Tobi. He succeeded where so many others failed. That toy got made, and it sold, by the millions. And gave Tobi this life; the chance to find himself in a home like this. Hell, to own one not too dissimilar.

His argument with Sarah over dinner the previous week came flooding back to him. Was he destined to follow the same path that his father had before him? He thought of Lily and her earthworms. His failure to record them for her, though he promised he would. He reflected on the pressures that his life had created for him. The ones that they had created for Simon. And how men act when pressed by stresses they can't articulate. He thought of Simon and Jennifer's two children, who must wonder when their father might return home. If ever.

The sound of Clara's voice shook him from his runaway train of thought, bringing him back to within Simon's grand walls.

"Sorry for imposing. We've been trying to track down Simon. Only he wasn't at his office," said Clara. She knew Tobi's silences inside out, but when he indulged in them around strangers, they left her feeling uncomfortable. And with a need to fill them.

"You won't find him here," she replied in a definitive tone. "God knows where he's hiding but I imagine what's left of his family would know a few good spots."

Her green eyes appeared grey in the sunbeam's inconsistent light. Jennifer had been happy for Simon to leave behind what, in her eyes, was a history of petty criminals and welfare indulgers. Simon had put up little resistance. Tobi had spent enough time in the house to know that family photos of Simon's side were stashed in obscure corners of their home. He flicked his gaze to a dark nook over her shoulder where one used to lie, but saw it now had a fresh vase of colourful flowers in its place.

"We won't keep you any longer, Jen," said Tobi, meeting her eyes but turning away from them straight away.

She eyed him before she spoke again. "I spoke with our lawyers yesterday. They said that you had been in touch regarding control of the company."

"Yes, I hope that wasn't too intrusive, but given the, uh, delicate state of where we find ourselves, I thought it best to make a short-term call." When had Jennifer last blinked? "Of course, the interim control of the company will only last until the next meeting of the board. It's then that we'll be able to make formal decisions about the future of the company." Jennifer knew this already. Simon had signed the company into her name when they'd started out as a way of separating their financial assets. Despite Tobi's urgings, he'd never changed it.

"Very kind. You've always taken such an interest in us, Tobi." Had she finally blinked as she spoke? She must have. Or was Tobi's mind playing tricks on him? She continued, "But I rather think I might want to rid myself of the whole thing. Think about a fresh start." She trailed off with her words and at last lowered her gaze to her hands, which were clasped together, fingers out and pointed downward.

In any other setting, the silence would have begged to be filled. But within the open air of the hall and falling light, it settled itself on the floor. It lay under Jennifer's downward pointed fingers. Until it lifted its head and nodded to Clara.

"I'll schedule an appointment with your team to discuss this further, Mrs. Pentworth."

Jennifer raised her head and met Clara's gaze with a fullness one might reserve for sweeping panoramas. "Please. And I won't be going by 'Mrs' any more."

Tobi stalked to his seat while the train ratcheted sideways, gaining pace over the tracks.

"What am I missing, Clara?" He looked up with wide eyes, palms held out across the table towards her. "Why was she so quick to make up her mind? How did she seem so calm? And why the fuck does she never blink?"

Clara left him to reel while she composed her thoughts. The train had slowed to crawling speed, dragging itself through a station that it wasn't scheduled to stop at, and hauled its weight across the tracks one rotation at a time. After a minute, she felt the renewed press of her back into the cushioned seat as the metallic beast gained force once more.

"She's angry. Somewhat at you," she said before adding more quietly,

"She couldn't care less about me. She expects me to do what I'm told behind the scenes." She took a breath, her hands balling up, and continued, "But mostly she's angry with him. With an anger that has been there for a long time. Since well before he stepped into that lorry's cabin. But-" she paused, "- something about what's coming has excited her."

"Excited her?" Tobi's arms crossed over his chest as he slumped back into his seat. His right eyebrow arched upwards. Clara couldn't help but think of a hapless puppy trying to puzzle something through. She resisted the urge to smile and pat his head.

"Yes. The way she held her hands together, pointed down. She was controlling them."

Tobi nodded slowly. "Uh huh...to stop them shaking? I don't blame her given the situation."

"No. Controlling them from raising up too quickly. They were held down, not clasped together."

Tobi's face bunched together, full of uncertainty. "And what does that mean?"

"Trust me, Tobi. She's hiding something."

"And do we need to be worried about what she's hiding?"

"That's the part I'm not sure about, yet."

This was no way to run a multi-million-pound business. Hand gestures, grey eyes, the trickery of light within a hall. None of it had any place in the world of high-flying venture capital. In that world, he preferred to be the turnstile operator at the fair ground. He was happy to let others board the rides while he sat at the entrance, deciding who got on and when they got off. But that was why he had Clara. Because when fresh problems kicked off outside the fair ground, he needed someone he could trust to step in and quieten them down.

The train pulled into the station at King's Cross. Tobi needed to figure out this mess, but first, he needed to visit somewhere he knew was pulling him in. Somewhere he didn't visit often enough, but always when he needed clarity.

Tobi. Tuesday. Afternoon.

A light rain fell from the high, white clouds. The drops worked their way through Tobi's hair and into his scalp. He glanced up and ran his fingers through his styled mop. He felt the moisture soaking through the knees of his suit trousers as he pressed them into the turf below.

Crumbling walls covered in green ivy surrounded him. Behind him lay the central knave of what was once a grand old church in the middle of London. Bombed during the second World War, it was left in this damaged state; missing a roof, but with most of its walls still standing. There had once been plans to restore it to its former glories, but a combination of uncertainty, hesitation and bureaucracy had seen lengths of green vines take control instead. They crept and rolled over each crevice, abandoned window and gaping doorway, determining their own paths across the once sturdy structure. It was hauntingly beautiful to Tobi.

He was in a small courtyard to the right of the main building. In front of him lay a simple bouquet. It comprised just one type of flower: bright, bulbous yellow tulips inside thin green veils, its flowers on the cusp of breaking through. Above them was a small, faded and weather-beaten brass plate that was screwed into the wall. The screws themselves were uneven, secured by hesitant hands. On it, an inscription: *Here lies Monique van den Berg. Wife of Pieter and mother to Tobias and Yorick. Missed by all. 1959 - 1987.*

His mother's ashes were in a small red clay urn buried a few inches into the soil. On it, her first name was inscribed on the outside in white handwritten paint. It wasn't the original resting place of the urn, but it had become her final one. After their father died, Tobi had moved her ashes to this treasured spot, away from Plaistow Park. That had never been home to her.

He thought back to how, in the years after she disappeared, one of the few activities that he and his brother shared with their father was to walk through the streets of Plaistow. It took took them past the local crematorium. She had officially been taken from them at that site. Tobi and Yorick hadn't been allowed to attend that day. Their father had forbidden it. In the months that followed, Pieter relocated them to that intimate community. Perhaps he felt closer to her there; if he did, he never admitted it to them.

Tobi touched the metal plaque and wiped away the drops of rain that had gathered across the letters of her name. The reflection of the tulips in the dulled brass reminded him of their childhood home in Den Bosch. It had been a simple, two bedroomed terraced structure. Alongside their blue front door, their mum, known as Kikki to most, had hung a simple plaque. It was the colour of a rusty clay. She had brought its earthy redness to life with greens and yellows of acrylic paint. Thin, pointed leaves reached upwards towards petals at their tips, as if reaching towards the sun. It was a delicate depiction of a simple tulip in full bloom and had the number 24 stencilled alongside it. All by his mother's hand, all those years ago.

That home held only a few memories for Tobi, but they were strong ones. He remembered Kikki's long, dark and thick hair that fell in great volumes of curls around her shoulders. Like a velvet blanket, he would bury his small head amongst it, engulfed by her flowing locks.

He cried a lot when he was young. He had been a child prone to searching. Sometimes it was among the small stones of their little front yard. Hands dragging across alternating smooth and jagged stones, sifting and sorting for the feel of wriggling worms or the coolness of the first shoots of spring weeds. The textures of the dirt that filled those precious years with his mother had stayed with him. The days of wandering fingers and toes finding something alive were good ones. But the failed pursuits that yielded only cold and dry trails of nothingness led him to seek the comfort of his mother's embrace.

From what he remembered, Kikki's hands and fingers were always busy. They always moved with a purpose, whittling away at objects to create something unique. Sometimes her tools of choice were hard, pointed needles that worked feverishly among soft strands of thread. At other times, a robust wooden-handled knife ground away at a piece of timber that she had found in the nearby forest. Transformations took place quickly; from a forgotten and discarded piece of family furniture into a charming resemblance to a woodland creature, a mouse or rabbit, that could be sold to a family with a small child of their own. Amongst all the activity, though, there was one constant that could force those hard but supple fingers to pause and put down their tools. The sight of Tobi running towards her, hands stained with spots of dirt, and eyes that were wobbling.

Yorick had been born eighteen months after Tobi. By comparison, he had been a quiet and cautious baby. Unusually so, many of the neighbours had said. Tobi had assumed the role of noisemaker for both. Their father, Pieter, had worked tirelessly in their hometown. He was the only recognised bookkeeper in the small district and his work was unglamourous, for little reward. The sight of him hunched over a small desk was a common one, alongside the light of a small lamp and the shadow of his pen and papers moving on the walls. Frustrated and furious, the actions were all too often in direct contrast to those of their mother's. But then, as the industries had closed around them, the papers had grown less. His pen had lain still for extended, barren periods. The rapid privatisation of companies across the Netherlands in the 80s saw the smaller provincial towns, like theirs, struggle to keep pace as the big centres grew away from the rest of the country.

He ran his hand back across the plaque, removing the fresh batch of rain droplets that had gathered around his mother's name. They fell from his fingers like cold tears and his mind flashed back once more. But not to the touch of the earth or soft curls of dark hair.

The piercing cuts of hard whispers and sharp emotions were rarely heard within those tulip-decorated walls of Tobi's youth. But in the months before they left their homeland, they had crept through the floorboards incessantly. Their parents railed against each other for weeks. It happened over the remnants of a meagre dinner once the boys were in bed. By the time the sun had shone with the warmth of Spring, their little family was packing up that small house, with its garden of hidden treasures in the dirt.

They gathered what they could fit into the small suitcases they owned. The furniture stayed. As did the needlework, ornaments and assorted crafts that had remained unsold at the local markets in the months before. They bundled their suitcases towards Amsterdam's port, loaded them onto the boats and set course for Dover in the month of May 1985, in the hopes of better times.

Back in the church's yard, an icy wind had worked itself around Tobi's shoulders. It sent a shiver down his spine, and he plunged his hands into the pockets of his trousers. His fingers stroked a carved child's toy in his left pocket. The smoothness of the cool wood brought a quietness to Tobi while the rain grew heavier on his back. He flexed the movable limbs of the figure, feeling a strain of resistance as the bolted elbow joint of the otherwise anonymous figure flexed under the pressure of his fingers. He pulled the toy from his pocket and touched it to the tulips. The green heads, with their shy flowers tucked inside, now sat bowed under the weight of the rainwater accumulating within them. He rotated the figure upwards, head over heel, until the feet were visible to him. There, printed in plain black ink and stained onto the soul of the right foot were the words blazoned on his mind; "Pieter's Play. Established, 1988."

This particular figurine was eight years old. It had come off the production line in May 2012, nine weeks before the birth of Tobi's daughter. The supple, in parts, yet firm toy had taken the world of child rearing by storm in the early 2000s. Child psychologists had attributed its calming powers to the softness of the wood balanced against the strength of resistance that lay within its moveable limbs. Small inquisitive hands fiddled and twisted for hours on end, interwoven with bouts of smoothing and caressing for the minutes of boredom that lay in-between. Yorick and Tobi's father had poured more than a decade of all of their lives into creating it. And then almost a decade more after its launch.

Around the height of the toy's success, newspaper articles carried the story that it was the memory of his departed wife that gave him the strength to persevere. Others hypothesised it was raising two sons alone that led to him finding that perfect blend. Tobi knew the story better than anyone. It was his stubborn nature, something he knew he had inherited. But buying the company eight years ago had meant he'd gone from being at the heart of that story, whatever the truth of it was, to owning it.

The gate to the old courtyard creaked against the patter of the rain. Two sets of shoes crunched on the gravel path in the far-left corner from Tobi. He slid the toy back into his pocket, brushed his knees free of the scraps of grass that had gathered, and tucked the flowers up against the brass plate. He wiped the cool metal one last time as he mouthed a plea for forgiveness to no one in particular. The gravel twisted beneath his feet as he made his way past the strangers and out into the cavernous mouth of London's banking district.

Tobi. Tuesday. Early Evening.

Scents of Spring filled the London April air. As quickly as the clouds had gathered, they were lifting and fleeing the scene.

The moment his foot hit the pavement outside the church's ground, Tobi removed his smartphone from his pocket and flicked through his contacts. The name he needed was near the top of his 'Recent' list. His hand moved to the text message icon and his fingers pecked out a brief message.

THE TRACK. ONE HOUR.

He snatched a parting glance at the church's grey bricks, speckled with green vines as they tangled their way towards the light wherever they could. He hadn't bothered to return the phone to his pocket. As his gaze trailed up towards the sky, he felt a ping in his hand. He glanced down at the screen and saw what he expected.

A single letter response, K.

He stowed his phone and set off south towards the Thames river. He let his feet guide him as his mind noticed his body passing Old Billingsgate, a grand old fish market.

The smells of shorn fish guts, scales and flesh had left the area in the early 80s to move east to the Docklands. The original Billingsgate fish market had been on the banks of the Thames between two of the capital's most famous bridges, Tower and London Bridge. The market had been forced from the area by the finance houses once Tobi was born. The hard-working fish mongers were forced to find somewhere else to set up shop every morning before the sun rose. They moved three miles east to the area known as Poplar, close to Canary Wharf.

At the time, the land was cheap. It had taken a hammering during the blitz of the Second World War and had been ignored since. That made it affordable for an immigrant family of four from the Netherlands. Tobi had grown up with the zingy aromas of fish filling his nostrils in the morning. The sounds of stall owners setting up for the day woke Tobi and his younger brother every morning of those first two years in London. Those were the days before they'd needed to move even further east to Plaistow - when there was just one earner in the family.

Each morning, when he would wander into the kitchen bleary-eyed, his father and mother had long since beaten the fish mongers to starting their days. He'd find them tinkering away at something in silence. His mother focused on painting and restoration. His father whittled away at pieces of wood and links of metal. They would fashion something that would be handed to Tobi and Yorick to play with. If they took to it, they'd make more and move into the markets to sell what they could. Then his father went to the first of his jobs at the surrounding businesses. He would visit three to four, checking in on their finances, signing off invoices and clearing cheques, allowing the traders to focus on the dealings of the day. After a few hours at the local nursery school, Tobi and his brother would spend most of their days with their mother. Late at night, Pieter would return, eat a simple supper that Kikki had prepared, and head to bed soon after. Only for the routine to begin again the next day. Tobi thought things might change after his mother was gone, and was surprised that they didn't.

The smells weren't the only thing that Tobi grew up around in those early years. All around the lands of Canary Wharf, buildings had sprung upwards. Unlike the weeds that Tobi used to forage among while he looked for worms, the buildings proved far more robust. They grew in large numbers, spurred on by each other to greater heights. He would track their growth at the start of each school holiday. During those breaks, his father sent him out in the early hours of the morning to find odd-jobs with the local sellers. Their single father had always impressed upon them that everyone needed to do what they could to contribute to the family. Maybe it was a few pennies one day, or a free fish the next; it all counted.

On his way, he took stock of the towers that had shot up in the previous weeks. They fascinated him, causing him to wonder as to what activities could need so much size and space. When he found a task for the morning, he'd look at the tables before him, in and among the discards of hake tails, salmon guts and cod heads and remember how little room they needed for someone to hand over hard-earned money and get sustenance in return. But the buildings continued to grow and influence his life. He took comfort in the cooling touch of the concrete. Their smooth, untainted walls drew his wandering hands to them. The firmness that met his fingers, as they ran along for yard after unbroken yard, calmed him before he headed over to the stalls for the morning. Once there, his fingernails were filled with slippery scales as he shifted fish from counter to counter, running down the seconds until he could feel the unshifting concrete on his way home. He thought of his daughter once more, before his mind came back to the present day.

He turned away from the old fish market and towards the river. He followed the road until it broke onto London Bridge itself, crossing over the waters of the Thames, and hurried across the bridge. A set of stairs led him into the underground system, where he jumped on the silver Jubilee Line. He continued past his favoured Green Park and all the way north to Baker Street. He popped out onto busy streets, continued further north and found the canal system that tracked through the north edge of the city. Another staircase took him to the water's edge. As he drew level with the canal, he slowed his gait. A walk that should take him fifteen minutes gained an extra ten. He adjusted to the new rhythm as he made his way east. The odd ambler came and went. He trained his eyes on the water as he walked, thinking.

At the north end of Regent's Park, alongside a canal, lay The Track. It was a cinder running path with long straights followed by tight bends. A favourite of over worked city executives looking for a quick blow-out.

Tobi made his way to the centre. He looked around as the first of the post-work warriors limbered up under the trees alongside the pressed dirt surface. A pair of feet was making its way around at a constant pace. Tobi followed the movements of a heavy-set woman in her late thirties while he waited, his gaze fixed on her feet as they prodded their way towards the first of the bends. It wasn't long before a figure joined him in the middle.

A short man pulled up alongside him. Tobi spoke first. "Mikey. Our last project - we're not done."

"You heard something?" Mikey said, pronouncing each word.

"Not yet. But something doesn't feel right. And we need to make sure we're ahead of it, so that we don't hear anything. It's the wife. I need you to do a full history," continued Tobi as his eyes focused on the now empty corner of the track.

"The redhead? Alright. It'll be extra on top of what we already did for the main job."

"We'll pay. And I need it quickly." He felt Mikey's shoulders hunch up and down alongside him in an exaggerated physical tick. The corner of the track was filled by the same heavy-set woman, rounding it at an increasing pace.

"I can get you something tomorrow," said Mikey, a hint of hesitation in his voice. "How quiet do we need to be on this one?"

"More so than usual. Keep your distance for now. No unnecessary risks."

The little man ran his fingers through a head of thinning hair that was styled bolt upright at the fringe. The only quirk of an otherwise unremarkable appearance. With his other hand, he brought an electronic cigarette to his lips and took three quick jabs. He exhaled before he continued, punching the words out in a slight stammer. "Nothing definitive came up in the briefing work we did on her. But we found interesting links to a government agency. Surprised us. Unrelated to the husband."

"Government agencies? Which ones?"

Mikey toed the ground, working his shoe in small circles as if putting out an imaginary cigarette. "She was a caterer. Figured she used some of her fella's money to land her something sweet in the public sector. Enough fat to keep everyone well fed and better paid in those circles. But she had plenty of correspondence that went above and beyond a supplier's duty. Minister of Health is involved."

Tobi heard the methodical thudding once more cascading into his right ear. He thought his mind must be playing tricks on him, but the woman was there again, going faster and faster towards the bend. Things weren't as he'd thought this evening.

"As early as you can tomorrow, Mikey," he said as he moved off, leaving behind a pair of twitchy feet and a thinning cloud of raspberry scented smoke.

Yorick. Tuesday. Night.

Rikki pushed the main door of The Rams & Lion and felt it click into place with a little encouragement from her shoulder. Gabbi emerged from behind the bar with a broom. The shards from a broken glass lay at her feet.

"Won't be a minute, Riks," she sighed. "Why do they always wait until the end of the night to smash the glasses?"

"Most likely time, luv. Makes it easier for me to get them out the door, mind."

Gabbi gathered the shards into a neat pile as Rikki came around with the pan. Together, they dragged and harried the pieces together, ready to be cast out into the bins out back. It was a Tuesday night, about to turn Wednesday morning. Gabbi seldom felt exhausted, but tonight she did. Trying to keep a London pub running had taken its toll. The incessant thirst of the city had lapped at her like a drunk sips late night whiskey; relentlessly and without stopping to count the number of times the glass had been topped up. She watched Rikki slip through the back door and reminded herself that she wouldn't survive without her. She wouldn't have accepted the pub from her foster father if Rikki hadn't been part of the deal. She had made the hard toil bearable.

The door clanged shut behind the pub's matriarch as she re-emerged next to the bar. "How'd it go tonight?"

It had been a 'new material' night for Gabbi and those in the basement. The members of her group were all chasing the same dream of one day beating the odds and making it as a paid comedian. Gabbi believed that if you stood up in front of people, on a stage, and attempted to make them laugh, you could call yourself one. That first brave step earned you that right, regardless of whether anyone found it funny. It was in the trying. She had learned not to trust every laugh, too. Alcohol, stress relief from a work day, attempts to impress first dates and remorseful thoughts all created mirth in that room. But sometimes the comedian was the sole source. She knew the laughs weren't always all about her, in the same way that the hanging silences weren't either. New material nights were a free hit. A night spent with fellow strugglers. They were all secure, knowing that it was a testing ground to see what landed and what missed. It was a rare chance to take a plunge, knowing there were others around you waiting to pull you to the surface.

"There's something in there. It was refreshing to break away from politics," said Gabbi, as she reflected on the six minutes she'd delivered earlier. Most of her routines centred on scathing social commentaries, but for this week she'd allowed herself to wander off on a tangent. She had enjoyed herself.

"Referencing 80s kid's cartoons was something different," said Rikki, smiling to herself as she lifted chairs and placed them on the tables. Gabbi expanded her broom sweeping landscape to cover the areas vacated by the chair legs.

"He-Man was just the most wonderfully ridiculous concoction, wasn't he? Big muscular stereotype, but with hair any woman would kill for." She ran her fingers through her own hair, smoothing down her natural curls. "And there he is, flaying danger while dressed in a loin cloth trying to sneak in as many dance-moves as possible along the way!" She punctuated her account with a waving of the broom and a jig of her hips. "Not to mention his sexually repressed yet fabulously skeletal arch-nemesis, Skeletor. It writes itself. Who could ever believe such a thing?" She looked up from the broom at the squat figure of Rikki, who had paused a few feet away, both legs of an upturned chair clasped in her hands above a table. Gabbi was used to Rikki's powerful use of silent moments, but hadn't expected this to be one of them. The spell broke as the seat of the chair clattered down with a bump onto the table's surface.

Rikki moved onto the next and last one. "Irony's always been at the heart of the best comedy. Tragedy, too, I guess," she added.

Gabbi followed up behind her as she finished the night's sweeping. "Be nice if it paid the bills. God knows there's plenty of irony rolling around for free out there." She looked up from the floor and rushed forward as she shouted into the empty bar, "Careful, Riks! God, are you alright?"

It had happened so quickly. The last chair had slipped from Rikki's grip as she'd raised it to the table, causing her to lose her balance and tumble to the floor alongside it. Within a moment, Gabbi was kneeling next to her, comforting her. Rikki tried to steady the shaking in her hands she knew wasn't from shock. She pressed them to the floor before allowing Gabbi to help her back to her feet. Gabbi righted the sideways chair and settled her into it. This was the first time she'd fallen in front of Gabbi. But she didn't want to cause her worry. It wasn't her burden to bear.

"I'm alright, hun. Thanks for the hand. You know me at my age, getting clumsier by the day. I'm alright. Honest."

Gabbi bent down alongside her and took her hands in her palms. She must have felt the twitching of her fingers. It would have been impossible not to. But she'd only assume it was the shock. "Honestly, I'm fine, love. That's why I keep a strong, young one like you around me."

A knocking on the front door interrupted them. The frosted central pane hid the identity of the knocker. A pair of flat shoulders filled the small square where a head might appear. Rikki paused as she looked at the door. "Speaking of which," she said, standing and moving towards it.

His knuckles rang from the rap on the door. His skin was always more sensitive when he was this tired. Yorick put it down to his own form of survival instinct. The entrance to The Rams & Lion remained closed.

But then the door emitted muffled sounds of struggle, and sprung open. Her cropped red hair appeared first as Rikki's eyes focused on the door jamb. They remained there as she spoke.

"We just closed up," she said, unsure whether to add to the sentence. She let her instincts guide her. "But what can we do for you, my young man?"

He wasn't in the habit of apologising at the outset. It was a local trait that he had tried to weed out of himself. But this time, he lost the battle and offered a soft response. "Sorry, yes. I... I just felt like some of that chicken." He, too, left his sentence hanging.

Rikki picked up the baton of what had become a stunted race. "Gabbi, I've got a confused young man here. He talks of chicken, but he looks for you. Can't imagine he's confused the two." Her reply was neutral, containing neither malice nor congeniality. Gabbi appeared from behind Rikki, glanced up at Yorick and then to his feet where a small bag lay.

An amused grin spread across her face, "A weary traveller seems to think he's found an inn," she joked to Rikki, while keeping her eyes locked on his tired face.

She fiddled with the gas knobs of the grill behind the counter. The cool, flat surface flared into life.

He took a seat at the table, facing the counter and its secret sauces that stared lazily back at him. His bag lay at his feet with his coat crumpled on top. The old fluorescent lights above flickered into action as they warmed up. The 'closed' sign faced out into the street, unchanged since Sunday night.

Gabbi splattered oil onto the metal plate and reached into the fridges below, pulling out a large tub of marinated chicken. She chose two quarter pieces with her fingers and dropped them onto the grill with a satisfying thud. They sizzled. She ran her hands under the tap and turned her attention to the array of spices that lay in front of her. She removed the lids of three of them. "Chicken is on you this time," she said. "Ten pounds to cover the food and late-night fee. And your story to take care of the labour."

He produced a half-laugh as he responded, "I'm not very good at stories."

She splattered and splashed her three chosen spices across the chicken pieces and they argued back at her with assorted fizzes. "I'll help. Where've you come from?"

He glanced down at the bag beside him. "China. It's already tomorrow morning there but somehow I haven't had today's lunch yet."

She flipped the chicken pieces over and viewed him through the glass partitioning erected on the countertop. "Not visiting family, I'm guessing?"

He laughed with her through the glass. "No, not visiting family. That's not much of a story."

"I'm cooking a suited stranger jerk chicken at- " she glanced at the old, tattered clock above his head, "- twelve past midnight on a Wednesday morning. Try me."

"My father raised the two of us - my brother and me." He undid his tie and added it to his heaped coat. "Back in those days, he was just a little bookkeeper in a small village." Yorick felt himself drifting into what felt like another life. The creeping sensation of self-indulgence washed over him as he spoke and, for once, he let the waves crash into him, flowing with not against them.

"He lived a steady but unspectacular life. He met and fell in love with our mother. And they tried their best to make a life together, I guess. But we always knew they struggled," he said into the table. "The sad irony was that he only made a success of himself after she was gone," he continued, tapping the table. "Still, it was a quiet and stable enough life."

Gabbi added strips of plantains to the grill. The chicken was pushed to the side, away from the flames. She grabbed two plates and flicked the fried fruit onto them before placing the quarter chickens on top. "I wouldn't knock a quiet and stable life. Try being born in Zimbabwe in the mid-nineties. We saw some things." She emptied the pre-cut mix of a simple lettuce and tomato salad alongside the chicken and brought the plates over. She placed the one that looked like it had a larger piece of chicken in front of Yorick and grabbed the tray of sauces. He eyed the cream coloured one with scepticism and reached for the red bottle.

"Thanks. Is that where your grandmother is from?"

"Grandmother?" she replied with a raised eyebrow.

"I assumed-"

"Rikki?" she said as her face split into a wide grin. She tore off a chunk of chicken at the same moment. "I guess she is like a grandmother to me, but her history is her own story. She keeps to herself, a free spirit, and I respect that." She shovelled a hot, wet piece of flesh into her mouth.

"And your parents?" he ventured. The second the words left his mouth, he regretted asking the question. As someone who'd lost his mother so early in life, he'd always had a sense of that sadness in others.

"Both dead," she said, staring at him, her eyes not running anywhere. "Zimbabwe was a violent place to grow up. It's why my parents moved me across here as soon as they could. Old family friends took me in and ended up fostering me." A small tear formed at the corner of her left eye, which she wiped away. "It took all their savings to do it just for me. They ended up paying a lot more for it." And there was the sadness. But laced with strength. She carried on picking away at the chicken, but at a slower rate.

"I'm sorry," he said, as they ate in silence for a few mouthfuls. "I lost mine, too. My mother a long time ago, when I was just a little boy. My father when I was a man, but a young one."

Minutes stretched out between them, but neither felt consumed by the awkwardness. The warmth of the spices filled Yorick's mouth and offered a soothing glow as they made their way down the back of his throat.

He picked up the only napkin on the table and slid it towards Gabbi. He reached to grab another from the counter, and a thought flew into his mind. "Want to go to China?"

Gabbi couldn't help but splutter out the last mouthful of spiced chicken. "-I'm-" she coughed, "- sorry. What?"

"China. Big country. Strict rules. Far, far away. That place."

"Cheers," she pinched the napkin and raised it to her mouth. "I know it."

"Go with me sometime?" His hands hovered, gripping the napkin halfway to his mouth, flecks of chicken skin hanging from his fingernails.

She finished wiping her mouth and folded the napkin before dropping it back onto her plate, watching it as it landed in a pile of the hot sauce. "This part of London is far enough east for people like me."

"People like who?"

She grabbed both of their plates and moved behind the counter, tipping them into the trash. "People who are happy in their place."

"I feel like I'm being put into mine," Yorick replied, flashing a quick grin through the glass shelving towards her. It hung in the air, unreturned.

Gabbi twisted and turned the edges of the garbage bag as she lifted it from within the bin's rigid metal casing. "I'm ok with where I am right now, Yorick - are you?" she said with a soft smile as she moved through the back door.

A sharp silence dropped around the small, forgettable little cafe. The smell of the blackened chicken skin on the grill hung in the air. Yorick stood and put his jacket on, straightened it at the front and buttoned the top button. He reached down and draped his coat over his left arm, and picked up his bag. He pulled himself up to his full height and squared his shoulders as Gabbi emerged through the back door.

"Go out with me then. I can pick somewhere closer than China," he said.

She didn't break stride and moved behind the counter, grabbing a blue washcloth on her way. She dampened it under the tap and turned to the grill, looking at him with her hand hovering above the warm surface.

"I try to avoid making decisions after midnight. They're usually no good," she said.

"I'm not very good at waiting. Stops me sleeping," he said, shifting his weight to his right foot and drooping his shoulders as he did so. She dropped her hand to the surface and began working at the gristle and grit with the damp cloth. Her eyes remained fixed on him.

"That shouldn't be a problem on a stomach full of London's best chicken," she said at last, smiling as she turned to rinse the dirtied rag.

"Alright," he said, "can I at least get your number. In case of an emergency?"

She expelled a short, gruff laugh and looked down at the griddle and the smooth concentric pattern she'd been making in the grease. "Huh. And what kind of emergency could a girl like me solve for a man like you?"

He paused, still stooped. "Needing a laugh?" he said, but with no hint of a smile.

The wiping paused. The stillness of the moment settled between them once more.

Gabbi broke it. "The number on the flyer in the window is mine." She went to wet the cloth once more from the tap.

He turned to the window, seeing only the white on the back of the leaflet. He spun back with a fifty-pound note in his hand and tucked it under the corner of the rack of hot sauces on their table. He called out over his shoulder as he made his way out. "Thanks for the chicken. Another life saved."

She wiped down the grid once more, satisfied with her efforts. "Goodnight, Yorick," she said as the door closed behind him.

She watched as he took his phone out, noted the number, nodded at her once with that blank expression that she'd come to recognise, and moved off into the night. As she brought her gaze back down to the counter, she caught sight of the orange note on the table. She moved over to collect it, paused with it in her hand, before slipping it into her pocket and flicking the light switch, showering the little cafe in darkness for another night.

Tobi. Wednesday. Early Morning.

Tobi emerged from the sloped exit of Green Park's underground station and turned right. He approached his regular kiosk with a five-pound note in his hand. He paused when he saw the lights were already lit on the cash register. The man offered a friendly, wagging finger and head shake towards him. Tobi followed the Turkish man's eyes as they flicked towards the Big Issue seller. The trader wasn't alone this morning. Through the light fog, Tobi made out the figure of Clara in one of her fitted skirts. The hemline stopped just above her knees before faultless black stockings carried the rest of the look to the ground. As he approached, he noticed two steaming cups as both women were locked in bubbly conversation over their hot brews. A mix of the sweetness of hot chocolate and strength of coffee crept over Clara's shoulder towards him.

"Stealing my number one client?" he said as he punctured their chat.

They turned towards him together. Clara broke into a smile, revealing a trace of dark red lipstick on her front tooth. "Malala was just keeping me up to date with the real economics of London."

The weathered face of The Big Issue seller raised her eyebrows in innocence towards Tobi before settling back into a familiar grin. He stayed silent.

"To be continued," said Clara with a wink as she rotated Tobi's left shoulder to point him away from the park. "No time for the office. We have other business to attend to."

"Must be pretty important to steal my morning thunder," he said with a friendly nudge of their elbows. Her emerald eyes gave away nothing in response but twinkled in the light of a passing car.

"I've cross-referenced your diary with Jennifer's, and it makes for interesting viewing." Clara set their pace in a westerly direction alongside the perimeter of the park and towards Hyde Park Corner. She had a way with diaries, particularly ones that didn't belong to her. Tobi remembered he hadn't yet checked his own emails since emerging from the disconnected underground system. He pulled his phone out mid stride and swiped down to check for new items. No word from Mikey.

"What have you found?"

Clara detailed that each time Tobi and Simon had a meeting scheduled or a work trip planned, so did Jennifer. The titles and locations of her meetings had little consistency about them except for the timings; they followed an obvious pattern that matched to Tobi and Simon's activities. In addition, the day after those meetings, there would be another at a coffee shop, bakery or other nondescript high street outlet. But all in the same area. Westminster.

As Clara spoke, they reached the end of the park's boundary and altered their direction of travel left, heading down towards the river and into the neighbourhood of Victoria as it rose for the day. Tobi's thoughts were trying to keep pace with their strides. "Westminster? Not inherently suspicious. What am I missing?"

"Nothing, yet. I've not presented the last piece of the jigsaw. The diary references that bring the story together are when the meetings don't happen. There's no rendezvous scheduled for this week, for example."

Tobi racked his brain over what was happening in the world of politics. Nothing of significance came to him. It had been a quiet week; parliament was on recess. Ah. "Because parliament isn't meeting this week?"

"Exactly. It seems like Jennifer's charitable actions have a very public interest component to them. But I'm highly sceptical it's in the public's interest at all. In fact, I'm guessing it's very much a private affair."

Tobi's mind sifted through the information. He pulled his phone out once more and swiped down. Still nothing. They walked on in silence for another fifty yards. "So, where the hell are we going this morning?" When in doubt, he preferred to stick with the facts that were right before him, however literal they might be.

"I said a meeting was unlikely. I didn't say there wasn't one happening," she said with a smirk. "We're heading to a coffee shop on the South Bank. I presume you fancy a cup?"

Tobi's smartphone buzzed. It was out of his pocket before he'd thought the action through. There was one notification on the screen with the word 'Mikey' in bold letters across the top of it.

Tobi. Wednesday. Later that Morning.

Tobi and Clara arrived at the coffee shop at seven AM. It was the sort of place where commuters drifted in and out, collecting takeaways to fortify themselves before heading into the surrounding skyscrapers.

Clara carved a path through the mass of people queueing in front of the main counter. She chose a table flanked by a bookshelf on one side and the staff's service station on the other. The positioning meant no one could take a table next to them and it gave them a wide view of anyone looking for a spot. She motioned to a member of staff behind the counter, who nodded and began preparing two coffees. They waited.

As they sat, Tobi reopened Mikey's email to find a file attachment which contained several photos and high-level facts about Jennifer. Most of them were known; they involved the lists of charities she volunteered at, previous addresses within the Yorkshire area where she had grown up and bounced around in her youth and old work contacts. She and Simon had met and been together since high school. Both had left once they'd gotten their GCSEs. Tobi knew this from working late nights with Simon. He paged forward in the document until he got to the most recent year. Simon's indiscriminate activities were known, if ignored, by Tobi. What he needed was something about Jennifer's. He came to a section at the end of the file labelled 'Political Interests'.

Jennifer had signed up to become an official member of the Conservative party eighteen months ago. Fellow attendees at a charity dinner she had organised encouraged her to join. It was an event sponsored by Simon's company. And it wasn't a solely charitable evening. She had curried favour with political connections that night. In particular, those who had influential, and favourable, views on the laws and taxes of moving pharmaceutical goods across borders. She had learnt how the game was played. There were pictures of three Conservative MPs. Each middle-aged, grey-haired and male with blue ties. A list of bullet points that outlined their political views and ambitions accompanied the little images. And then a picture on the following page, marked out on its own.

An Asian man with a thick, groomed beard stared back at Tobi. His eyes reflected the small grey flecks in his beard. He appeared younger than the rest and had an energy about his appearance that the others lacked. His headshot leapt off the page. Tobi recognised the face of the current Minister of Health. 'Fazir Khan' was stencilled below the image.

There was a lack of text but in its place was a series of screenshots from email exchanges between the two. They started out innocently; pleasantries back and forth following the initial meeting at the charity dinner. They were planning to set up a subsequent event with the language of 'quid pro quo' sewn into the seams of their exchanges.

And then the tone of the messages changed tack. Business parlance disappeared as emails signed off more informally. The pages of the e-doc switched from screenshots of emails to private mobile texts between the two. Interspersed within the shorter messages were images of each of them. A variety of creative angles, taken using a smartphone, was on display across the series. So, too, was a lack of clothing.

"We're looking out for Fazir Khan," said Tobi as he flicked his eyes across the room. A steady tide of people flowed up and against the counter before retreating out of the doors. Two other tables were now occupied. One by an elderly couple who looked like a pair of bewildered tourists, in need of a break from the torrent of the early morning crush. At the other was a young, single woman in her mid-twenties, settled down in front of her laptop, with a croissant. There was one other table available which lay beyond Clara's back and up against the far wall, tucked alongside another bookshelf.

"The Fazir Khan?" said Clara, unable to conceal a rush of excitement in her voice. Tobi nodded and handed the phone over to her. She ran her finger repeatedly up the screen, catching her movements with every odd swipe for a brief review before following with another upward flick. "That's interesting." The server leaned over the counter and placed the coffees alongside them.

Tobi's mind was off and racing. He had come across the political ambitions of Fazir before. West & West always had to take MP's dreams into account when scoping out their clients' business interests. Fazir had long hinted that his aims extended far beyond the role of health minister and to the top job in the land. He had been a Conservative loyalist for years and achieved an impressive amount in the health sector. He'd taken the national health care scheme, perceived as inefficient, and shaken up its ideas so effectively in the past six years that the constant rumblings around it had receded into the distance for a few brief months. That was no small feat. The man with an immigrant history and a bright future was well positioned to keep climbing the political ladder. But his background would require bold moves to scale the obstacles in his way.

"What does he stand to gain from Simon's fall from grace?" he mumbled under his breath. Before Clara could answer, he held up his hand to halt her thoughts. He was looking over her shoulder. A woman in leggings, a workout top and a peak cap had just wormed her way through the crowd and towards the only available table. She took a seat facing away from the pair and towards the door. Jennifer's unmissable flowing red hair fell in neat curls from beneath the cap. The same woman that had served them made her way over and placed two cups at her table, one in front of her and the other opposite. Tobi leaned down and pulled the seat of Clara's chair towards him. She followed his lead and nudged it along until he pushed back, leaving the back of her head obstructing Jennifer's direct line of sight towards him. "He's just arrived, too," he whispered.

Fazir was dressed in a long tan spring coat with the collar turned up against the morning chill. The coffee shop was warm inside; the heat of the ground coffee and constant ebb and flow of people and electronics kept it toasty. And noisy. Fazir sat down with his coat on, in front of a drink that steamed towards Jennifer. Clara adjusted the mirrored serviette holder in front of her. She could see the figures, but they were misshapen from the warped metal surface. Tobi would have to be her lookout. She craned her left ear towards them, but the conversation was too far away, drowned out by the hiss of the espresso machine. She searched for Tobi with her eyes, her frustration at the lack of information written across her face.

Tobi sensed the activity across from him, but kept his gaze fixed on the small gap over Clara's shoulder. His face was concealed by her falling black hair. Through it he saw nothing more sinister than a casual coffee catch up. If he hadn't seen the images on his phone just a few moments ago, he would have thought nothing of them. There had been no signs of physical contact between them, but that tension was soon released. Fazir broke cover and reached across and towards her under the table. Something white in his hand. Tobi's view wasn't clear enough to decipher what it was. He was too exposed to shift any further to adjust his view. Jennifer's hand met Fazir's and the white object passed between them. A folded piece of paper? Their hands lingered. His on top of hers. He stroked the tops of her knuckles once, and then again, before hers lifted first, as both went to the sanctity of their warm cups.

"He's handed something to her under the table, but I don't know what and I can't hear a damned thing," Tobi hissed to Clara. A rush of conspicuousness rose within him as he spoke. At that moment, Jennifer swept her gaze across the room towards them in a slow arc. Tobi reached for a lock of Clara's hair, as if to brush it away. He let his hand rest there for a second to ensure it blocked any glimpse of him Jennifer might have had. He completed the motion, and Clara followed his lead as she readjusted her hair behind both ears. They laughed and reached for their cups, dipping their heads down as they did, mirroring each other's movements. They toyed over their cups as Tobi gathered the courage to peek back over her shoulder once more, but lost his nerve. A second later, from his bowed position, he spotted movement. Fazir's coiffed collar reared into sight as he saw him stand. A curt smile flashed across his face, and he turned to leave. He willed for Jennifer to do the same and kept his eyes fixed down. His fingers fidgeted with the spoon resting on his coffee saucer. Clara reached out and put her hand on his, halting the metallic clicking. With her spare hand she pinched a magazine off the bookshelf and placed it in front of them. She flicked it open to a random page in the middle. She directed their gazes down towards it, allowing Tobi to lose himself in an article on the wine lands of Tuscany. They mimicked travel plans that would never come to be. His fingers stopped their fiddling and settled into a brief calm. She withdrew her hand back across the table towards her and pointed to the many Tuscan towers of San Gimignano that were highlighted on the pages in front of them. More movement caught his eye. At last, he could allow himself a furtive glance towards the now empty table, save for two coffee mugs. The steam was still rising from them. Beyond it, a tight ponytail, hidden beneath a baseball hat, made its way through the crowd and out of the main entrance.

"Thanks," Tobi said to her, as his shoulders sagged back into his chest.

"For someone who trades on information, you are astoundingly bad at acquiring it," Clara said, as she tucked away another strand of hair behind her ears, along with the moment. "Always let me be the lookout, we've spoken about this." Her reproachful words fell from her lips too softly to land with any menace.

His mouth cocked up on the right before his lips pursed together. They parted in admission. "I don't think I learnt anything more than Mikey, and you, already know." She smiled back at him. He continued, "But one thing I know is that MPs passing written notes under coffee tables to beleaguered, attractive wives of another man have something to hide."

Clara spoke, summarising her own thoughts, "Well, the wife of a very wealthy pharmaceutical entrepreneur takes the Minister of Health as her lover-"

"-a minister who is very clearly set on becoming the next man in Number Ten," Tobi interjected.

"A very ambitious Minister of Health," she corrected herself before continuing. "Who has stated running for office in what is an election year."

"And who will need to fund that campaign somehow."

"Said minister seduces the entrepreneur's wife, who looks set to become a wealthy ex-wife in the near future."

"Through an unfortunate tabloid leak," he added.

"Through a leak," she confirmed. "But a convenient one for them both. It leaves them open to carry on their budding romance, but also gives him access to funds to have a run at PM. Is that what we're saying?"

"What we're saying," he leaned back in his chair, rocking it back and catching himself on the table before continuing, "is that it puts us right in the middle of something. Something bigger than West & West."

Yorick. Thursday. Morning.

Yorick sat in a large, comfortable armchair in a private airport lounge. He waited for the flight team to make their final preparations and turned Gabbi's question over in his mind: *I'm ok with where I am right now, Yorick - are you?*

He knew he had walked away from something the previous night. It wasn't his usual style. At work, Yorick relished confrontation. He thrived when given the chance to outshine young upstarts who thought they knew their business better than he. But in his private life, he found no satisfaction in the fair exchange of ideas, particularly when emotions were involved. That way messiness lay.

He cast his down eyes to the small personal tablet in front of him, docked in the front corner of his private waiting booth. A soft orange glow flowed from its corners; passengers could begin boarding. He stood and scooped up his suit jacket, shrugging it over his shoulders, enjoying the ease with which it settled onto each curve and dip of his torso. He snatched the whiskey tumbler in front of him and brought it to his lips, pausing to breathe it in, before tipping the remnants down his throat. The mixture of the sweet caramel and a crisp nuttiness warmed the top of his lungs. He exhaled and felt his phone jolt to life.

Huang.

The screen pulsed back and forth at him, just below the time; 09.35. He was due to land at four the next morning in Guizhou and be in Huang's office before six. He debated ignoring the call. But when Huang rang, he answered.

"Huang, I'm just about to step on board-" he began, eager to cut off the inevitable inquiry at its source.

"Don't."

Yorick waited for some sign that Huang would carry on. Silence.

"What?"

"Change of plan. Plans are moving more quickly than we thought. We're coming to you."

His mind was racing with questions. He wanted to fixate on the word 'we' but knew Huang wouldn't give him any more information. He changed tack and attempted to wrestle back control of the conversation.

"What do we need to have in place for when you land?"

"The new business, remind me of the name?"

The fumes from the whiskey sat at the back of his throat, burning with a stale ferocity. "FORT-ify," he replied through gritted teeth.

"Yes, Mr. Ben." Another interminable pause. Yorick steeled himself to wait this one out. Half an agonising minute later, a reply came. "We need to step it up significantly. Our schedule."

"Huang, listen - these things take time."

"We land in two days, Yorick."

"We only signed the deal last week, for fucks' sake." More silence engulfed the line. He knew he had to break it this time. "At least a week, Huang. I need more time to work, Ben."

"Two days, Yorick. And we need the others, too."

"Others?"

"All of them, Yorick. 48 hours."

The click of Huang hanging up rang inside Yorick's ears long after his phone had faded to black.

He buttoned his jacket, picked up his leather briefcase and headed towards the exit. In the distance, he heard footsteps treading behind him. He inched his pace up.

"Mr. Van den Berg, sir. Mr. Van-" A confused voice limped ahead of the chasing feet.

"Cancel the flight," he called out over his shoulder without breaking stride. The feet drew alongside him, and the face of a pensive young man hovered to his left.

"Sir, we need to remove your bags and security will need to process the change. Please, sir, it will only take a minute."

Yorick stopped himself short. He held his gaze dead ahead. "Just sort it out," he picked up his stride, but this time unaccompanied. "And send my bag to my office." He ploughed through the exit and back into the heaving hum and mass of Luton's public terminal.

There was no time for anger as Yorick's taxi streaked through the outskirts of London. Huang had warned him this day was coming. Their previous investments were designed to get them to this point. He ran through the concluded deals in his mind. It was thirteen confirmed and signed, with

Ben's FORT-ify making it fourteen in total. Fourteen entrepreneurs he had helped along the way to build their dreams. Or so they thought. But today, with Huang on the way in 48 hours, he needed them, and he needed them quickly. He'd have to call a meeting with all of them by tomorrow. He dialled Ben's mobile number.

After four rings, a husky voice stammered, "He-hello?"

"Ben. It's Yorick. We need to meet tomorrow."

"Sorry, Yorrie," said Ben, causing Yorick to bite down hard on his lower lip, "No can do, pal. I'm skiing in Val-de-Saire. I'm back on Sunday so let's do Mo-".

"No, Ben. It's tomorrow. Get the next flight back and I'll send the details later."

"Yoric-" Ben started, but Yorick hit the red button and ended the call. He was in no mood to entertain pained responses.

His driver wound the sedan through north London. The ride had been smooth, but they faced constant interruptions of stop and start traffic building up all around them. It held them at an intersection outside Finsbury Park underground station. Yorick lost himself in the weaving sea of legs that flowed back and forth while he let the wheels in his mind spin. The light turned green, and the car leapt forward, causing the last of the legs to hustle through their paces.

Yorick flicked his phone to life and found a list with the thirteen other contacts. He scrolled to the bottom, letting the names wash over him. Then back to the top. And down again. He started from the bottom and worked his way up. That meant the first call would be to his longest investment contact.

He was the founder of a technological innovation in the dentistry space that had seemed simple and straight forward at the outset. It allowed local small businesses to compile and schedule patient information all into one neat, convenient space. It saved the reminder calls, the chasing of overdue accounts and the mundanities of small business life. And it worked for thousands of dental practices across the United Kingdom. A harmless innovation, on the surface.

"Hugh. It's Yorick. We need to meet tomorrow."

An educated and well-bred voice chimed back, "Yorick, mate." The middle letter of the word 'mate' elongated itself into the air. Yorick bit down once again on his lower lip and felt the salty release of a crack of blood rolling onto his tongue. "Great to hear from y-".

"Tomorrow at midday. I'll send the details." Click. Twelve more to go.

He bullied and blustered his way through the rest of them. Ben's security app and Hugh's dental service were soon joined by the remaining twelve digital breakthroughs that had made everyone's lives easier, more convenient, and safer in the past decade.

A digital network for pet owners to connect and socialise, a food delivery service that prepared and distributed ingredients for meal kits, a music app designed for sharing workplace appropriate recommendations. On the list went, populated with a disparate collection of unrelated ideas and people. The only element they had in common that they knew of was Yorick.

He clicked off the last of the calls. He stared at the screen of his phone after it faded to black and the reflection of Wellington's Arch flicked across it. They were in the heart of royal London. The monstrous marble-coloured structure loomed over them, away and to the right. On top of it, a huge bronze sculpture caught the beaming sunshine. The arch represented victory - designed and created following the defeat of Napoleon by the Duke of Wellington almost two hundred years before. The figure reflected into Yorick's eyes. It sat in the early morning sun, depicting the Angel of Peace as it descended on the 'Quadriga' of War - a four-horsed chariot. Their car inched forward, and the ray of sunlight faded away from Yorick's eyeline.

The rolling lawns of Green Park stretched out beyond the sculpture. The main entrance to the park was at most a ten-minute walk from Yorick's Mayfair apartment. A walk he could barely remember. It must have been well over a half a decade since he last strode along it. His driver adjusted his position in his seat and nosed the hulking metal forward.

"Smalls, I'll get out here," said Yorick, as he pulled on the lever of his door.

The mass of his driver craned his neck in his direction and caught his eye in the rear-view mirror. "Alright, boss," was all he offered in response as Yorick slipped from his view and out onto the pavement. He darted across the road and made his way towards the arch, feeling it pulling him towards it. As he did so, he ran through the phone calls in his mind. He prepared for the next day, when they'd be assembled in one place for the first time. He emerged from underneath the arch, felt the sun strike him on the back of his neck and moved towards the soft, cut grass of the park.

Tobi. Thursday. Night.

It was deep into the night. Tobi and Clara had spent the rest of the day analysing details, looking for the one thing that continued to elude their grasp: Jennifer's ambitions. Bits of information had trickled in from Mikey during the afternoon. Each new document sent over, scraped from another digital source, built the picture of Jennifer and Fazir having established a long-term relationship behind Simon's back over the past year and a half. Mikey hadn't been able to hack into Fazir's diary, though. Tobi was surprised and annoyed at that detail, despite the wealth of information they had unearthed about the pairing. There was little Mikey hadn't tapped into over the years, and government officials were not beyond the limits of his abilities. But this time, it had been different. "Squeaky clean," Mikey had said, aside from the obvious Jennifer material. But even that had been lifted from her various devices and accounts, not his.

"What if it is just the relationship, Tobi?" said Clara.

He lifted his head from the scattered pieces of paper that lay strewn across the large wooden table in the centre of his expansive dining room. It led off the kitchen in an open-plan layout.

The table had been a wedding gift from his in-laws. Large family gatherings were a centrepiece of his wife's childhood, and Sarah had been insistent on having a table of stature to do the same in their home. She hated it when he brought work home from the office at the best of times. Scattering it across their dining room table a couple of hours earlier had meant she had put their daughter to bed early, along with herself. He reached for the bottle of wine he'd opened ten minutes earlier and topped up the glasses that sat on the paper trails.

They'd been circling back to the same point during the day; something was telling him it couldn't be that simple. There had to be more to it. He looked into Clara's eyes as he handed her the freshly stocked glass. They were both exhausted. Clara never looked tired. But after a day of foraging down too many alleys to count, and returning empty handed save for the alcohol in front of them, she had lost the shine that he thought lived perpetually in her eyes. He took a sip of the merlot, breathed in hints of an earthy flavour and pressed on.

"There are just too many things that line up for it to be pure coincidence," he said with a shake of his head. For once his lips settled in a straight line, not a hint of their usual crookedness.

Her eyes drifted to the walls around her as though she were taking in the unique pieces of art, but she spoke with a frustrated tone. "People like her are ambitious, Tobi. She knows what it would mean to be a future PM's wife." She reached for her glass of wine and brought it to her lips. "People can be vindictive and maybe she wants to hurt Simon publicly. She must have known about his post-work activities, women always do." She drew long and hard on the glass. He let her continue. "And people can simply just fall in love with someone else for just that. With nothing else to gain. No one to hurt. Maybe it looks all too convenient from the outside because it really is."

They faced off against each other in silence. The stubbornness between them stretched through a series of sips, as if in a poorly structured game of chess. He broke the rhythm as he reached for a random piece of paper on the table in front of him. As if by a hidden force, his movement towards it ejected Clara from her seat. She pushed what remained of her wine away from her and stood.

"I'm done for the day, Tobi. If you want to continue to chase shadows on this, you can do it on your own time." She grabbed her coat from the back of her chair and folded herself into it, flicking away the sections of hair that were caught inside it. "We should focus on what we're going to do about the situation instead of why we think it's come about. That'll get us nowhere." She moved past him.

His hand dropped the paper and shot out to intercept her path. But the gap between the table and wall was large. She breezed past it with ease and called out over her shoulder as she left the room, "Call me tomorrow when you're ready to make an actual plan."

He didn't bother to chase her. She was gone and most probably right. Instead, he looked down at the discarded piece of paper in front of him. A copy of an old electronic receipt from another coffee shop that contained nothing more than a low tip on the bill. He pushed it off the table and watched as it gathered a few comrades with it, losing pace as they fluttered to the floor. He reached for the bottle and poured the rest of its contents into his glass.

Tobi's head snapped towards the ceiling. He had caught it falling towards his chest. The effects of the red wine had long since taken hold, and he was filled with the familiar sensation of chasing reality for hours on end.

Darkness folded around him and papers were scattered on the floor at his feet.

But they weren't the receipts of the trail that he and Clara had been tracking earlier. The fuzziness of his head, caught halfway between drunkenness and the start of a headache, made him question if it was still the same night.

These papers were yellowed. Boxes that were old, brown, and crumbling were littered around him . The strange darkness brought some light to where he was. He had stumbled up into the attic of their narrow, four storey home.

There was a flashing memory of the sound of crying. Ah. Sarah had been angry. He touched the pit of his right arm where she had pulled at him to stop him from going up. The crying had been Lily's, their daughter. It had stopped at some point as the intensity of the silence in the cramped space welled within him.

He didn't know how long he'd been slumped in that position, but it had been long enough to make his back hurt. He attempted to twist upwards onto his knee to relieve the pressure of something angular digging into his right shoulder blade, but a blunt pain struck him just above his left eye. From inside of his head. He sighed and slumped back, unable to fight the incapacitating powers of his impending hangover. The sharp edge settled back into the groove it had created in his right shoulder. He let the numbness of familiar pain wash over him for a few more minutes. What the hell had he been doing up here in the first place?

As soon as the thought entered his mind his right hand shot out across the floor to the side of him. His fingers danced across the ragged boards, controlled by a power of their own. Until they hit something smooth. And wooden. He felt his fingers fold over, and then encase, the small figurine in his palm while a wave of reassurance flooded through him.

He remembered now. He followed his mind as it retraced his footsteps from the hours before.

Predictably, it had all begun with him spilling his wine. Clean-up operations were second nature to him. He'd grasped the sturdy armrests of the chair with both hands, and had stood poised, half standing, half stooped, ready to spin around to head into the kitchen. But he'd stopped. He had been held in place by the sight of the thick, red liquid seeping out over discarded papers. Papers that he couldn't make sense of, yet still they held him in a trance. The liquid hadn't so much pooled as lurched. Monstrously. It cascaded across, through and down tiny rivulets created by the overlapping papers and uneven surface of the table. The individual reaches would peter out, only for a fellow stream alongside to extend an arm and pull the disparate courses together. In those small, isolated actions, the entire mess had roared back to life and surged forward once more, its momentum having grown.

And then, as quickly as it had sprung to life, the spill crashed to a halt. A ragged outline of shapeless edges and depths lay before him. He felt its stillness mocking him from the chaos it had rained down upon his night's attempt at progress. From that stillness, a memory had erupted. He was back in the hot balmy months of June ten years ago. The details of quite different papers flooded his head at that moment. He held the specifics of them fast in his memory. They were title deeds to the first company that he'd held under his control. The toy company that his father had started all those years ago, Pieter's Play. The company that had carved and then churned out millions and millions of the figurines that were like the one in his hand. That never left his pocket. And so, instead of cleaning up the stagnant pool of red wine, which by now had seeped further and further into the mahogany of the table, he had aimed his sights on those long-neglected but often remembered papers in the attic. That was why he had come up here.

A spark of sobriety reared within him and he used it to flick on the torch of his smartphone. He ran his hands over the piles of paper beneath him, but none of them held any relevance to his father's old company. His legs were cramping in the tight space, and that damn box was still digging into his shoulder blade. He lost his patience with it, twisting to his right to dislodge it. He felt the pain increase with a flash, but the box gave way, teetering as it did before it fell over. The weight of the papers inside caused the lid to cascade forward, showering the floor with more old and discarded documents.

From beneath the mess, a batch of crusty papers emerged. His fingers moved to scoop them up. He brought the torch across them and at last found what had driven him up into this place.

"Van den Berg & Sons" was written across the top. Below it lay the commonplace details of a simple title deed document. The listed address of the company itself, details of the financial particulars and, finally, signatures at the bottom. One of which was Tobi's. The year listed was 2010.

In the dankness of the attic, Tobi felt himself welling up. Jennifer's ulterior motives were far removed from his mind as he found his hand shuffling the papers beneath the title deed. They lay at an odd angle, propped up by something irregularly shaped beneath.

He pulled the sheets away until he came across a brown padded envelope. There was nothing remarkable about its appearance. It was the size of an A4 piece of paper and bulged outward, an inch and a half thick. The back of it faced up towards him and he could see that it had never been opened. He turned it around in his hand and shone the torch on the details on the front. The handwriting stood out to him. His brain searched for past connections and made one. The writing belonged to the lawyer who had executed their father's last will and testament. Tobi had handled all the last affairs, just as he had cared for their father in his last days. Yorick had kept his distance.

But it wasn't addressed to him. Yorick's name was on the front. At the bottom of the envelope, stencilled by the same hand but in neat block capital letters, was a plea; PLEASE READ, YORICK. THESE CAN'T REMAIN UNOPENED FOREVER.

Tobi thumbed the back of the envelope nervously, feeling the stale glue cracking open under his influence. He felt a torrent of emotions raging within him but the thumping in his head, frustration at a night of wasted effort and his innate protective spirit for his brother, saw his thumb run along the flap. His eyes remained fixed on the name on the front, and he felt the fold spring away from his thumb with little persuasion. He reached inside and used his right hand as his eyes, feeling his way through the contents.

The dulled corners of multiple bits of folded paper worked away at his fingertips. He pinched a small cluster between his thumb and forefinger and extracted them from their sheath. He placed his phone's torch at an angle and pointed the wad of papers towards the light.

He was holding a stack of smaller envelopes, all identical in size and shape but with differences in their degrees of ageing. Some corners were more battered than others, the writing on others had faded more clearly. But they were all old, that much was clear. The handwriting on the front of all the smaller envelopes was identical. But different to that on the front of the brown, padded envelope. He recognised it straight away. It was his father's.

There were two other consistent details across them all; they were all addressed to Yorick. And they were all unopened and marked 'Return to sender'.

Tobi stirred. His eyes opened, painfully taking in the sun's light that poured in from the window opposite him. He was in bed, alone. Lying flat on his stomach. He couldn't remember the last time Sarah had got out of bed before him. He reached out behind him to the bedside table, scrabbling across it until his fingers found his smartphone and he brought it to his face. 09.17. Shit.

He'd only ever overslept once before in his working life. And that was 15 years ago. That time, it had been as if his bedsheets were electrified and he'd been doused in cold water, given the time it took for him to get ready and out the door. But this morning, he let the realisation sink into his bones. He pressed himself into the rumpled linen and dragged himself up and away to the large adjoining bathroom. His pace was measured as he showered, brushed his teeth, combed his hair, and got dressed. He picked out a clean outfit that consisted of the nearest to hand for each item. He plodded down the stairs.

Sounds of Sarah chatting away with their daughter floated back up at him. He stepped off the last stair and turned into the kitchen, taking in the sight of the two of them at the far end of the room. He could see the corner of the dining room table from this angle and his gaze wondered over to it sheepishly. It was clean. Except for a stack of papers arranged in its corner. Some were stained red.

There was a place set for breakfast at the island counter in the middle of the wide kitchen. He moved towards it, and Sarah looked up as he did so. Lily's eyes remained focused on the book in front of her. Her hesitant index finger continued to trace across the page. Sarah moved towards him. She met his gaze fully, and asked, "Coffee?"

"Thank you." It was all he could offer in response, as he moved to the place set for breakfast. For one. He watched in silence as she poured a fresh cup of coffee from the filter machine. With the hot mug in one hand, she opened the oven in front of her and pulled out a plate, having tested its heat first with her fingers.

"Mummy?" Lily called from away behind the island.

"Mummy's coming, darling," she said, knocking the oven door shut with her hip as she turned to Tobi and brought the plate and mug over. She set them at the table. The mug didn't make a sound as she placed it on the marble counter. Tobi felt his fingers drawn to the plate. He pulled them back as he felt its heat. "But first we've got to look after daddy, haven't we?" she asked to the room at large.

A pause played out as their daughter hesitated. And then, in a singular note filled with excitement, "Yes, mummy!"

Tobi felt Sarah's warm hand settle on top of his as his daughter's voice rang through his head. She squeezed his fingers in a grim grip. The softness of his wife's eyes brought a tear to his. She watched as it rolled down his cheek before catching it with her thumb and wiping it away into her palm. She patted his hand as she moved back towards Lily. "It's what we do, isn't it, sweetheart?"

Yorick. Friday. Midday.

Yorick watched as the clock that dominated the room ticked slowly, making its way towards midday. He sat back and pressed his shoulders into his favourite leather armchair. It was deeply set, causing his knees to float up to the level of his chest as he settled into it. He held his right hand to his shaved chin. His fingers ran across the superficial cut from where he'd lost control of the blade that morning.

He watched the seconds tick on, one precise movement at a time. He gathered his thoughts. His words. His approach. The clock's hands came together. It rang out with a purposeful chime. The sound didn't fill the room with its reverberations, but punctured it in one conspicuous jab. It could be heard through the wall.

The adjoining room was also simple, but different. Rather than being rectangular, two long, diagonal glass walls encased it. The enclosure formed the tip of a triangle where they met. It was a unique aspect of the building's design that allowed for this feature on only one floor of the thirty-storey structure: the top one. There were two entrances to the triangular room. One of them lead in from the reception lobby. It was through this door that fourteen pairs of feet had shuffled five minutes ago. Some of them were housed in sneakers that weren't as comfortable as they should have been for the prices that had been paid. Others sported brown loafers, without socks, that rubbed enough to keep the wearer on their toes. They had made their way around the large wooden table in the centre of the room.

Specifically carved from one singular redwood tree, the piece dominated the room in a way that none of its current occupants could. Concentric circles spread out across the plain of deep brown, drawing the eyes of the room into its centre. It was Yorick's pride and joy of the office, chosen by his own hand on a trip to California five years previously.

Seven chairs lined each side of the table, all occupied. One chair lay empty at the head. The climactic point of the room framed it and it was aligned with the centre of the redwood. The table lay bare. The room was silent, save for the readjusting of feet on the muted grey carpet.

Yorick ran his hands over the smooth contours of his head. He reached into the inside pocket of his midnight blue suit. It was single breasted, tapered at the back and with a faint pin stripe pattern, each line stacked next to its identical partners. He pulled out his phone, tapped it to life, and loaded up an app on the device. It brought up an image of an eye. It was outlined in green on a black background. He held the phone's small camera to his right eye. The outline of the eye flooded with green. It blinked into Yorick's retina and the screen flashed white. Yorick lowered the device to his lap and looked down at it. There was a single header at the top, and it read: Partners. It held only one name: Huang. He pressed the name with his right thumb.

His fingers moved across the screen.

ALL HERE. READY FOR YOU. He clicked the envelope icon on the top right, the only image on the screen.

A small lock appeared and simulated the motion of locking and unlocking. It faded away and simultaneously closed the app. The encrypted message was released and Yorick sat back to wait. His eyes settled on a piece of brick on the wall in front of him that jutted out from the smooth surface.

A ping sounded. He unlocked the phone and brought it to his right eye once more. A quick glance down was all he needed to confirm what he was already thinking.

12.05.

The app shut down on its own and his phone flashed the large digital time display at him. 12.03.

He dug his heels into the thick carpet, pressed down and unfolded to his full height. He moved to his right and reached out for a hidden door handle set within the faint outline of a door frame. It slid from right to left without a sound, and he stepped through it. He emerged from the small room and into the large glass triangle. He caught the assembled group unaware. Those that faced him drew themselves upright. The other half emitted a series of sounds as their chairs spun around in attempts to face him. Yorick kept them swivelling as he walked to the head of the table, his feet clicking on the carpet that wasn't as thick as it looked.

12.04. He had no intention of inviting discussion today.

"Hey, Yorick-" started Ben. Of course, it would be him. No one followed his lead.

Yorick offered him a silent, tight-lipped smile in response.

"Some of you know each other," he said and paused as some exchanged a few nods across the table. The rest sat in stillness. "For others, it's the first time you've met." He reached into his pocket and pulled out his phone. He placed it in front of him with its bottom edge squared against the rim of the table. "As of today, you all have at least two things in common. Me. And my firm's money." He broke into a grin and lowered himself into his chair. A few expressions relaxed and smiled back, while others stiffened, pressing their necks into the tops of their high-backed chairs. "Today, I present a third to you." An identical clock to the room in the back was on the wall opposite Yorick. He followed the slow arc of its second hand as it made its way around to complete the fifth minute past twelve. With ten seconds to go, he brought his phone up to his eye and waited for it to complete its authentication. He brought it down as it lit up with a single word pulsing back at him in green in the centre: Huang. "Everyone, please meet Huang." He slid the green flashing name to the right of the screen to begin the call, pressed the button to turn the phone into its speakerphone setting, and let it connect to the surround sound system of the room via Bluetooth.

The next words the room heard were Huang's.

The intoxicating lilt of Huang's accent, familiar to Yorick but new to this crowd, flowed from the room's powerful speakers. They filled the awkwardly shaped space with a thick, unexpected timbre.

"Good afternoon, everyone. Let me start by saying what an honour it is to meet all of you." The group exchanged confused glances across the table. Some craned to get a closer look at the screen, but those closest to it indicated that this was a wasted effort - there was nothing to see except a name. During Huang's opening exchanges, Yorick had taken the chance to swing his chair around, turning himself towards the apex of the walled triangle. He alternated his focus between the reflected expressions in the glass and allowed his gaze to settle into the middle distance, beyond the encased walls and out east over the rooftops of London. Yorick felt the familiar twitching in his fingers and clamped them to his thighs. He'd be damned if he was going to let those around him glimpse his weakness. Not when he was this close to securing his ambitions with Huang.

Around him, his Chinese partner's voice continued. "You may be wondering who I am." A couple of chairs shuffled in and out, readjusting their position in the silence that followed. "I am sitting in Guizhou, China. And all around me are hundreds and hundreds of servers. You see, Yorick and I have been partners for a long time and together we've had the aim of supporting all your entrepreneurial dreams however we can. For Yorick, that's been on the financial side, and for me it's been providing you with the best data storage systems anywhere in the world." Yorick felt the mood in the room behind him change. A new atmosphere expanded into its open spaces. The bubble of curiosity and confusion, which contained little pockets of wounded pride, had burst. In its place was recognition as cogs clicked together.

Every deal signed between Yorick and the room's seated legion had one core tenet at its centre; Yorick securing Huang's prized data warehousing services. They featured the latest in technological advances, meaning that they could house all app developments and data in a unique virtual cloud. This agreement allowed them fast, reliable and convenient access to all their data whenever they needed it, without the risk of running out of server space. It sounded too good to be true to them all - server space was a key and expensive concern of all growing developers - but engineer tests consistently sent back the same data. It worked. Better than they could have hoped. It provided the platform for them to grow faster than they could ever have expected, adding users as and when they needed to, not when their systems allowed. It had been the key factor that had secured the deals with Yorick. The access was unprecedented for the prices he could offer, making his financial investments even more lucrative for them all. Once the technical specifications had been proven, the questions had dried up from that side of the table. And quick success had come for each of them. But within their agreement lay a clause that no one had commented on. One that Huang was about to bring to their attention.

"So, you must be wondering what you're all doing here today," Huang said, homing in on the question that hung over the room. "First, let me offer my personal recognition for everything you've achieved so far. Yorick?" The Dutchman turned and tapped a button on the underside of the table. The door in the bottom left of the room sprang open. Through it came Craig in a pressed suit. He had seen little of Yorick since they had returned from China. He held a pile of stapled papers in his right hand and placed a copy in front of everyone. Except for Yorick. In front of him, he placed a fountain pen. Craig gave Yorick a curt nod and a barely perceptible smile and left the room through the other door. The one Yorick had used to enter.

A murmuring broke out as sets of eyes sought reassurance in those around them. *Were they all on the same page?* Yes, a quick nod from someone else appeased the few who were worried that they might be alone in their concerns of the unknown. *OK, we're in it together.* Next, the eyes switched from searching to interrogating. *Who around the table was worried, or looked at ease?* The impact of everyone casting their eyes around at the same time had the unexpected effect of calming the room. No one knew anything more than anyone else. *I'm not the only victim of some sort of scam that's about to fall out from underneath me.* A steeliness took root amongst the group.

"I want to make an additional investment into each of your companies. We like what we've seen. But we want to see it happen even faster." Huang offered the last word with what sounded like a broad smile. Greedy hands pawed through the investment papers. It didn't take them long; it was just two pages.

"Mr. Huang, a pleasure," said Ben. His eyes searched the room, unsure where he should be focusing. Yorick watched his ferreting glances darting about. "It's Ben, from FORT-ify," he tried once more, eager to carry on.

"Yes, Mr. Ben. I remember you from my short visit. Do you have a question?" Huang said.

"Well, uh, no, I just wanted to express my gratitude for what you've done for our growth so far. Remarkable work you're achieving out there."

Yorick could feel Huang's glance shifting elsewhere in the room. His voice was flat as he carried on. "Thanks. So, all that's required is your signatures. Unless there are questions."

At this prompt, Yorick stood and offered his pen to a woman to his right. She accepted, before extracting one of her own from the inside of her casual, floral-themed jacket pocket and passed the pen down to her right. She paused, poised over the bottom of the second page.

Tessa had been one of the better negotiators Yorick had dealt with over the years. She'd successfully set up and run an online pet food delivery system, allowing for tailored food packets to be made up and distributed across the UK. People loved their pets more than sense itself. The only thing they might have loved more? Taking pictures of those pets. And then submitting them to the pet food company out of excitement, showing how much more energy their aged Labrador had got back. It was cute, he assumed. But less so when you stripped away the images of the dogs in the frame and pooled the images of insides of thousands of UK homes. Which, when placed into skilled hands, could reveal a lot of information. "And we're expected to sign this today? Now?"

Yorick chose that moment to break his silence, addressing Tessa while staring at her short, cropped blonde hair that had a playful curl to its fringe. "Everything would run a lot more smoothly, if you would, Tess. Isn't that right, Huang?"

"Precisely, Yorick. It would be preferable for all concerned."

A key proprietary system lay at the heart of the data warehousing agreement. It was called Yulü. In Chinese folk religions, there existed a pair of divine guardians. They oversaw doors and gates, acting as protectors against evil influences. Yulü was the name of one half of the couple.

Once logged into the system, all the different companies were separate. The engineers from all fourteen had been invited to hack into it, but none had succeeded. It had passed all their tests. And housing them all together was integral to the savings that each of them enjoyed.

During the exchange, Yorick noticed that more pens had appeared from various bits of clothing. Of the fourteen sets of documents, he had counted a half dozen so far that had been signed. Six other partners were poised, with pen in hand, including Tess's. While two younger men towards the back remained empty-handed, trying to catch the eye of their temporary colleagues around them to borrow a pen. Even at this level, those types existed, Yorick sighed to himself.

And then one of the pens raised into the air, drawing Yorick's eye. "Rob?" Yorick asked, raising his eyebrows as he did.

A black man with a manicured beard straightened himself in his chair and met Yorick at eye level. He started speaking with an accent Yorick had heard plenty of in the northern areas of London. "Yorick, Huang. There are some generous numbers on here. Significant growth capital, for what is only a negligible increase in shareholding. So much so, that it's almost a gift," Rob said. He shuffled the first page behind the second and ran his finger down the top few lines before bringing it to an abrupt halt. "So why do I feel like agreeing to this is a present from us to you?"

Yorick opened his mouth to speak, but the room was filled with Rob's voice once more, "If we accept this money, this investment, then all the data that you're holding in your magical warehouses, you're allowed to collate it? Aggregate it across all of us?" Rob said, opening his palms across the room in a circular motion.

Huang met the silence before it had a chance to settle. "I think you misunderstand us, Rob, is it? Rob. Our warehouses make use of efficiencies.

That means some of your data will be run across the same systems. There is an exceedingly small chance data might run at the same times across your businesses, and an even smaller chance that this might mean it could become vulnerable to a breach. But risks are part of every business, are they not?"

"You're telling us you can't guarantee the safety of our customers' data, right? We can't guarantee it if we agree to integrate our data onto these new systems of yours." A few chairs were readjusted in the room, from those with pens already laid on the papers in front of them.

"Nothing is guaranteed in the world of business. I don't need to tell you that. You wouldn't be at this table if you hadn't learnt that lesson. Who around it hasn't had a data breach yet on their systems, the ones based internally here that we don't currently hold?" The entrepreneurs exchanged sheepish glances across the table. One lonely hand went up, Yorick's most recent investment, before going back down again. "I'll take your silence as admission. We're talking about acceptable risk, Rob. We're not naïve to think that we can talk in absolutes."

Rob's eyes scanned the room and as he caught Ben's gaze, the floppy haired millionaire jolted into action as though he was a coiled spring. "I can't speak for all of you, but I wouldn't be where I am without Huang's help. Surely you can all recognise that? Nobody else can get a deal like this. Not possible. You want to give up growth, Rob. You go for it. But I'm signing." And with a flourish, he whipped his pen through the air and scrawled across the bottom.

Slowly, four others around the room took his lead and lowered their pens to the papers on the table. Rob watched each of them. Yorick watched Rob. Until he, too, picked up his pen, placed his left hand across the top half of the page, to stabilise it, and made his mark at the bottom.

He placed the cap on his pen and let it roll towards the centre of the table, but it was snatched up by a bald, short figure next to him, who hurriedly added his own signature at the bottom of his own document.

"Right, thank you all. We'll get copies over to you tomorrow morning," said Yorick, placing his middle finger under the table once more. "Craig will show you out." The door in the bottom right of the room slid open, allowing Craig to slither out and open the door in the opposite corner. He stood by as the pairs of feet shuffled out.

Once the last pair had drained from the room, Yorick tapped the table.

Huang's voice filled the room once more. "And my copies?"

Yorick's gruff laugh felt alien within the glass walls. "What?" he said.

"We're doing this one by the book, Yorick. No stone and all that," said Huang.

"First time for everything, I guess. We'll get them right over," said Yorick.

"Yes, Yorick. Please see that you do." And with that, the line went dead, casting a soft crackle across the room's speakers.

Craig came back into the space, a bottle of dark whiskey in his left hand. He took large strides towards the door in the bottom right corner of the room. But was halted in his tracks by Yorick's booming voice, "Contracts, Craig. Now."

The bewildered face turned to him in a shrug, "But you said tomorrow morning to that lot?"

"Huang's contracts. Now."

The young man's shoulders sagged as he realised he would not be included in the celebrations. He turned back but was interrupted again, "The whiskey. Leave it, Craig."

Yorick plucked up the bottle, pulled back the sliding door of the den and stepped inside, taking in the soft, brown colours that flooded towards him. He closed the door behind him and settled into the same armchair. Next to him was a table with a record player. It was styled to the 1960s but had been produced on the high street earlier that year. He flicked the needle into its groove and picked up the glass tumbler alongside it.

He emptied an inch of whiskey into it and placed the bottle at his feet. The sounds of an angsty punk rock band from the late 90s filled the small room.

Yorick soaked up the first sips and then reached for his smartphone. He brought it to his eye once more, allowed the protected app to open and typed out a terse message to Huang.

AND MY MONEY?

The start of the song's chorus rang out as the Sent message disappeared from his screen.

I never conquered, rarely came
16 just held such better days
Days when I still felt alive
We couldn't wait to get outside

The buzz of his phone brought him back into the present.

H: PAYMENT MADE. CONGRATULATIONS, YORICK.

He knew he didn't need to check. Job done. His biggest to date. He closed his eyes and for the first time in what felt like weeks, relaxed.

You'll close it off, board it up,
Remember the time that I spilled the cup,
Of apple juice in the hall.
Please tell mom this is not her fault.

Slowly, his eyes folded open. He reached for his phone and flicked it to life. He went to his sparsely populated photo gallery and viewed the most recent image. The outside of a chicken shop reflected at him. He noted down the number on the poster in the window and dialed it.

Tobi. Friday. Midday.

It was seven minutes to midday when Tobi cracked the doors of West &
West and made his way slowly up the stairs. He hadn't planned on going in
at all, but a barrage of missed calls and emails from Clara had made it
impossible to ignore the day.

He stepped out of the lift and made his way towards his office, dragging
his toes lightly with each step. Clara wasn't at her desk and he silently said a
small prayer of thanks as he slipped past, closing his office door behind him.

He sensed something was off before he turned around. Technology had
helped Tobi in a lot of ways in his career, but none more so than its ability to
declutter his life. He operated a 'clear desk' policy; no excess paper in and
around his office. He saw it as in the best interests of his clients; loose lips
may sink ships, but stray paper was the work of the devil in corporate
finance. But, in reality, it provided the order and structure around him that he
craved.

So, when he turned back to the room to find his desk covered with every
newspaper rag of the day dotted across it, it was enough to make him forget
about his throbbing headache. Briefly.

He made his way around to the other side of the desk, taking in the
words that were screaming at him from the headlines; "China", "NHS",
"Connections", "PM" and "hot water". Before he got there, his door flung
open and in strode Clara. No knocking this time. Her matching skirt, jacket
and stockings painted her in a formidable armour of dark grey as she stood at
the threshold, arms crossed.

Tobi cracked off the first shot of friendly fire. "Before you start, I don't
know what any of this-" he waved his hand vaguely across the expanse of
tabloid and mainstream papers in front of him, "- any of it means. I've had
my phone off all morning. Sorry."

"No time for apologies, and you look like absolute shit by the way. But
all of that," she darted her eyes at the papers in front of him, "All of that has
given us what we wasted our time looking for last night." Her eyes flicked
back to his face as she raised an eyebrow. "Assuming you didn't find
anything about Jennifer, of course?"

He slumped into his chair and rolled his eyes towards the ceiling, allowing himself a moment of self-pity but knowing she wasn't about to let him dwell in it. "No, I didn't." He snapped forward, slapping his palms down flatly onto the piles before him. "What do I need to know?"

"Let's start with the boring stuff," she said as she took the seat opposite him and used her index finger to punctuate her words, pointing to specific images as she spoke. "The country's going to shit again, of course; it's all the PM's fault because he's been caught dealing in corporate favours at the expense of the public. Nothing new there, but in this case it's the NHS involved and, that's important."

The images swam in front of Tobi's eyes, blending into one. "And this time it's different, because?" he trailed off.

"Well, for most people, it's the same old bullshit. But what makes it different for us, is this," she said. She moved her index finger across to an image of a Chinese woman that Tobi didn't recognise. She was featured prominently across most of the papers. "This is Zhi Ruo Yang. She heads up a medical supply factory in Guizhou province in China. Her factory has been providing surgical masks, gloves, other bits of protective equipment for the NHS since winning a new contract from the PM last year. Turns out, they contain dangerously high amounts of perfluorinated chemicals."

The swimming in Tobi's head started to speed up. "Perfluoro-whats? They sound...bad?"

"With long, close exposure, yes. Especially if you're around pregnant woman. Like people in the NHS tend to be when wearing surgical masks and gloves."

"Jesus."

"Yes, but unfortunately that's not our focus." She was now dragging her index finger across other bedraggled images of the PM as she continued talking. "The PM is being raked over the coals for approving this deal in the sake of cost-saving, the usual story. But I thought I'd remembered seeing Zhi's name somewhere else." She paused to pull out her iPad. When she turned it towards Tobi, he could see that she'd opened it on the latest report they had received from Mikey on Jennifer.

"This is linked to Jennifer?" The fuzziness inside his head subsided momentarily.

"Not directly, but I'll get there," she said, swiping left to right on the screen. She arrived at the image of Fazir and his piercing blue eyes. She paused and scrolled down, before enlarging on a section titled, *Known*

Commercial Associates. Even in this state, Tobi was able to pick out the same name of Zhi Ruo Yang amongst a long list.

"Fazir is the Minister of Health, after all, so it doesn't seem out of the ordinary that he would have a connection to Zhi. What am I missing?" said Tobi.

"The prominent line in all of the news coverage is that the PM has been thrown under the bus of this exposé by a fellow party member." She pulled the iPad back towards her and opened what looked like her email account. She clicked on the top item and turned it back towards Tobi. "And Mikey is certain that Fazir is the leak."

Tobi scanned through the email, including some notes from a highly questionable mobile phone tapping device that Mikey had collected just two days prior. It hadn't been part of the brief, but Mikey was the type who did his work, billed you afterwards, and expected you to pay. And you did, because it was worth it. "So, we were on the right track with thinking his political ambitions went straight to the top job."

"Seems so. But that's not the only place that Mikey came across Zhi." She delved back into the document on the iPad. This time she brought an image to the screen and it was one Tobi finally recognised. It was from a charity event that West & West had arranged in the early days of HEAL-y's success. It had been their attempt at a form of guerrilla public relations. Prominent health industry leaders from across the world had been invited to raise funds for third world benefactors; those that could now be supplied with medical drugs thanks to Simon's creation.

The image that Clara brought up was of the main table. The table itself was circular and the focus of the image was Simon and a couple of notable pharmaceutical CEOs, set to the left of it and posing casually. But to the right of the image was Jennifer, deep in conversation and unaware of the photo being taken. She was listening intently to an Asian woman. Zhi.

"But this image was taken four, maybe five years ago? We're not suggesting that this has been that long in the making?"

"Unlikely. But what we do know is that -" she started listing factors on raised fingers, a trait that charmed Tobi, given her fierce intelligence, "- Jennifer knows Zhi from years ago. There's not a lot of love lost for her soon-to-be-ex husband Simon. She's more than just a fan of Fazir's health policy recommendations. And he's gunning for the top job in the land. I don't know about you, but the fact that Simon's business lies at the heart of all of this makes me more than just a little bit nervous for us." She drew her fingers back into her palm, made a small fist and lowered it to the table.

Tobi dropped his face into his palms and used his outstretched fingers to slowly massage his tired eyes, working his way up towards the top of his head. He ruffled his hair back and forth. He combed it back into place with his fingers by feel and said, "You're right. West & West doesn't get involved in politics publicly. The partners won't stand for it. It's time we step away."

Clara bristled at his words, pulling herself upright in her chair and arching her back defiantly. "Running has never been our style, Tobi."

He shook his head slowly while pawing at the papers in front of him, shifting them back and forth before finally losing his patience and sweeping a clutch of them to the floor. "Maybe there are different ways to fight, Clara," he said, aiming the words down at his desk.

He heard her rise to her feet opposite him, button up her jacket, and then she asked, "What the hell happened after I left last night? Drowning your sorrows and ability to retaliate?"

He brought himself forward to face her once more, looking up at her. "No. I..." he tried to find the words but realised there was nothing to grab onto. He'd pored through the contents of those hidden, aged envelopes for what had felt like endless hours and, for all those words, he was left without any of his own.

Rikki. Saturday. Morning.

The sun found its strength and winter's weak rays had been replaced by the fullness of spring's. They filtered through the windows of The Rams & Lion in dulled patches, fighting through clusters of grime on the glass. The brightest rays caught small dust particles on their way and illuminated them in a twisting dance.

Rikki could smell the new season in those movements. She brought a coffee mug to her lips, drawing in the flavours of the rising steam as she did. It was a few minutes before seven. She had always been an early riser, and a poor sleeper. Especially when news loomed on the horizon.

On the table in front of her was a canvas with faint tracings marked out across it, showing the start of a new creation. Alongside, a painter's palette sat unopened. She held a pencil in her hand in the air, trapped by the sun creeping in. She looked down at the jagged lines on the paper in front of her. She'd been attempting to draw a smooth curve for an hour. But each effort ended the same; the pencil's nib shaking across the page, tearing the arc off into untamed directions. She threw the pencil down in frustration. While she knew these days were coming, the realisation of her disease taking hold at last shook her with a deep sadness. She had been in a state of trapped fear for decades, waiting for the day when it would overpower her. She regretted that it hadn't happened when she was younger, when it should have. It would have made her decisions easier, she knew that for certain. The years of waiting should have prepared her for these days, for the start of the end. But it had created the opposite effect. She was frozen with uncertainty, afraid of the unknown.

The main door rattled as a set of keys searched for the lock. The door gave way and through it stepped Gabbi. The horizontal rays danced off stray strands of her hair. Framed from behind, her hair was like a mane on fire at its tips. Rikki pulled her inner strength to the surface as quickly as Gabbi had appeared.

"Morning, hun," she called out.

"Morning, love," Rikki replied.

"God, sun feels good this morning, right?" she said, dropping her bag and coat onto the bar's surface.

"Better each day. The day I stop enjoying that feeling is the day I'm done down here."

Gabbi cocked an eye and stared at Rikki from across the room. "Plenty of life left in you yet, I hope? Can't be doing all this shit on my own." She helped herself to coffee and moved across the room, pulling up a chair at the table by the window. She placed a stack of papers alongside her on the remaining chair at the table.

"It's been a while since you made us one of those," Gabbi said, her eyes directed towards the canvas in front of Rikki. "We'll have to make space for when it's done." She looked at the pieces of art on the walls and then at Rikki, her face showing a new softness to it. Her lips were parted as she sat transfixed, staring out of the window and up the street that ran past The Waldorf. She tried again. "Rikki? You ok? You're lost in another world."

The older woman shook her head as she brought her gaze around to Gabbi. "Sorry, sweetness. Lost in another time," she said as she bundled up the materials from in front of her and stashed them at her feet. "Don't worry about this, just keeping old hands busy. Shall we get right to it?"

"No time for a girl to even relax," said Gabbi, hauling the modest stack of papers onto the table in-between them. "It's all here, I think." She placed a tentative finger on top of the stack. "Financial records from the past five years. My best guess at an inventory stock count, and what I think they might value the rest at."

"The pile's bigger than I dared guess," Rikki said with a gentle grimace. She reached for the top piece of paper, which was a summary of the most recent financial records. She let out a long sigh, causing what remained of her coffee's steam to drift towards the window and fade into the sunlight.

Gabbi paged through the pieces of paper, pausing over the latest valuations of the property. "Reality says we're going to have sell, and based on these-" she tapped her fingers at the bottom of the page in front of Rikki. "- we'd get enough out for each of us to make do for a little while. I think."

Rikki passed the papers back to Gabbi, her interest having faded. "I've lived most of my days with not very much, dear. I don't need any more now. Whatever you can raise, you take it. We had a good run. And we gave it what we had. That's all there is to do with your days, if you ask me."

Gabbi lifted her eyes from the stark numbers at the bottom of the page. She'd run them through her head enough times to know that after taxes, lawyers' fees and whoever else would try to lay a claim to selling the place, she'd have enough to survive a couple of years. Enough for one last throw of the dice at the comedy dream, while studying something sensible to prepare for a stable future. The thought terrified her. "There may be one more option."

In all the years of knowing her, through all the protection Rikki had given without wavering an inch, Gabbi had never seen her lose patience with her. She had seen it happen with strangers plenty of times, but not with her. She saw it now. Rikki lowered her coffee mug to the table, placing it with a finality on the surface. It came to rest on top of the most recent financials.

"Sometimes in life, you gotta know when to fold 'em, love. You're young, but knowing that, well," she paused, lost eye contact with Gabbi and then pulled back into her. "I learnt that lesson the hard way. There's no going back, but it doesn't change the decision." Her shoulders softened as she reached across and placed her hands on top of Gabbi's. "We've had a good run, sweetness."

The sun had risen a few more degrees into the sky. It streamed at them, showering their faces. Gabbi steeled her gaze directly into it. She hadn't budged as Rikki had spoken. Her steadfastness stirred Rikki into more words, against her better judgement. "Alright, try me; one last time."

Gabbi didn't turn back to her, but spoke to the sunlight, blinking her eyes as she did, feeling the warmth on her eyelids for a brief beat each time she closed them. "What if I think I've found an investor? One who might let us run it our way."

Rikki stiffened in her chair.

"I'm serious. He's just one guy. He's not attached to some company and their rules. I don't think he'd care about the place, to be honest, but I think he'd listen to me. He has so far."

Rikki stood and turned back to the window, her gaze wandering the streets outside once more. They avoided Gabbi. "Wouldn't be a tall, bald man with all this money, would it?"

"And if it is?"

"I don't think it's a good idea, honey. Can you just trust me on that?" she replied, refusing eye contact.

Rikki's disinterest in the conversation unsettled Gabbi. She sought to bring her attention back the only way she knew how. "Come on, Rikki. You know he's the one who would have to watch out for himself," she joked.

The hard lines across Rikki's cheeks sprang to life for a brief flash.

"Didn't say I was worried about you." She looked down at the folded canvas at her feet, fiddling with the corner of the paper. "I'm not ready for that, Gabbi."

"Ready for what?"

Rikki reached for her coffee, drinking from it before she spoke again. "To go back. To the past."

Gabbi pushed her own mug aside and reached out towards Rikki, who had an agitated look on her face. "What do you mean, the past?" she asked.

Rikki straightened herself up and at last looked into Gabbi's face. "To a time when it was anyone else but just us, love. But you do what you feel is best. This is your home."

Gabbi took hold of the old woman's hands and patted them. "Well, he can't seem to say no to me. And I'm not done with this old place yet. Plus, I think he's looking for something. Something to save a wandering soul."

Rikki held a long silence. At last, she spoke, "Wandering souls are wild and unpredictable beasts, sweetheart. I hope you know what you're doing." Rikki stood and walked back to the bar. She retrieved her own coat and wriggled her way into it, adjusting her bag over her shoulder as she did. "This is your journey. I'm just trying to make sure you get through it OK. You let me know what you decide, and we'll ride it together. As we've always done." She made her way to the entrance and swung the door open. "Sounds like I should see you back here later?"

"Thanks, Riks. I'll call him this morning." said Gabbi. She watched the matriarch head across the street before she turned and disappeared. Their exchange left her confused, but she knew better than to probe any further with Rikki. If she wanted to talk, she would.

She reached down and pulled out her phone. She went to her call log and scrolled across the section titled, "Missed Calls". There was a number she didn't recognise at the top, from yesterday afternoon. But she knew who it belonged to.

Yorick. Saturday. Morning.

Yorick slept better that night than he had for weeks. He'd made his way back to his two-bedroom loft flat in Mayfair and logged into his internet banking. The account was not registered in the UK but confirmed Huang's payment.

Craig had finished the paperwork quickly and Yorick had dismissed him and his crew into the clutches of Soho in the early afternoon. Three of them had the decency to feign disappointment when he said he wouldn't be joining them. Whether that was to him, or his company card, he didn't much care.

He woke with a minor headache from the whiskey and enough vigour to seek exercise. His apartment was above a small yet exclusive workout studio on the ground level. His spontaneous decision meant that the spin classes would be full. He knew he could talk his way into one, but didn't have the heart. A slight pity, he admitted to himself, as he glanced at his watch. 09.15. He knew the current class would be packed with toned, experienced women of his age. With their hair pulled back into taut and serious bundles, focusing on their younger instructor in front of them, they would pedal against her for 45 minutes. After which, they would greet her fresher face with a forced high five by the door, taking her congratulations on a 'great effort' with the condescension with which it was served.

He greeted the gym's receptionist with a nod and motioned to her he was headed for the weights room, not to worry about him today. He skipped down the stairs and past the line of class attendees as they prepared for battle. He offered a knowing smile to a couple of familiar faces as he weaved down the corridor and through the crowd.

Just over an hour later, he re-emerged. He felt strong and in control; there hadn't been a hint of his condition that morning. It was in-between classes, and the hallway was empty. He soaked up the view of himself in the mirrors and then strode upstairs and to the breakfast bar. He lingered and made small talk with the young, petite barista, cajoling her as she threw assorted green ingredients, along with a generous scoop of whey protein, into a metal cup and blended them together. A pressed fruit bar was added to his order. He paid, and threw a parting grin to the girl, causing her to blush, and headed for the couches behind him.

They were all low to the ground; made for perching, not lounging. Yorick settled onto the arm of one, refusing to lower himself down into the seat itself. He sipped at the smoothie, his body gobbling up the nutrients. This was a good start to the day.

In front of him lay a small selection of the morning's papers, stacked and squared against the edges of the table. He reached down, plucked the top one between his fingers, and set his smoothie alongside the pile. He ruffled the familiar pink pages of the Financial Times with both hands, giving himself a full view of its front page.

They had led with an image of the Prime Minister, sweating and red faced, his hand raised to his foppish fringe of hair as if to brush it away from his face. In the bottom left corner of the square frame was a nurse in scrubs, mirroring the Prime Minister's hand movements, but standing over a gurney with a patient in it. In the bottom right was a smaller circular image of a headshot of an attractive Asian woman with dark, sleek hair and strong features. Yorick didn't need to read the caption to put a name to the face. It was Zhi.

"Morning, Yor-eeey," said a tall, blonde woman with a bob cut so sharp it could have been used to slice the produce behind the fruit bar. She had a thick, American accent straight from the west coast. "You look happy with yourself this morning!"

He glanced up from the pink pages with the realisation that his smile must have broadened while reading. He dialled it back. "Hey Ash, you alright?" he said, dropping his eyes back to the pages.

"Great, love. You have a great day, OK?"

"Uh huh," he said without a glance.

His eyes darted across the remaining details on the front page. He didn't need to read the further context on the inner ones. Snapping the pages together, he drained his smoothie and grabbed his fruit bar, taking a bite as he stood and made his way from the reception. He was flush with energy and took the stairs to the seventh floor, ignoring the doorman by the elevator, who beckoned him in. He bounded up them two by two but slowed as he neared the end, walking the final two flights at an ardent pace. He took a few steps inside his apartment, and dropped his keys, gym towel, water bottle, and phone to the table. As he did so, it rang.

Gabbi. He remembered calling her from the secluded room in his office the day before. She hadn't answered. A little more hazily, he also recalled trying again a couple, no, a few hours, later. Maybe more than once? He winced at the thought.

He closed his eyes, took a couple of deep breaths to slow his breathing and slid the green circle to answer the call, bringing it to his ear. "Yorick speaking."

"Hey stranger, it's Gabbi. From The Rams & Lion. And your favourite chicken shop," she said, her voice higher than Yorick remembered. She carried on before he had a chance to interject. "Sorry I missed your calls, lack of hands down at the pub at the minute." She took a brief pause and a breath. "How are you?"

"Don't worry about it. I'm a night-owl myself," he said.

"Sounds like you're having a busy morning. Have I caught you on the move?"

He took another deep breath. "Not at all. I've just finished up at the gym. All work and no play, that's what they say, isn't it?"

She exhaled in a short, punctuated laugh before continuing with a breezy tone. "We've got very different ideas of play. So, what was the emergency last night?"

"Emergency?"

"I thought that's what we'd agreed, a number to be used for emergencies of levity?"

He thumbed the edge of the counter's surface, forcing it to dig into his skin. "Ah, yes. I... it was nothing. An indulgent dial after a celebratory afternoon."

"Cheers to you, Yorick. You've earned that gym session."

He stiffened his back before he replied. "Look, I really should get on to some work. Maybe I'll call you another time."

"Of course, but before you go, Yorick, it's actually me who is looking for a bit of help."

"Yes?"

"Perhaps the next time you come to The Rams & Lion-" she started to say.

He cut her off as he responded, "I don't make that trip very often. Best to ask me now."

"Alright. Well, I wanted to ask for some... guidance. Advice. Financially, speaking. You see The Rams & Lion," she began once more.

"Is cutting back? Struggling? Folding?"

"Well maybe a bit of the first, and I'm trying to stop it getting to that point, but-"

"Gabbi, listen. I know how this goes. It starts with advice, but we both know how it ends; with asking for my money," he said, loosening up his back and sagging his shoulders.

"Yorick, that's not-" she tried once more.

"And it ends with me saying no."

The abrupt lack of words seeped from both phones into sad ears.

"I guess no call to an emergency line is ever a happy one. You take care, Yorick," she said, before ringing off.

He surprised himself. There was no urge to slam the phone down. He lowered it to the surface of the counter, placing it down with a light click. He made his way to the shower, dropping his clothes into the wash basket along the way. He turned the taps, adjusted the temperature, and waited for the steam to rise. He stepped under the powerful stream of water, feeling it pierce and puncture the skin on his head with a thousand tiny hot stabs. After a few seconds, he ran his fingers up his forehead, brushing the water away before continuing across his scalp, forcing the water to part and cascade down along his arms. He held himself in that position, arms up and fingers interlaced at the back of his skull, thinking to himself.

They're all the same. Back to business.

Tobi. Saturday. Midday.

Tobi didn't know how many laps of Green Park he'd completed. All he knew was that his feet had taken over, and answered a primal need for the feel of a dirt path grinding away at the soles of his shoes. They had taken him on alternating tours of the park. He'd started in a clockwise direction from his office, which took him past the grand buildings of Buckingham Palace and then looped up and around towards the hulking presence of Wellington Arch. When he reached it, he spun and sent himself back, in an anti-clockwise direction, alongside the palace and the doors of West & West. He carried on past the hot chocolate kiosk, and Malala with her Big Issues, for the half a mile that led back to the arch. Where he would spin around once more. The route took him 25 minutes.

It drove Sarah mad when they had first met. His need to walk and talk. Almost twenty years prior, he would grab their cordless landline phone and pace. Back and forth, in circular directions, his feet with a mind of their own, while his mouth ran through the inner monologue in his brain. The two were indelibly synced, mind and feet.

He'd just begun another clockwise loop, the hot beverage kiosk in the distance ahead of him, the arch behind him, when he was stopped in his tracks. His eyes were trained on the ground, taking in a few feet ahead at a time. But were soon filled by the robust frame of his brother. He was grinning.

"Just as well, you're rich, Tobi. God knows how much you spend on shoes," he said.

Tobi shook himself into the moment. "What?"

"Come on, bro. Carving another Tobi Track? I'd know that pacing anywhere," Yorick said.

The reference to their earlier years jolted him. He had picked up the habit from their father's walking trails through Plaistow Park. Around they would go, looping in and among the trees and paths, the metal framed jungle gym, in a far more criss-crossed pattern than he tended towards now. But always circular, always reversing on himself.

"What are you doing here, Yorick?" said Tobi as he glanced at his watch. It was after midday.

"A rare day off for me. Thought I'd take a wander, see where it led me," his brother replied.

"You don't take days off, even on Saturdays," said Tobi.

"Earned it after the deal I closed yesterday," said Yorick. His hands were in his pockets, his stance relaxed.

Tobi noticed a young woman with a stroller making her way towards them and steered Yorick to the right, moving them both out of her way. "This deal wouldn't have anything to do with your late-night TV appearance last week, would it?" he said as his eyes trailed on the wheels of the stroller, watching them as they bumped over the path's surface.

"Maybe. But I won't be needing your PR associate's help, judging by the papers. Perhaps you can recommend her to the PM," he said with a chuckle. His line of sight settled above the young woman with the stroller, into the distance where the large arch stood. He could tell Tobi had drifted off again, his words falling to the surrounding path. "Brother, you look like you could use a drink," he said, as he jerked his head back over his own shoulder and toward a pub he knew.

Tobi stirred. "Maybe."

They made their way back along the same path in silence. Tobi's eyes searched for the kiosk owner as they passed, but he was busy with a customer. As they crossed in front of Malala, he threw a glance in her direction, but she was readjusting items in her bag, unaware of his presence. They slipped in between slow-moving traffic and, two blocks over, found themselves outside a traditional looking pub called The Clarence.

It was styled with a nineteenth century appearance; wooden floors, except near the bar where a black and white tiled motif was prominent. Framed prints lined the wall and an out-of-date sign advertised an old-world dining room as available to hire. It had the same air as The Waldorf.

They moved to the bar and Yorick ordered two pints. The barman poured the first, letting the large foam head run off into the drainage tray before placing it down in front of Yorick. He had poured a third of the way on the second when Tobi interrupted him. "Cancel that one. I'll have a soda and lime."

Yorick and the barmen turned to him, both speaking.

"Tobs-" said his brother.

"Mate, I've started this one, so you're getting charged either way," said the barman.

"Fine, charge it. And leave it. I just want the lime and soda," Tobi said to them as one. Yorick grabbed his drink and headed to a tall table behind them with two accompanying stools. Tobi threw a cash note on the bar counter, retrieved his clear drink, and went to join his brother.

"I thought we were going for a drink?" said Yorick, taking a large sip from his pint.

They drank a few sips in silence, the barman looking their way as he cleaned glasses behind the counter. Tobi relented and met his brother's gaze for the first time that day. "I'm sorry. I've just got a lot on my mind."

"From the office? Or home?"

"Somehow both, at the same time," said Tobi. He felt his feet growing restless as they rested on the wooden strut halfway up the stool. They tapped against it, striking up a rhythm. He knew what was on his mind. "Why didn't you tell me about the letters, Yorick?"

"What letters? I haven't read a fucking letter in years."

Tobi's feet stopped tapping as he spoke. "All the letters that father sent you. The ones you never read," said Tobi. His hands closed around the tall, slim glass in front of him, feeling the condensation cooling against his fingers.

"I don't know what you're talking about, Tobi."

Tap-tap-tap went his feet once more. "I found a bunch of letters, twenty, maybe thirty, all written in his handwriting, sent to your home, your first one in London, and they were all marked 'return to sender'. And unopened. I'm just supposed to believe that every single one somehow unluckily avoided your attention? Your doorman just got it wrong, or maybe it was the postal service?" Tobi's voice rose as it increased in volume. The barman paused his cleaning, watching the pair more closely.

Yorick held his tongue. He drowned it in his beer, swallowing large mouthfuls as he drained the glass. He turned to the barman, squared up, and thrust a finger into the air.

"Don't do table service, mate," said the barman, placing the cloth and glass he was cleaning on the counter as he returned the stare.

"Christ," Yorick muttered under his breath. He levered himself off his chair and towards the bar, a crumbled note already in a balled fist. He dropped it on the counter from the height of his chest and watched as it bounced towards the barman's damp rag. The barman shifted the clean glass from one hand to the other, hesitated, and reached for the tap. He ran off another large foam head from the top of the glass and placed it down onto a coaster in front of Yorick.

"Cheers," said the tall, bald man, towering over him before heading back to the table.

As he did so, a pair of elderly gentlemen entered the pub. One of them, the larger of the two with a closely cropped shock of grey hair, called out to the barman in a sing-song tone. "Alright, Marty. Two pints of bitter, if ya don't mind."

"Coming right up, Robbie. Grab a seat, gentlemen," said Marty, motioning at a table towards the back of the bar.

Yorick waited as the elderly pair shuffled past their table, staring into his drink as they passed, and then turned back to his brother. "How did you find the letters?"

Tobi lowered his voice and slowed his pace as he spoke. "They were bundled up with the title deeds from when I bought his toy company. I was scratching around old papers, trying to piece together some loose ends on one of my clients. It doesn't matter how," he added, waving away his brother's raised right arm. "I just don't understand why you never even read them. Not one?"

Yorick took another deep draw of his drink. "There wasn't anything I wanted to hear from him. There was nothing he could teach me. After a lifetime of not having him around, him always working on those fucking toys instead of, I dunno, maybe spending some time with his real-life sons. Like some modern day Geppetto. Taught me everything I needed to know about putting success first, right? Worked out alright for us, didn't it? His two immigrant offshoots from Plaistow running this goddam town." It was now Yorick's voice that was raised. Yet it was muffled by the two old men laughing together. Yorick heard them and rolled his eyes to the ceiling, pouring more beer into his mouth.

"Jesus, Yorick. Get your head out of your own arse. If you'd bothered to read just one of the damn letters, you would have seen that he was trying to make amends. Don't you get it, the toys were always for us?"

"What a load of shit, Tobs. We'd outgrown those stupid wooden things by the time he had something he could sell."

It was Tobi's turn to roll his eyes towards the ceiling. "Drop the stubbornness for once. Everything he built with that business was to give us a life that he never had. That they never had."

"Don't bring her into this," said Yorick, before slamming back the rest of his second beer. "We didn't need him to be a fucking millionaire. We needed him to be around." He turned to the bar once more with his finger held up, muttered 'fuck' under his breath and stepped away from the stool towards the counter.

"Nah, mate. You're done here," said Marty, his arms folded across his chest, the damp, dirty rag still held in the fingers of his left hand. A glass in the other. In the corner, the two older gentlemen rotated towards the commotion.

Yorick threw up his hands, to the room at first, but then to Tobi. "I don't fucking need this. Today is a good fucking day for me."

Tobi called out from his seat as his brother marched towards the door, "I've forwarded the letters, Yorick!" All he received in response was the sound of a sad door hinging itself shut.

He lowered himself to the ground from his stool, held his palms upwards in apology first to the grey hairs at the back, and then to the barman, as he hung his head low over the tall table.

Rikki. Saturday. Midday.

Rikki left Gabbi with the paperwork at The Rams & Lions in search of some better news to add to her morning. One bus ride and a couple of underground exchanges later, she had arrived at the Blue Cross Animal Hospital in Victoria. She had a powerful love for all animals. Especially ones that were foreign to her. She'd felt the urge to return to the animal hospital more strongly than ever over the past fortnight.

She wasn't on the volunteer's schedule for the day, but she had rushed a small tabby cat to the hospital a week before and it was due for a second operation. She knew it was silly, but she wanted to be there for when it woke up. She needed the peace of mind that everything had gone ok, even though she would have been the first person called if it hadn't. Everyone knew Rikki within those halls.

The operation had gone as expected and once she'd satisfied herself that all was well, she treated herself to a rare walk in one of London's central parks. Usually she rushed to and from the place, eager to get back to the sanctity of Plaistow, but a restlessness within her urged her to let her steps guide her. She left the hospital and headed east towards Hyde Park.

She refused to rely on phones to find her way. Gabbi had consistently tried to get her to upgrade to a smartphone with all its features. Maps being one of them. But Rikki hadn't budged.

"It'll make it so much easier to stay in touch with you, Rikki. Come on, for me?" the young comedian had pleaded. But to no avail. She was lucky enough that she had agreed to even carry a mobile phone. Rikki lived next to Gabbi and didn't have anyone else in her life that she felt needed to be in constant reach of her.

"Being able to contact someone at a moment's notice means that's what people will do, Gabs. Make your plans and stick to 'em, that's how I am, how I've always been. Won't change me now." Rikki's steadfastness was what Gabbi's foster father had first liked about her.

She had been the only applicant to apply to the original 'Help Wanted' ad he had placed in the Newham local newspaper. "She had the look of someone searching," he had said to Gabbi. "If you can help a fellow searcher in life, why not do it?"

As Rikki walked, her mind toyed with her conversation with Gabbi that morning, but soon drifted to the words of her foster father. He had been right; she had been searching. Her search had brought her to Plaistow almost two decades ago.

It had been the one untouchable rule between herself and Gabbi; not to ask about her past. And Gabbi, true to her word, never had. But the pair shared the same eye for spotting wanderers. She would feel her presence when her own thoughts cast over the streets of the neighbourhood that surrounded their pub. And now, with Gabbi's call to Yorick, those wandering thoughts were stepping out of the shadows and into Rikki's line of sight.

She looked up to find her bearings and realised she had walked too far, finding herself outside Apsley House. It was the site of an old lodge that belonged to the monarchy. Its most notable inhabitant had been the Duke of Wellington. The same Duke to whom the monstrous arch across the road was dedicated. Rikki had taken a tourists' walking tour many years ago and had learnt the disputed origins of his nickname, the 'Iron Duke'. The colloquial interpretation was that it referred to his character, in particular, his uncompromising style, disposition and attitudes towards Catholic emancipation in Ireland and the Reform Bill. More popularly, though, many believed that it came from the fact that rioters and demonstrators over the same bill broke the windows of the royal home by throwing rocks at it, forcing him to erect iron shutters to barricade himself inside. With men, Rikki knew which theory was most likely to hold the truth.

It was then that her phone had sounded, a shrill and tinny ring screeching out of every seam of the bag around her shoulder. As she answered, a crowd of youthful backpackers made their way across the large intersection when the pedestrian light turned green. Rikki felt her feet follow them as they drifted towards the north-west entrance of Green Park.

Gabbi spared no details as she recapped the phone call from earlier that morning. She berated herself for being stupid enough to think that a man like that would ever be willing to help them.

Rikki fought a rising tension within her. No one treated Gabbi like that, no exceptions. But.

No, first things first.

She reassured her, confirmed she would see her later and hung up after just a few minutes. The backpackers had drifted ahead along the path that led towards the main gates of Buckingham Palace. Rikki lost her desire for walking and steered her own track towards the underground station that she knew lay at the far end of the park.

Her abrupt change of direction took a young woman with a stroller by surprise. The inexperienced mother jolted the pram to the right with a slight bump.

"So sorry, love. Didn't mean to startle you. Are you both ok?" Rikki said, bending over to peer inside the pram.

The young girl, barely out of her teenage years, glanced over the top of the stroller at her resting baby, who lay beneath a pile of shaggy blankets. "No harm at all, dear, don't you worry. You alright?" she said.

Rikki stole a glance at the small bundle of rags and the contented, scrunched-up face nestled amongst them. She offered a weak smile in exchange as she moved off. "Just fine, thanks. You take care," she said, picking up her stride.

It was when she lifted her head to the path ahead that she saw them. The lanky but sturdy frame with its gleaming, shaved head, catching the weak sun as it tried to break through the thickening clouds. It was Yorick. Alongside him, a shorter man she knew was Tobi. She fell into step behind the pair, fifty yards behind, as they headed towards the underground station. They carried on beyond it, however, to a nearby pub. A tension within her bubbled to the surface as she walked. She couldn't stay silent any more. She ignored the station and continued in her pursuit of the pair.

Her coffee steamed up against the window. The order had specified 'extra hot' and the letters 'E' and 'H' were stencilled in clear black letters on the front of the disposable cup, above the misspelled name; 'Ricky'. Not that it mattered; it wasn't her real name, anyway. The Rams & Lion's guardian shrugged off the lid and investigated the dark liquid below, taking a second to let the wave of heat hit her nostrils. Outside, the clouds gathered and deepened in colour overhead.

She sipped the coffee. It was black, no sugar, and she savoured the bitter taste at the back of her mouth. The wisps of steam danced and swirled in front of her, mirroring her thoughts.

She wasn't an impulsive person. The decision to follow the pair had been years in the making. It was what she had done for decades, but always from a safe distance. One where they could never discover the truth. But close enough that she could always assure herself that they were safe. Especially after Pieter had passed away. They didn't need her, of course, but a mother's instinct never dies. Even if her former life had.

She brought the hot drink to her lips once more but swore under her breath as the shaking of her left hand took control of her. It sent rivulets of the scalding liquid across her fingers and she dropped the cup to the table, spilling more. She grabbed two paper towels and held them to her hands, wiping away the heat. Then, just as suddenly as she had burnt herself from the drink, she felt hot tears falling down her cheeks. She brought her hands to her face, the wet lines of her tears leaking through fingers that still tingled.

She had been diagnosed not long after they had moved to London. They'd fled their homeland in search of a better life. But those early days had been harder than either of them imagined they could be. They had no support, mentally, financially or physically. It had started with her crafts. She'd always been so adept with her hands. But then, while whittling at an old footrest, the distinctive jerks had first appeared. She'd nicked herself lightly that day. But it wasn't long before the convulsions became much worse.

"Huntington's disease." A rather attractive if boring doctor had said in a bare white room, from behind his clipboard. She'd never heard the term before. It almost sounded fun, like a summer activity you might seek with friends and children. But as he had continued to describe the degenerative nature of the disease, nothing could be further from the truth. "Life expectancy can be up to fifteen, maybe twenty years from diagnosis, in most cases. But your symptoms will deteriorate towards the, um, the end." She remembered that stammer as honestly as anything in her life. It had sounded so final.

That conversation had been not long after her 26th birthday. Tobi was five, Yorick, just three and a half. She would be lucky to see either of them make it to adulthood. It felt like someone had implanted a stone boulder at the bottom of her stomach, one that she could never dislodge. The waterways of her life had flowed over and around it from then until now, changing its shape in small ways over time, but never reducing its weight. She and Pieter had struggled on in the wake of the news, neither able to grasp what it meant for them. Then, one day almost a year later, she had been boiling milk on the stove. Tobi was perched on a stool next to her, Yorick playing with a toy car near to her feet. She remembered the coloured tiles around him that were typical of the 80s. They looked like molten lava that had been left to harden. As she'd gone to remove the pot from the stove, it had happened. The moment she had always feared. It was as if she'd been hit by lightening, the force with which the pot rocked and jumbled out of her hand, and crashed to those burning tiles. The hot milk spread itself everywhere, catching both boys across their arms and legs. As a small tribe, they all erupted in a shrieking panic.

She had reacted quickly, her spasms having subsided, and covered them in cooling rags. No serious harm had come to either. But the shock lived long within her. And Pieter. That was the start of the end. The thought of turning into an active threat to her sons was too much.

The doctors had feared that with the worsening impairments, her expectancy was likely to be shortened even further. And that news had made her mind up. She remembered how that day, the stone at the pit of her stomach had felt as though it had been set alight. It burned with a white-hot heat, eating up every other emotion within her. She'd told Pieter that she couldn't go on; she couldn't be the one who put their children in danger. She couldn't be the one that forced them to live with a mother that they would have to care for, and watch wither away, in the years - possibly months - to come.

She knew how resilient young children were. That they played at her feet in the kitchen the very next day was proof of that. Perhaps the lack of knowledge, or fear, is the key to trusting the unknown. Something that had become impossible for her. Walking away at that age gave them a chance to live a life that would be hard, but not as traumatic as watching their own mother emaciate before their eyes. They were young enough to spare them that future, she'd decided.

In those years, she had always asked herself the same question, over and over, "Why me?" Of course, there was no answer. There was just life. The life that hers had become, and would be. Through no fault of her own, she had fallen victim to the randomness of existence. And was left to deal with the consequences as best she could. The one solace in her decision had been that she wouldn't have long to live with it. But life hadn't finished with its tricks, and exceptions, for Monique. The hands of fate had wrung their fingers and chosen to deal her with a flush of irony. Her disease stalled in its progression for almost 30 years. Too long for her to go back on her choices. "A medical anomaly" the men in the white coats had said, with confusion.

"You're lucky."

But one person's luck was another's pit of stone.

The window she sat behind was opposite the pub that the brothers had slipped into fifteen minutes ago. The building itself was shorter and squatter than the ones that surrounded it. The top half was a uniform face brick design. Set within the brick were three attractive trellis-styled windows, each with overhanging flowerpots. The lower half of the building advertised the pub itself and was painted a stern matte black with gold lettering spelling out the name; 'The Clarence'. There was a small awning that extended a couple of feet over the pavement and was supported by two gold coloured metal stanchions. Each of them had several pockmarked dents in them, catching the falling grey light of the clouds in different patterns.

There was a sudden tapping at the window. It was sharp, distinct, and scattered. It took her a moment to realise that large raindrops were falling and battering the glass. They were gathering pace. It didn't take long before the road outside became slick and transformed the day.

Beyond her wrinkled and stubby fingers, now wrapped around the warmth of her temporary mug, a burst of movement caught her eye. She looked up to see Yorick moving with a sharp step. He took awkward strides that were too short for his legs and ploughed beyond the awning and into the full strength of the rain, dipping his head to the drops that pelted him from above.

She rushed to grab her bag and coat, dropping the warmth of the mug onto the surface once more, and stormed out of the coffee shop. Her short legs moved at double the pace to keep up with the strides that stretched out in front of her. She ducked and weaved in and out of on-coming pairs of feet, their bodies hidden behind dipped umbrellas that were weakly fighting the aerial bombardment. Yorick's hairless dome floated above them all, bobbing to the left and right as he headed towards the park.

As they neared it, the smell of churned and disturbed turf flowed through the air, heavy and full. It brought renewed energy to her legs, imploring her to quicken and strengthen her stride. He was moving past the line of street vendors outside the station, many huddled within their makeshift stalls for shelter. He plunged to his left as if to enter the park, but then turned right, towards the ramp that led into the underground station. Concerned that she might lose him in the crowd, she called out to him, throwing off the shackles of forgotten memories as she did so.

Yorick pulled up at the sound of a voice. He couldn't have heard what he thought.

"Skeletor! Skeletor!" There it was again, this time closer.

He turned, aware of the shifting rain as it went from striking his forehead to the back of his head. His eyebrows relaxed at the respite and, as they inched upwards, he looked at an average height woman stuttering in her steps towards him, but progressing. Her ashen coloured hair, pockmarked with red, was pinned against her scalp. A wrinkled and crooked index finger was held aloft. But her hooded eyes peered out with clarity through the rain. "Excuse me?" he said.

"Yes, sorry. It just came to me, no offence meant," said the woman, her index finger transforming into a swift hand waving gesture. Up and down. She looked flustered. "You know, tall and bald. Anyway," she said, her voice tailing off as if confused in thought.

The recognition hit Yorick as she dropped her hand to her side; the old woman from Gabbi's pub. His shoulders sagged as he felt a burst of temperature surge up through his chest and neck. "Ah. Right. Shouldn't you be haranguing designer suits out of a warm pub?"

The top of her head came up to his shoulders, but she met his eyes with a softness that caught him off guard. When she next spoke, it was with a tone of voice he hadn't heard from her before. "How about getting a suit into a pub, permanently?"

He sighed as the call with Gabbi came back to his thoughts. He breathed out as he spoke. "I know times are tough, but it's just not my scene, alright? It's her problem and yours, not mine," Yorick said, turning on his heel.

"You know she's not just doing it for herself, right?"

Reluctantly, he felt his curiosity bite. "What do you mean?"

"You don't know me, but I know you. Your kind, at least. They've filled that place and my life in this city for almost twenty years; the wanderers, I call 'em," she started, with no sign of letting up. At this last word, he turned to face her. The rain had dropped off into a gentle drizzle around them as she continued. "I know them because I am one. I'll tell you where it's got me; alone and wandering for too long. The first time I've paused for long enough to stop myself from wandering was when I met Gabbi. Sure, we both want that pub, but she doesn't need it. Not like I did, like I do. Like so many others like me do. It gave me a home. But she doesn't give that chance to just anyone."

Yorick ran his hand up from his forehead to the base of his skull, removing as much water as he could. "It's a nice pitch. But roots aren't for everyone. Good luck to you, but I've got actual business I need to tend to," he said with a series of clipped words. He turned and headed off down the ramp, into the crowds of people gathering at the turnstiles, leaving Rikki standing in the rain.

Tobi. Saturday. Afternoon.

"You're soaked," said Clara, with a neutral tone, rising from her chair as Tobi stepped into the office. Water dripped from every part of him, the tips of his shoes, the hem of his trousers, his sleeves, his hair.

He breezed past as if he hadn't heard her and headed straight for the airing cupboard. He had expected her to be in the office today; she couldn't resist it in times of crisis. He ran a towel through his hair and over his clothes, damming the dripping flow as best he could. He looked up at her while brushing down his shoes.

The rain had been just what he'd needed to free himself from the week's confusion. "Can you get me a 'walk and talk' with Fazir? The sooner the better," he said, stripping off his wet socks and stepping towards the small shower cubicle next to his office.

"Health Minister, Fazir, yes? The one at the heart of the shitstorm that's just erupted, that one?" came Clara's response with the same neutral tone.

Tobi paused for a second before replying, "That one," he said and pulled the cubicle door shut behind him.

He switched the shower on to full blast and waited for it to get to its full heat. After a few seconds, he stepped into the harsh stream, allowing his tensions to melt from him. He'd done what he could for Yorick and had bigger problems to confront on his own doorstep. He allowed himself another minute under the jets in silence, before shutting the water off and changing into the spare set of clothes he kept in the cubicle. He ran his fingers through his hair, ruffling it into his preferred broad side parting, although not as neatly as he would have liked, and stepped back out.

Clara's voice fired at him as soon as he slid the door open. "I've got you ten minutes with him at three. He wants to meet on the bridge in St. James' Park." She glanced out through the window behind her as her sentence tailed off. The rain had subsided. The park was next to Tobi's favourite. It would take him just under ten minutes to get to the meeting spot.

"Thanks. Did he put up much of a fight?" asked Tobi. He moved over to her desk, placing his hands palms down on the edge of the surface opposite her.

She paused from a maze of spreadsheets, put down her glasses, and looked up at him. With neither of them smiling, she said, "I should never have been able to get through to the Minister of Health on a day like today. Let alone have him readily agree to an impromptu meeting within the hour," she said and picked up the pen. She twisted the nib mechanism back and forth. "I don't like this, Tobi. You need to be careful."

He reached over and placed his fingers onto hers, wrapping them around the pen, bringing her movements to a halt. "I'll update you straight after."

Tobi took himself into his office and pulled the door closed. He had just under thirty minutes before he and Fazir were due to meet. He should have targeted Jennifer as his next move. But the memory of her eyes and words from Simon's house still coursed through him. He couldn't read her. It didn't feel safe to approach her again until he felt he had nailed down her motives.

Background politics was a realm that he was far more comfortable in. While the players traded places, the issues rarely shifted from a single constant: personal motivations. Power, greed, legacies.

He used the remaining time to research the latest headlines and articles that had been written since the NHS story had broken. He stood hunched over the keyboard at his desk, stabbing away at it as he scoured different sources. He took in a cross section of the media of outlets, left-leaning, right-leaning, and social media. The names of the Prime Minister and Fazir were trending, along with "PPEEVED". The public, and media, had latched onto the Personal Protection Equipment acronym. He tutted to himself and brought up a selection of brief video clips. He wanted to get a sense of the governmental response so far.

"Thoughts go out", "tireless heroes of our country deserve better", "launch of a full investigation." The usual empty soundbytes that Tobi had expected.

Then he came across a piece that caught his eye. It was titled "Health Minister throws unprotected PM under the bus". He clicked into the article. Scattered within it were prominent quotes from Fazir, showing that he had broken party ranks and pinned the final decision on the PM. In fact, the article said, Minister Khan had recommended against the contract and highlighted some concerns that he claimed to have surfaced earlier that year as to the legitimacy of the supplier's business. Fazir was making his moves more public, which meant Tobi's picture of him became that bit clearer.

Tobi settled into his seat. He pressed his feet into the carpet, enjoying the solid pressure beneath him. He looked down at his watch. It ticked over to eleven minutes to the hour. He shot to his feet, like a spring uncoiling. He gave a curt nod to Clara, grabbed a light rain jacket, and made his way out of the building.

Cutting across the south-east corner of Green Park, he indulged in the chance to dash across its lawns for a second time in the day and exited all too shortly afterwards. He crossed The Mall and slipped into St James' Park via a small iron gate. A quick check of his watch and he estimated that he was ahead of schedule and slowed his pace to a measured stroll. He arrived at the north side of the bridge at exactly three PM. He looked across it and saw the side profile of a tall, dark haired man with a prominent and clipped beard. He was staring out across the water. The Minister of Health was facing west towards Buckingham Palace. The water was calm, despite the deluge of rain that had fallen so recently. Small pieces of debris from the surrounding trees floated towards the bridge before passing underneath and slowing their trajectory once they got to the other side.

Fazir didn't turn as Tobi approached. But he started speaking when he got to within twelve feet. His tone was deeper than Tobi remembered from the conversation they had overheard in the coffee shop. "Mr. van den Berg, good afternoon. You'll excuse me if I dispense with pleasantries. What can I do for you?"

Tobi was quick to register the confidence in Fazir's voice. It was unsurprising given a man of his stature, but still impressive after what had unfolded. Tobi matched the tempo of his words. "Minister Khan, call me Tobi. I appreciate your making the time in what I imagine must be a busy day for you."

"All the more reason to make this efficient," said Fazir, turning to Tobi. His moustache connected to his beard and hung over the tip of his upper lip, making it difficult to discern his facial expression.

"I want to help you, Mr. Khan. By helping Jennifer. Sorry, Mrs. Pentworth," Tobi said, letting the words float over the lake in front of them. Both men fixed their gazes out over the ebbing water.

"I've heard of your thoughtfulness towards your clients. Jennifer has gone through a lot of late, it's true. So why are you out here, on this bridge, talking to me, instead of her?"

Tobi pressed his weight forward onto the balls of his feet, the stippling of the bridge's surface needling at his soles, before swaying back. "Mrs. Pentworth has instructed us she wishes to dispose of her interest in her husband's business. I believe you've come across it," said Tobi, turning to Fazir, who nodded. He had been part of the regulatory board who had approved the pharmaceutical app's application to be allowed to export British-made medicines to Africa. "In times of grief, it's easy to make rash decisions. Stability is important. For her, for the children. The business is growing, and I've lined up a successor. On top of that, we're willing to divest our stake in it to her at an attractive price." Tobi now turned to read Fazir's face, but the man next to him held his focus on the water below. "She's going to be very wealthy once the divorce goes through and the financial opportunity for her is ripe. I was hoping you would help me to persuade her to see that. Because of your, shall we call it, special friendship that you've built. One that a minister might prefer to keep quiet in times like these."

Fazir placed his hands on the thin metal railings in front of him. He gripped them and then released them just as suddenly, turning to confront the Dutchman. It was only then that Tobi appreciated his full height; he was at least two inches taller than he. Fazir brought his hands together with a steepling of his fingers. "Jennifer very much intends to dispose of all dealings with her ex-husband's, including his business interests. So, it is you who will stand to benefit from the financial ripeness, as you say, when you buy her stake. Because-" he reached into his inside left pocket and pulled out a manilla envelope with the flap closed, but not sealed, along the top. "-Mr. Pentworth's, shall we call them, indiscretions, are a cost you will have to carry."

He pressed the envelope to Tobi's chest and stepped back, resting his hands on the rails once more. Tobi peeled back the envelope and pulled out a small sheaf of papers. The textures across the paper varied. Some had a standard matte feel, while others were glossy.

The first was a printout of a string of text messages. There were no names listed but two different mobile numbers, alternating back and forth in digital conversation. Tobi recognised his own at once, and his heart skipped a beat as he connected the other a second later; Mikey's. They were inconsequential words to any casual observer, vague discussions of logistics and meet up times and locations at a track. He flicked through more of the same on matte paper before he came to the first feel of a glossy page.

It was a picture of a vehicle, a large lorry. The one from Simon's fleet. The next page was also glossy, but featured a registration plate. It was the same as the one from Simon's fateful morning. Except this time, it was not on a vehicle but in a pair of hands. Hands which belonged to a man Tobi recognised as part of Mikey's crew. A dizziness descended on him, and he reached out to steady himself against the railing with his right arm. Fazir knew all about how Tobi had orchestrated Simon's fall from grace. If word got out about his role in all of it, no one could trust West & West ever again. Everything that he'd built would come crashing down.

Fazir straightened himself up and glanced at his watch before turning his gaze on Tobi once more. He watched as the shorter man's combed hair hung across his forehead in the breeze as he stared past the papers in his hands and towards the ground beneath him. It had just gone ten past the hour. "I must be going. It's getting windy now, Tobias. And I hate the wind, don't you?" He said as he turned to leave. He took two paces and glanced back over his shoulder before landing one final blow. "When you ask yourself how, Tobias, and I know you will, I suggest you and your brother have a chat. My Chinese associates and I will always be many steps ahead of the pair of you, because your brother has given us more information about everyone than even he will ever know," he said, smoothing down the front of his tie. "Jennifer and I thank you for your help. Both of you." He resumed his stride and headed south towards the banks of the Thames where the Houses of Parliament stood in the distance, waiting.

Yorick. Saturday. Afternoon.

Yorick stormed out of the elevator doors and collided with Craig, who was carrying a takeaway cup of coffee. Milk frothed through the protective lid and over his hands. He winced and swore but caught himself, "Fu--sorry, Yorick. Alright, boss?" he said with a high pitch.

Yorick ignored him and continued on his forceful path to the main conference room. He slammed the door shut behind him, hammered Huang's number into the keypad next to the door and slumped into the nearest chair.

The old woman's attempts to tell him what to do with his life had been the final straw. He'd lived his life how he wanted to. Don't expect others to look after you if you don't look after yourself, right? Isn't that what his father had taught them? It had hit like a punch in the face; for years, he had been dancing and singing along to Huang's tune. He had earned his chance to call the shots for once. To leave his mark. Enough was enough. Time was running out.

The dial tone of Huang's phone filled the speakers in the room. The vast table disappeared into the distance, dropping off a cliff into the glass walls The ringing went on and on and then clicked off. There was no option to leave a voicemail. Yorick bellowed into the surrounding room, "Redial!" The ringing started up again. Another click at the end, followed by silence. He repeated the process five, six, maybe seven more times. He wasn't counting, just listening. The loop came to an abrupt halt, but this time not with a click.

"Mr Huang's line, how may I assist?" said a female voice with a faint Chinese accent. He didn't recognise it. Yorick glanced at the array of clocks that lined the wall nearest to him. There were six, each displaying a different time and fixed with a small metal plate beneath. The plates held the names of corresponding cities, running from left to right; Los Angeles, New York, London, Paris, Guizhou and Sydney. The fifth clock along, Guizhou, showed it was past eleven in the evening. Throughout their relationship, Huang had existed in his own time zone.

"I need to speak to Huang, now," Yorick barked into the room.

"I'm afraid Mr. Huang is not in Guizhou, Mr. Yorick, so this is not possible on this line," said the voice.

Yorick pursed his lips and shook his head. He muttered into the empty air, "Where the hell is he?"

A silence greeted him. Yorick spun round to look at the call panel by the wall. It was still green. After a few seconds, the voice crackled back into the room. "Please, sir. He landed in London this morning."

Yorick bolted out of his chair and slapped the panel as he exited the room, changing the screen from green to red. By the time it faded to black, he was in the elevator heading to the ground floor.

On the rare occasions he spent the night, Huang only ever stayed at one place during his visits to London. It wasn't a hotel, but a collection of serviced apartments. The property that housed them was on a quiet lane running off the dominant roundabout at Old Street in east London. From the outside, it looked like a typical building of the area; a light brown brick face with tasteful but recessed, white trellised windows. It rose up six storeys and was topped with a couple of chimneys poking out into the sky. It was the tallest in the lane, and could have been mistaken for a refurbished warehouse. A simple black door, flanked by two white pillars, hid the elegant opulence within. Yorick rang the bell.

A pleasant young male voice came over the intercom and greeted Yorick by name, having already identified him through the door's pinhole camera. Yorick stepped inside and took in the atrium that greeted him. Above him was a vast glass ceiling with its panes tilted at various angles to regulate heat and transfer light. It made him feel as if he'd stepped into a greenhouse. But one with refreshing, and rarefied air. He breathed it in and felt his heart rate slow. The young man with the practised voice came to meet him at the apex of the room. He informed Yorick that, while he couldn't divulge information about any of their current or past guests, as he was a friend of The House, they'd be more than happy to let him make himself comfortable at the upstairs bar where he could wait to see if anyone appeared.

A circular metallic staircase rose from the middle of the floor near to where they were standing, inviting Yorick to ascend into the light of the bar above. He reached the top of the stairs without breaking stride. As he emerged from the staircase, soft textures of pastel coloured couches and foliage of green, pink, and white plants greeted him from every angle. The centre of the room housed a circular bar. Yorick caught the attention of the young woman behind it. Her arranged blonde hair and defined jaw took him back to the girl from his gym's breakfast counter. He nodded in her direction. She set to work on a small bronze tumbler, filling it with ice and mint. He settled down into a peach-coloured couch with a view over the surrounding lane. The varying heights of the neighbouring buildings afforded broken views of the city's banking district. The blonde girl approached him with the confidence of someone far older. She placed the drink down in front of him, told him it was nice to have him back, and moved back to her position. He was the only one in a room that seated twenty, but spaciously. He brought the metal cup to his lips. The coldness of the iced drink hit him hard. But then the warm flow of the bourbon calmed and smoothed his tongue. He waited.

Two hours passed. Yorick flicked through the magazines and newspapers that were scattered on a table. He ordered a couple of items from the small plates section of the menu. It described itself as being inspired by both California and the Mediterranean. He knew the combination was odd, but didn't question it any further. When the food arrived, he realised how hungry he had been. In between mouthfuls of a ricotta herb salad, he assaulted a nduja arancini, barely registering the scented truffle pecorino on top. The spicy sausage within the rice crust met his primal need for meat and carbohydrates. He could have ordered the same again and demolished it. But he resisted. He lost his edge once he felt he had eaten enough.

He used the remainder of the time to think about what he wanted to say to Huang. The old woman's words ate away at him. But there was a truth in what she had said. It was time to make his move. He was tired of being the big fish in a moderately sized pond. Craig and his band of brotherly idiots were no match for him. He knew he could swim with the sharks, and Huang needed to know it was time to give him that chance.

The soft clinking of footsteps ascending the winding staircase broke Yorick's chain of thought. The sound infiltrated the silence of the room. Yorick craned his neck over the couch to take in the figure. From above, he spotted a thick mass of dark hair advancing. A tailored, dark grey suit jacket encased a set of wide shoulders and was combined with short, purposeful steps. It gave Yorick all the identification that he needed.

Huang rounded the top of the staircase with his back to Yorick and made his way over to the bar. The barman placed a hi-ball glass packed with ice, black cola and a slice of lemon in front of him. As he turned, he fixed his eyes on the gleaming dome of the Dutchman. Yorick remained in his seat as he approached.

From ten feet away, Yorick spoke, "You didn't tell me you were coming to London." They were alone in the room. The thought registered in his mind that he had been the only customer all afternoon.

"I'm here for other business, Yorick. May I sit?" said Huang, lowering himself into the teal coloured, deep-set armchair opposite his business partner.

Yorick offered his hand towards the chair as Huang completed the motion. "Business, or politics?" he said. "Our Prime Minister has found himself in a pickle."

Huang placed his drink in front of him on the glass-topped table. It didn't make a sound. He leaned back into the support of the chair and placed his hands together. The protruding wingbacks above his shoulders made them appear even wider and more prominent to Yorick's eye. "This is a busy time for me, Yorick. What is it you want?"

Yorick's long limbs manoeuvred him forward onto the edge of the couch, his suit jacket silhouetted against the soft colour. "To be on the inside, Huang. Fiddling about with these-" he waved his hands in the air, weak at the wrists, "- these technology firms, getting them to sign away their data to you - it's child's play," he said, before inching further forward. He lowered his voice. "What's happening in the warehouses in Guizhou? I know you, or your bosses, were involved in yesterday's news. And I know the warehouses are connected. Join the dots, circles, triangles and hexagons for me. Let me in. I've been loyal to you, haven't I?"

Huang met him eye to eye. He studied him for a long second. Unblinking. "We don't just let someone inside, Yorick. They have to buy their way in."

Yorick mirrored Huang by leaning back. But the support of the couch was too low for his lengthy torso, leaving him perched at an awkward angle. "What's the price?" he said.

Huang's eyes roamed the room, starting and ending at the bar, which stood empty. He adjusted the hem at the front of his jacket, ironing out a small series of non-existent creases. Satisfied, he laid his hands on his lap. "Yorick, when I visit these shores, I do so quietly. Like a soft breeze in the shadows of a large tree.

"I drift in, and I drift out. You see, back in Guizhou," he said and reached to place his hands around cola in front of him. The condensation had melted away. "In Guizhou, the climate is temperate. Neither severe winters nor hot summers," he said and returned the glass to the table. "I feel comfortable to venture more freely there. But here, it is in the shadows that I can find that temperate climate. That is where I live and work when I am here. Do you understand?" A small strand of jet-black hair had fallen across the left side of Huang's forehead and he used the silence to tuck it back into place, undisturbed once more.

Yorick bowed his head an inch and ran his own hand over the top of his scalp. He looked back up as he spoke. "I'm a rich, orphaned immigrant who hasn't been back to his home country in almost three decades. The shadows of this city, any city, are the closest thing I have to calling a home. Living in them is all I know. If it means I can pull the strings from there, then it's a price I'd happily pay."

The soft ding of the elevator rang out, bouncing off the glass panels above them. The young man who had greeted Yorick stepped through and moved behind the bar. Huang nodded in his direction and stood. A bottle of whiskey made its way to them, the amber hue caught in a shaft of light that fell from above. "First, turn off your phone, Yorick," Huang said and waited for him to obey. "Now, let me tell you about our warehouses, Yorick. The ones you've helped to stock, more than anyone else."

Tobi. Saturday. Night.

The meeting with Fazir had sapped Tobi's strength. He couldn't return to the office and face Clara. Instead, he had spent the afternoon chasing shadows, looking for his younger brother. He couldn't get through to Yorick's phone, and he'd never known him to switch it off. But he needed to find him - he was at the heart of all of this.

He had checked at his office. No, the young men there, working on another weekend, didn't know where he was. Yes, it was unusual that his phone was off. He had been past his properties; the robust and convenient Canary Wharf flat, the crisp, modern loft in central Mayfair and even his original, brick-faced and ignored property near Elephant & Castle in southeast London. Few knew about that one. He'd come up empty-handed at all of them. The neighbours couldn't offer anything useful about "the tall, bald man who's always rushing about". The Mayfair doorman had at least confided, with the help of a small wad of cash, that he'd seen him that morning on his way to and from the gym.

His frustrated efforts had taken him eastwards. He had continued in that direction, more in hope than purpose. A mix of his feet, public transport, and a raging mind led him to a park. He was back in Plaistow, but the scene was one he no longer recognised. The park bore little resemblance to his childhood memories. It was established around a renovated playground. Fresh white sand marked out a large sandpit in the middle. An arrangement of kids' climbing equipment, a metal slide and a small wooden hut, sat on top of the beachy surface. It gleamed in the early evening light. Tobi's mind drifted over his own daughter playing on similar playgrounds. Those warm memories had replaced his own, where playgrounds like this one had never featured.

The Waldorf was a short walk westwards. He wound his way around the circular sandpit, looking on at a young family of four. A mother and father were playing hide and seek with their two boys. The children shrieked with delight as they darted in and among the simple structures built on sand.

Tobi breathed in the scene and moved beyond them, where his feet took him to The Waldorf. Their father's pub. The familiar sounds of karaoke crooned out from under the door. Voices sang from inside that were full and vibrant, but also relaxed and calm. They represented the unique energy of a gathering of seniors. He hesitated, sensing a feeling in the soles of his feet; they weren't done yet. He was on the move again, a further fifty yards down the street. He sighed when he realised The Rams & Lion was empty and closed.

But a movement behind the bar caught his attention. A round frizz of hair bobbed in and among the shelves, almost lost against the glass bottles and mosaic of liquid colours. The young comedian was making notes as she went along the racks. Tobi rapped on the central window of the locked door.

He raised himself onto the balls of his feet to peer through the glass pane. She made her way across the room and he rocked back onto his heels while he waited. He thought hard, willing himself to remember her name, but came up short. A key ratcheted in the lock and turned with a loud clunk. He readied himself with a smile, feeling the slight pull on the upper left corner of his lips.

He stepped back as the door opened outwards into him.

The realisation struck Tobi unexpectedly; she was beautiful. But in a way that he could not appreciate a fortnight ago. The light from the bar burnt at the edges of her round curls, framing her defined yet smooth features. They puckered into a set of thick lips that were full of a deep natural red. Her eyes told the truth to the lying features around them; she was tired. But a small smile offset them, forming a welcoming expression and one that Tobi hoped might be recognition.

"I... I'm sorry to disturb, but," he stammered. He hadn't done so for years, but his tongue had its familiar meaty feel to it. He felt the heat of embarrassment rising within him. He paused as a confused look marched across his face.

Her strong right arm held the door while she adjusted her body out of the way and said, "Yorick's brother, yeah?"

He breathed out, took her cue and stepped through the entrance. The room was cooler inside than he'd expected, and it helped him to settle. "You haven't seen him, have you? I mean, today?" He looked around at the closed bar and felt a flash of heat once more.

"I'm afraid not. I spoke to him on the phone this morning, but that's all. Is he ok?" she said with a softness to her voice. Tobi didn't pick up any affection, but no malice either. She motioned to a table in front of them, pulling back a chair. He followed her lead once more and lowered himself into it, feeling the weight of his shoulders sinking into his body as his lower body struck the firm wooden surface.

"That's what I'm trying to find out," he said with a sigh. "What did you talk about?"

She was back behind the bar, her notepad and pen in her hand. "Not sure it'll help you, I'm afraid." Her face showed genuine concern before she returned to her note taking. "He sounded busy. Maybe he's on a flight out to China? The last time he was in here he was talking about a trip out that way."

Tobi had run that scenario through his mind earlier in the day. It was plausible, rational even. But Fazir's warning had struck something within him. Something that had gnawed away at him throughout his search that afternoon. It was something that he hadn't been able to pinpoint, but he felt within his blood that his brother was in London. And in danger.

He looked up to find her staring at him. "Sorry, you're probably right. Thanks," he said as he stood to leave. She had turned back to the shelves, but he checked himself before heading for the door, kneading the hem of his rain jacket with his fingers. "Does the fact that you're closed on a Saturday evening have anything to do with what you two spoke about today?"

Gabbi continued about her work, twisting a bottle in her hand, making a note, moving on to the next one. She met his expression in the mirror behind the bottles. "Your brother was made for being on your side of the bar, not mine," she said, smiling with her eyes.

Tobi looked at his feet, scuffing his left shoe across the right. "We don't have much experience serving people," he said to the floor. "Can I help with anything?" he said, looking around the well-ordered tables and chairs. He placed the one he'd used back in its place with a louder scrape than he had intended.

"Just go on and find your brother. I hope he's ok," she said, turning her shoulders to face him. Tobi nodded in dumb response.

He leaned into the door, but it opened a moment before his shoulder made contact. "Shit, sorry," he said into a face he recognised. The older woman from the bar stared at him from the street, looking as if she'd seen a ghost. "I hope I didn't give you a fright," he said, extending his arms towards her before stepping back and freeing up the doorway.

She took a moment to gather herself and stepped through it, keeping her eyes on him. "Not at all, dear. Just wasn't expecting anyone else to be here this evening."

Tobi felt himself flush once more with the awkwardness of being somewhere he didn't belong. He nodded to the pair and said to Gabbi while holding a card in his hand, "Thanks again. Here's my number, and if you hear from him, please let me know."

It was the older woman who responded. Her eyes hadn't left his face. "Your brother?" she asked.

Tobi's face switched from resignation to shock. "Yes. How did you know?"

She fidgeted with the strap of her shoulder bag, clenching and releasing the leather strips. "I ran into him in a park this afternoon. Hard boy to forget," she said, lowering the bag to a table beside her.

"Which park? When?" asked Tobi, his brow furrowed, his eyes eager.

"Green Park. Somewhere between two and three. He said that he had something to prepare for tonight. He was meeting someone."

Tobi's eyes flared with wildness. "Who?" he barked out suddenly. Both women jumped with a start.

"I'm sorry, dear, I don't know," she said, placing her hand on his arm.

He felt the touch and looked down at her fingers, making no attempt to move. He looked up into her piercing eyes, and stammered once more. "I...I... Of course, sorry," he said through a set of clasped fingers as he pulled his face into his hands. "I can't shake this feeling that something is happening to him. That he needs help."

Rikki took him by the crook of his elbow and guided him to the table, pulled out a chair and cradled him by the shoulders as he sat. Gabbi walked over to join them, surprised by the sight of Rikki's hands resting on this stranger. She pushed the thought from her mind. "Let us help," she said. "Sorry, I don't even know your name. But let us help."

The words pulled Tobi back into the empty bar. He looked into the two faces, both full of resilience. His sight blurred with tears and in their expressions he saw Sarah's eyes, his daughter playing with her toys beyond their kitchen. His vision found its focus, and the kindly comedian reappeared. He shook his head and rolled his tongue around his mouth. His lisp resurfaced as he pushed the card across the table amd said, "It's Tobi. Tobias, actually, but everyone calls me Tobi."

Gabbi nodded but cocked her head at the sight of Rikki lifting her hands to an inch off the man's shoulders, frozen in the air.

Yorick. Sunday. Early in the Morning.

Yorick had lost track of the time he and Huang had spent talking on those couches. They had covered every detail with a fine toothcomb. Each time that Huang explained a new angle, Yorick countered with several questions. There was a level of patience between the two that Yorick hadn't experienced before. The conversation flowed thick and fast and Yorick switched to join Huang on the colas rather than the whiskey.

Hours later, he stepped out into a cold and black night. The moon had hidden itself within the buildings. With his head full of bustling information, he walked home. It would give him the chance to digest everything he had taken on board. But rather than heading west towards his Mayfair loft, he made his way south. He cut through the square mile of the City of London itself and continued his path across the Thames. After an hour, he arrived at the very first property he had owned in London, in the forgotten nook of Elephant & Castle. It was one that he had rented after university, before purchasing it for himself just a couple of years later. It hadn't taken him long to raise the funds on his first salary. Of the limited circle of acquaintances that Yorick kept, Tobi was the only one who knew about this flat. He cracked open the door and saw the pile of old packaged letters; he knew they were from his brother. He kicked them aside.

Huang had shared plenty of details in their conversation, but one point had not been up for debate. Over the next week, Yorick would need to go underground. To prove his loyalty to Huang's bosses, they needed to know that they could trust him completely. And his silence would pay for that trust. He would have to cut ties with his office for a week. They forced him to remove all contact from friends and family. The first part of that equation would prove tough but doable. The latter would be easy, he had said to Huang. They needed him off the grid and working solely for them for the next seven days. Beyond that, a new world would open for Yorick, Huang had assured him.

It was late by the time Yorick slipped into bed. He tossed and turned, plumped up the pillows and shifted beneath the weight of the unfamiliar duvet. Despite the foreign surroundings, it wasn't long before Yorick's over-worked mind shut down, his tired legs laid still, and the blackness of the night folded him into the depths of sleep.

Three hours later and his alarm pierced the quietness of the room. He woke with a start, slapped the digital clock to silence it, and took a second to remind himself of where he was. And why.

A quick, cold shower shook any lingering tiredness from him. He considered the clothes in the wardrobe and chose a pair of simple, fitted black jeans and a dark grey pullover that clung to his upper body. He brewed himself a cup of strong black coffee and perched over his laptop at the kitchen counter. He went straight to the national news provider's website. The time in the corner of his laptop screen read 05.45.

These days, the front page often featured a haggard photo of the prime minister, but in this case, it pleased him to see it. The first detail was playing out as Huang said it would.

The headline screamed of financial improprieties that had been linked to the PM. This was the next level of detail that had been unearthed by the investigative journalist. The writer had unexpectedly come across a swathe of documents that showed the PM as personally benefiting from the deal struck with the Chinese PPE supplier. It was to the tune of £3million, she wrote, with highly suspicious actions suggesting it was being syphoned off into personal offshore accounts.

The PM denied any knowledge of the financial transactions and claimed the offshore accounts were "the invention of a vindictively fictitious and imaginative mind". The quoted words caused Yorick to snigger. Huang and his bosses were many things, but imaginative was not a word he associated with them. But after last night's conversation, the level of planning that had been shown was undoubtedly creative.

The leaked documents were convincing. Yorick had seen enough funnelling of funds into foreign accounts to confirm that they would pass senior levels of scrutiny. Their authenticity was rooted in the real-life details that had been used to construct them. Many of those particulars had been signed over a week prior in his offices. If it were a boxing match, the blonde-haired, convivial yet ultimate rag of a man was up against the ropes. He was bloodied and weak and his opponents were moving in for the final blow. And Yorick was positioned in their corner.

Next on his list was contacting his office. He drafted an email to his partners and immediate team, citing that he'd be taking a week off. This introduced a degree of risk that Huang hadn't been happy about. Yorick never took time off. Unless the office was forcibly closed, he was working. Everyone knew it; hell, he was famous for it. But it was the one risk that they had been forced to accept. He framed it as boastful, wanting to enjoy the success of the deal he had just landed and hoped that would be enough to buy him the privacy he needed. It was more believable that way. The magnitude of the deal said that he deserved it. The email pinged off with a chime and it appeared in his 'Sent' items a second later with a timestamp of 06.02.

He clicked on an icon on his laptop's home screen. It was a simple black and white design; a shield-shaped outline that housed a stylised face within. The face had two distinct characteristics; eyebrows that arched downwards in two rounded 'Vs' and a moustache shaped in a defined and elongated 'w' shape. It opened a VPN software programme, a virtual private network, that allowed Yorick to create a highly secure connection. It would encrypt the data at the sending end, his end, and decrypt it at the other, masking his online activity. Part of Huang's instructions had been to use only this software for this week's work.

A red image of a lock shone, indicating a secure connection had been established. He logged onto the Yulii portal. An overview of all fourteen of his clients' data warehouse systems greeted him. He couldn't access any single account directly due to the security in place. As the sole administrator of the portal, however, he could open a set of developer's tools behind the system. As soon as he tried to, he was immediately asked for biometric confirmation of his identity. He pulled his phone from his pocket, opened the app that he and Huang used to message each other, and held the phone to his retina. The green light scanned across his eye and confirmation appeared on his laptop screen that his credentials had been accepted.

He pulled up a tall stool from his kitchen counter and settled onto it. He opened the developer toolkit and his screen flooded with information. He looked at the reams of code in front of him. It was made up of indexes and subcategories that felt like a foreign language to him. Huang had insisted Yorick wrote down nothing from their conversation.

His capacity for remembering details would be tested to its limits. After what seemed like an interminable period of scrolling, he identified combinations of letters and numbers that Huang had forced him to memorise. They appeared in little clusters. When he clicked on one, it revealed thousands of lines of code that were incomprehensible to Yorick. He opened a file transfer service that was included as part of the VPN encryption programme. He dragged folders into the file transfer system. Each time he did so, he double checked the digits and numbers three times, until satisfied that they were correct. It was painful and laborious work. It was the sort of task he would have told Craig to do. If it was official business.

Years ago he would have baulked at the idea of carrying out this type of work at this point in his career. But he'd come to realise that the ends justified the means. And recognition of his efforts finally lay in sight.

Tobi. Sunday. Morning.

Tobi spent the cab ride home firing off a string of questions and lines of enquiry to Mikey. It was the first time he had asked him to investigate for personal rather than business reasons. But for his own blood, he surprised himself at how quickly he could cast aside his rigid rulebook. Tobi had been explicit; Yorick was now his sole priority.

He arrived home and let himself in as quietly as he could. He made his way to the kitchen and dropped his wallet, keys and phone onto the counter, staring at the blank screen. He didn't expect any fresh developments until the next day. Beyond the counter lay the stack of wine-stained papers he had yet to clear away. The chaos waiting inside the halls of West & West mocked him from within the pile. A nasty tabloid scandal was spilling over, and the partners didn't do public politics. If he couldn't think of a way to rid them of their business interest in Simon's company, the mockery would become reality. And he and Clara might as well not bother turning up on Monday. The papers held one truth he was sure of; he was out of options.

He heard footsteps on the stairs and admonished himself. Lily was awake and investigating what her father was up to. He moved to intercept her, but it was Sarah who rounded the corner, treading slowly and with confidence.

"I didn't mean to wake you, Sa'. I'm -" Tobi started to apologise, but she cut him off.

She stepped forwards and drew him into her. He felt his face nestle into her hair as it wrapped around his cheeks. He breathed it in and softened into her embrace. She felt his tears dropping onto her bare shoulders, hot and wet. But still she held him. His arms worked their way up from his sides to around her back, drawing her closer still.

They spoke for hours, deep into the night. Like they used to do when they had first met. He was shattered by the time he pulled himself into bed, but Sarah had helped him to find the clarity he sought at last. It was time to stop running. He had one option left, and that was to front up and embrace the uncomfortable feelings he'd been avoiding. He needed to confront Jennifer to understand what was going on.

He woke early the next morning, took himself into the bathroom, closed the door and dialled Yorick's number once again. Still no answer. Same as the previous night. Thirty minutes later, he was boarding the first available train to Leicester. He took his seat and glanced at his watch. 05.42. He had ten minutes to spare. He tried his brother again. Nothing. He swore and his thoughts turned to the morning ahead. Clara's latest update of Jennifer's diary noted she was due to drop her children off at school that morning for their spring sports and culture day. Big money meant school activities didn't stop on Sundays - lucky kids.

He was due into Leicester just after 07.00, meaning he could make the short drive east and catch Jennifer as she arrived at the school.

He got there earlier than planned and set up camp in his rental car to keep a watchful eye on the line of vehicles trickling into the school grounds. A sprawling campus of stocky buildings among twisting, narrow roads greeted him. The main artery of the tangled layout fed off from the public road outside. His black sedan was parked inside the exterior walls of the complex, next to an archway. All around him were imposing and yellowed brickwork buildings, dating back three centuries. Tobi's car faced a courtyard that contained a generous rectangle of trimmed grass and a mature ash tree planted in the middle. The trunk of the tree was ringed by a thick iron fence with ornate finishings. There were two wooden benches set in opposite inlets in the fencing. A line of cars edged past Tobi, some stopping at the corners of the rectangle, others pressing on into the small side alleys. The notion of Simon and Jennifer's children attending a school like this without having met Tobi was fanciful.

The small electric clock in the car ticked over to 08.02 and the stream of cars had slowed. As the clock edged closer to five past the hour, a couple of cars remained in the courtyard. A silver Jaguar that Tobi recognised crept past the nose of his rented car, Jennifer's flame of red hair at the wheel. She rounded the first two corners of the rectangle, picked one of the many open parking spots, hopped out, and moved from the driver's seat to the boot. She offloaded a large guitar-shaped case to her son and a lacrosse stick to her daughter, together with a leather holdall. Tobi eased himself out of his own car, and looked up in time to see her giving each child a peck on the cheek, followed by firm taps on their lower backs. She watched her offspring scamper off while leaning against the body of the long, silver car. They disappeared into the nearest building as Tobi got within talking distance of her. She was breathing slowly, her torso rising and falling with a steady rhythm.

"They don't stop growing," said Tobi in a voice designed to carry the short distance between them.

She didn't turn to him or take any notice of the words. Her stare remained fixed on the tall, closed wooden doors of the building in front of her, as if she had been expecting him. The doors had large iron brackets adorning them.

"That's always the way when you see children infrequently. See them every day and you don't notice so much," she said with the same indifference that he recognised from his visit to their home. She began moving towards the driver's door and said, "I suppose your own daughter grows much too quickly for you, too, Tobi."

She didn't reach for the handle but kept going, past the front of the car and beyond. She crossed the barrier of the rectangular grassed area and set course for the eastward facing bench. Tobi followed. He made up the distance as she reached it. Jennifer took a seat, leaving her no option but to face him.

"Keeping your children here won't be a problem if you accept my offer, Jennifer," he said, as he waved an arm around the courtyard. "Or does Fazir have bigger plans?" he added.

Jennifer trailed her eyes upwards and away from him, into the reaches of the green leaves that were sprouting from thin, overhanging branches. "Is guilt your primary ingredient, Tobi? Mixed in with a bit of deception and topped off with a charm-laced icing to make your bitter little cakes go down sweeter for those who dare eat them?" Her eyes moved back to him. "Your guilt is no good here. Unless you're trying to shed your own."

"Mine?" he asked in response. His mouth settled into a thin line.

She was lost once more amongst the budding leaves above them as she spoke. "All those late nights, impromptu work trips, the little award ceremonies that Simon whisked himself off to over the years. Don't tell me you didn't know what they entailed, Tobi. Spare me the indignity of denying it. Simon and I were happy before all this," she said, and it was her turn to cast a look towards the bricked barriers that surrounded them. "I really think we were. But you changed all that. Your little dream, that only belonged to the two of you, became our nightmare. So no, your guilt won't work here," she said. She fixed her gaze downward at the trodden earth beneath her feet, smooth and brown, and stabbed the toe of her shoes into it.

Tobi shuffled in front of her before he spoke again. "I'm sorry, Jennifer. I chose to keep quiet. It was easier for me that way. I shouldn't have."

"It wasn't all you, of course," she continued, as if he hadn't spoken at all. "He was a weak man. I guess I always knew it. But before you, he was weak, but without options. You gave him some, and then, his weakness mattered." she glanced back to the wooden doors with their iron bars. "We won't make that mistake again. We won't go back to those dark days."

Tobi looked up to find her searching into his eyes. Their neutral expressions matched each other in a tiresome battle. But her emerald eyes were full to the brim with fight. The memory of his encounter with Fazir rushed back to his mind.

She stood, the redness of her hair eating at the green shoots of the leaves behind her. "And I plan to scrub our memories of those who brought those days to our door." She pushed past Tobi, made her way across the grass to her car, and left. Tobi followed her with his eyes from beneath the ash tree, standing alone on the brown patch of earth with more questions.

Tobi. Sunday. Midday.

The blaring of his phone roused Tobi from his muddled thoughts. The screen in front of him danced while his eyes steadied to read the name on it. Mikey. His focus snapped into place, and he answered it in a hushed tone. He glanced about the carriage. There was a group of men ahead of him in football shirts, each of a different vintage but in support of the same team, and a barrage of cans of lager at their feet. Two rows behind him was an elderly couple, ignoring each other with their noses in their own books. A teenager with bleached blonde hair sat opposite him. He had a yellow highlighter in his hand, a book packed with diagrams in front of him and thick black wireless headphones over his ears.

Tobi regretted not bringing a pair of his own as Mikey's voice filled his right ear. He lowered the volume and listened as his informant spoke. "Not good news. It goes deeper than we thought."

Tobi's heart sank as his thoughts raced to his brother. A memory streaked across his vision of the two of them standing in the front garden of their little yellow house in Den Bosch.

"Is he ok?" rasped Tobi, cupping his left hand over the bottom edge of his phone while pressing the top of it against his ear.

"Oh, your brother? We're not sure, for now. That's all I can say. But this goes way beyond just him. Or West & West."

The announcements started blaring over the PA system in the carriage; they would shortly be arriving at London Euston. Everyone was to please gather their belongings and prepare to leave the train. The chorus of men ahead shouted and jeered and the sound of cans being crushed and clattered raced towards Tobi.

"What?" Tobi said after the automated electronic message had died down.

"There's too much to tell you over the phone. We need to set up." Mikey's tone and choice of words created a clear picture. The last time they had set up, it had required Tobi to source an abandoned railway arch, empty tables, multiple computer monitors and a maze of cables to connect it all together. All within the space of a few hours. It had only happened once before. They had needed it then to keep Nanotech alive, and Tobi had little reason to doubt that they needed it now.

The elderly couple and student were gathering their items, retrieving bags and coats from the railing above him and blocking his route to the exit. He used the time to think. A calm patience seeped through his phone and into his mind. A loud double chime signalled the opening doors, and his fellow passengers made their way towards them. Tobi followed them, stepping off the train and away from the masses as they departed. The clutch of football fans sung from the door further down, and as they passed, Tobi rapped an address into the phone. He hoped he didn't need to repeat himself, and the sound of the call disconnecting confirmed that he wouldn't have to.

The headlights of the taxi reflected off the windows of the pub. Thick clouds had gathered on the drive from Euston. Tobi instructed the driver to nose another fifty yards down the road; this wasn't the right pub. She muttered a quick apology, covered up by an admission that The Waldorf was the only pub that appeared on Google maps. She pulled up outside The Rams & Lion, thanked Tobi for choosing to ride with her that day, and watched him step out and approach the door. He hadn't said a word for the entire journey. He hadn't noticed the loud shriek of the loose engine belt that needed tightening. She watched him in the rear-view mirror as she pulled away down the street. He had been difficult to pin down. Dressed in dark grey trousers, a navy round-necked sweater with a dark brown jacket on top and stylish grey and red trainers on his feet, he had sat looking out the window for the whole of the forty-minute trip. She knew the look of a man taking in the passing world while seeing nothing at all; lost in his own thoughts and feelings. Men matching his profile rarely got dropped off around these parts of London.

She reached the end of the street, checked her mirror once more to see him still standing there, motionless. She spied a gap in the traffic and pulled out into it.

The pub should have been open for Sunday lunch. But, again, it was closed. Tobi breathed a small sigh of hope. But the longer he stared into the darkness of the room, the more his optimism dulled. If no one appeared soon, he'd need to call Mikey, but he was out of ideas for where he would turn to next.

As he stared into the shadows, he replayed snippets of the previous night's events in his mind. They came to him in a series of feelings, rather than thoughts. The sense of welcoming that had come from Gabbi, someone he barely recognised, let alone knew, had stuck with him. The soft touch of Rikki's hand on him and comfort of their offers to help. He felt the awkwardness of his attempts to accept what they had laid out before him. The idea of two strangers who had extended themselves toward him, for no apparent reason other than to help, brought a unique calmness to him. There had been a connection that he felt compelled to pursue. His plans, thoughts and logic had been pulled apart by forces he didn't understand. All he was sure of was that within those walls lay something drawing him in.

From the far corner of the room, a door opened without warning and light spilled in. A warm yellow glow flooded the room as the lights flashed on and a figure moved towards the entrance.

It was a loud, intermittent whining sound that had drawn Rikki to the window of her small one-bedroom flat. The window was above the chicken shop, next to The Rams & Lion. She lived across the hall from Gabbi and her window looked out onto the street below. The comedian's flat had a view across the ragged gardens and allotments out in the back.

She pulled back the blinds and peered down the street. A silver sedan was edging its way down the street, rolling to a stop as if it had run out of fuel. It came to rest opposite the pub's entrance. Out stepped a man that she now could not fail to recognise.

She couldn't hide from the truth anymore. Two brothers, two sons, were hurting and in trouble. The time had come to step out of the shadows and confront her past.

The man beneath her appeared rooted to the spot as the crying taxi pulled away. She unlocked her front door as quietly as possible so as not to disturb Gabbi; the poor girl had faced enough reality this weekend. She crept down the stairs and out the back, skipping along the rickety fence until she came to the back gate near the pub's rear door. She eased it open, hoping it wouldn't squeak. When it didn't, she dashed across the courtyard and used her key to unlock the back entrance of The Rams & Lion. She gripped the handle and hesitated before twisting it.

Beyond that door lay a conversation she had held a million times in her mind, from every angle, but one she never thought she would have to face up to.

She twisted her hand and stepped forward.

Tobi wasn't surprised when it was she who opened the main entrance. She stood plainly and stepped aside, holding out her arm to usher him in. They locked eyes. He nodded to her and stepped across the threshold. He made his way over to the same table from the previous night. Its chairs were placed on top of it, upside down. As were all the others sprawled across the room. He lowered one. The sound of the legs tapping on the floor was matched by the firm click of her locking the door. He twisted a second one to the ground, removed his jacket, and hung it across the back of it. The arms of it dropped with a silky softness, the inner lining caressing the backrest of the chair as it slipped into place.

She moved towards him and the open seat. "Any word from your brother?" she asked.

"Still nothing," he said. She lowered herself, and after pausing for a beat, he followed suit. The oppressive air of unspoken words settled all around them. Tobi felt it and made the move to lift it. "This is going to sound strange, Rikki. But how do you know me?"

She shifted in her chair. She toyed with the floral scarf that was tied around her neck before letting it unravel and placed it on the table. The soft material folded into itself and settled in a small, neat pile. It was a soft beige, littered with a floral pattern that sported alternating shades of brown, burnt orange and yellow in an autumnal design. Without it, she looked different, and Tobi realised it had been a permanent feature each time he had seen her. She looked back up at him and said, "I knew your father, Tobi."

His eyes narrowed. The crooked slant of his mouth was etched on his face. There was no confusion, anger, or happiness, just a desire to know more. "You met him in London?" he asked, his lips unsteady.

She glanced down at the table. She fiddled with the edges of the small pile of scarf. "No... no. I've lived in London for many, too many, years. But I met your father back in the Netherlands." Her eyes flicked back to him. "When I was young."

He nodded, once. "In Den Bosch?"

She mirrored his nod.

"Where in Den Bosch? It's a small town," he said, as if trying not to scare a small child.

She pulled the scarf into her lap. Her fingers continued to work away at its edges. Her prominent and round cheekbones threw a natural shadow beneath her eyes. Tobi noticed them growing darker, soft tears forming and dropping across them.

One fell as she said, "In a small but beautiful home. It had a blue door. With a clay plaque next to it. And on that plaque, was the number 24, and a painted yellow tulip." Tears now fell freely down her face.

The air that had settled around the pair rushed from the floor to the ceiling in one sudden and violent storm all around Tobi. Shapes lost their edges. The stranger in front of him blurred in and out of focus. The only thing he could think of to make it stop was to clamp his eyes shut. But the feelings only intensified. When he opened them again, he felt the wetness and heat of thick tears of his own tracing paths down the sides of his face. Whilst his vision settled, the room turned. A cycle of confusion and disbelief rained down on him. He placed his hands on the table to steady himself.

And then he heard a loud series of hard knocks on the main door.

Tobi. Sunday. 17:00.

Tobi's mind swam with confusion. She couldn't have said what she did, could she? He peered through his tears, only to see that she was crying, too. The knocks on the door echoed through his mind and he leapt to his feet. Both pawed at their faces, dabbing their eyes with their sleeves in synchronised movements.

"You're not opening today, right?" he asked, the sense of urgency clear in his voice. Thoughts of Mikey and what needed to be done were the last thing he could manage. But he had no choice.

"No. We're closed indefinitely," said Rikki with a steady voice.

It brought Tobi back to the task at hand. "I need this space," he said, laying his hand on the keys in the lock. "It's for Yorick."

She rose from her chair, wiping her wet hands on the sides of her hips as she stood and said, "Of course."

Tobi stabbed at his face once more, threw back the lock, and swung the door open. Mikey was framed in the doorway against a large black truck. He carried a monitor under one arm and a computer tower under the other. He stepped through the doorway and surveyed the scene in front of him and its mix of tables and chairs. "We can use anywhere?" he said, his eyes scanning the windows and not noticing Rikki.

"All yours," confirmed Tobi.

From the shadows of the truck, two men followed their leader into the pub, carrying extra monitors, computer hardware, and cables. Mikey removed chairs from the tables, and Tobi and Rikki did the same. The mob of strangers worked in efficient silence.

"Windows," said Mikey, breaking the quiet atmosphere.

At this instruction, one of his men disappeared to the truck and returned with a long, thick roll of dark paper. He and his colleague measured sheets of the material against the window and then cut it to size. They fixed sections across the glass expanses with insulation tape. The room was thrown into a gloomy darkness, purging the light of the moody skies outside.

What looked like the main computer terminal lit up and Mikey called Tobi over and pulled a seat back for him. He threw a questioning glance back over his shoulder at Rikki. Tobi offered a nod of his head in response.

Mikey took the cue that he could begin and started speaking.

"We started by trying to figure out who hacked into your systems. Through geo-tagging, we could pinpoint the action to a network of decentralised computers across the Guizhou region in China." An image of red outlines appeared on a black background on the monitor in front of them. A series of blinking yellow dots glowed in small clusters within the red borders.

"That's the same region where that PPE factory is located, right? It's been all over the news stories about the PM's financial scandal," said Tobi, tapping the shape of the Guizhou region on the screen with his index finger.

"Exactly. You'll remember our last dialogue about Fazir and his connection to the factory's CEO, Zhi Ruo Yang," said Mikey, as he clicked on an image of the young woman.

"Fazir's leaning on his Chinese contacts to hack into our systems? Why us?" asked Tobi.

The speed of Mikey's speech accelerated. "It appears he needs a fall guy for the PM scandal, and he is trying to pin it on the private sector. In the chaos of Simon's disgrace and removal, they've been able to hack into medical practices' business documents that HEAL-y filed with the government. They've created a trail that links the supplier transactions to China with the PPE factory kickbacks. HEAL-y, and its stakeholders, is now in the eye of this storm."

Tobi leaned back in his chair. "Jesus," he breathed out. His shoulders touched the back of the chair and he sprang forward once more, his hands clasped together. "How have they done it?"

"Data. Reams of it. They've been tapping a wealth of protected public and private consumer data sources, coupled that with machine learning algorithms and set it loose against our public sector systems online. It's a powerful recipe for breaking in by sheer force."

"Is there anything we can do about it? To fight back?" asked Tobi.

Mikey swiped across the screen and brought up a fresh batch of documents and images. A leering grin from his brother leapt off the screen at Tobi. Around his face was a mosaic of company logos and tree diagrams that, Tobi guessed, represented the data flows that underpinned the different businesses. It was an endless mass of lines and shapes.

"I'm afraid this is where your brother comes in. He's brought all these companies together," said Mikey, the fingers on both of his hands tracing rough shapes across the symbols on the screen. "He's built a system behind all of their data networks. No prizes for guessing where that system is based," he said, turning to Tobi.

In turn, Tobi reached and swiped across the screen, back to the previous image with the red outlines. He tapped the region of Guizhou and the blinking dots.

"Correct, but still no prize," said Mikey. "In fact, it gets worse."

"Go on," said Tobi. His eyes were fixed on the screen, the yellow dots shimmering in his pupils.

"We've only been able to work this out because of what we know about you, your brother and our past work," Mikey said, slowing down his speech. "They need the PM to disappear, Tobi. And I don't just mean by a financial scandal."

"What?" Tobi hissed back.

"All of that data is giving them access to the PM, his movements and his security arrangements. A level of detail that should never be available to anyone outside of the government or Mi6. They want to make way for Fazir and his China-friendly trade policies and they're looking at assassination to make sure that happens." Mikey pressed on, not letting the enormity of what he'd said fester. "Yorick's digital fingerprints are all over everything." He swiped again at the screen and an image of the inside of an eye came up. "That's your brother's retina. He's been using it to log into systems in China that have been scrubbed of all other personnel data."

Tobi felt that familiar sinking sensation in the room returning.

"Whoever Yorick is working with in China is about to turn him into the greatest traitor this country has seen for over four hundred years."

When faced with unpredictable situations, Mikey's default behaviour was to act. And act fast. He set about explaining the two things that he needed.

First, he and his team needed time. Linking Yorick's involvement had meant fast progress, but there was an enormous amount left to do. Mikey explained they primarily hoped to use Yorick's data system to retaliate against the Guizhou-based behemoth they were up against. They needed to get inside it to have a chance of deleting the data and information being used against them. And the government.

Mikey's men were good. Maybe even the best. But the Guizhou gang had access to the one thing that they didn't. Yorick. He was the key to accessing the system. To giving them a fighting chance to repair the danger that was heading their way.

Tobi stood and looked at the other men in the room. Neither had said a word. They had set up their stations, connected the cabling and thrown themselves into the myriad of complex code that filled their screens. Neither had looked up from them since they had taken their seats. They would be paid handsomely for this, Tobi knew, but the energy with which they worked showed that they were driven by something greater. They had a steel to their focus and attention that Tobi had last felt many years ago, but was feeling again.

He turned to the room, desperate to get his feet moving, hoping they would spark inspiration as to what to do next. As he did so, Rikki stepped towards him. She had been listening wolfishly to the conversation.

"We need to find Yorick, right? Well, I've got an idea," she said, leading him away from the consoles that now dominated the room. Mikey and his men were now talking, oblivious to the pair. A foreign language of technical specifications, coding terms and the hammering of keystrokes filled the room, growing in volume. Rikki motioned to the staircase next to the bar and directed them down it. The noise dropped as they descended into the abandoned comedy arena. The rows of folded chairs were packed against the back wall, except for two. They were open on the small stage. They headed towards them and sat down, relishing the calmness of the setting, ignoring the flurry of activity that had broken out upstairs.

She leaned in towards him, taking his hands in hers. She felt them shaking. "Tobi, you have no reason to trust, or even believe me. But I'm here to help you find Yorick. Your words weighed heavily on me last night, and now more than ever."

He swallowed hard. His eyes searched hers. They darted back and forth, looking for something, but not knowing what that thing was. What choice did he have? "What's your idea?" he said, his tongue thick and cumbersome.

"I won't pretend to know anything about either of you. But I know the look of a man who's too stubborn to let someone help him. But even the most headstrong have that one person who can break in. I think Gabbi is that person to him. Let me talk to her, try to convince her to reach out to him, at least while we think of something else."

He nodded dumbly. He owed these two women a great debt. Yet they had now become indelibly linked to his past and his future. And still he wanted more from them. From her. His nodding morphed into a shaking of his head. The disbelief crowded his vision once more. Words from his father's bundled and previously unread letters flooded his mind.

I spent my life thinking my job for you and your brother was to provide, but it wasn't; it was simply to love. Your mother knew that instinctively. I learnt it too late.

Your mother loved you both more than you'll ever know. But her soul left us before she did.

I spent too long judging others, blaming others for the struggles that we experienced. Remember that you never know what decisions others may be facing. Especially those you love. It is a powerful but confusing emotion. You may never know the hardships that they're facing. So tread first with kindness, with love, not judgement. And remember, we always tried to do what we thought was our best for you, even when we got it wrong.

"So, why... why did you... abandon us?" he said, looking up at her, his eyes willing the words not to hold true. For some other story to be told.

The bags under her eyes filled once more and tears streamed down her face. She released his hands and lifted hers into the air. He watched as they shook before his eyes. She tried to close them, but the shaking grew more violent, as if she'd lost control. The sight threw his mind back to Yorick and their night in The Waldorf. The shaking was familiar. She lowered them back to her lap, retrieved the scarf and brought it to her face, crying into it.

"It was never meant to turn out like this," she said, in between deep sobs.

"Like what?"

"I wasn't supposed to live long enough for any of this to matter."

"I don't understand," Tobi said, as he felt the room spin once more. "Is this to do with the shaking?"

She drew the scarf away from her face and met his gaze with steady eyes. "Have you ever heard of Huntington's disease, Tobi?"

Tobi pressed back into his chair. "I remember it from a TV show. They made it sound awful. As though it was something taboo to talk about."

"It is. It's a terrifying disease. It starts slowly, with small shakes. And forgetting little bits. The sorts of things you think are just normal in everyday life. But then the shaking gets a bit worse. And your doctor tells you that's the beginning of the end."

"The end of what?"

"Your life, really. Soon you'll be -" Rikki paused took a deep breath before she continued, "- be dropping things. You become thick handed and a danger to yourself. And those around you." Her tears flowed once more, but she spoke through them. "And that's followed by the mental deterioration. It's not just forgetting things, your mind becomes thick. Just fuzzy all the time. You need to be cared for, a lot. That's what they said to me."

Tobi's heart sank in his chest. He felt distraught for this woman, baring her soul to him, but wasn't yet able to believe what her story meant. "But, I have to be blunt, apart from your hands, you don't seem to fit that picture?"

She lashed out at the microphone stand. It clattered to the floor with a bang, the sound taking them both by surprise. "Ain't life funny, isn't that what they say?" She watched the stand rock back and forth before it settled into a resting position. "They gave me five years, from my first diagnosis. Until I'd need full time care. What set the doctor off was an incident in the kitchen. I'd been holding your brother, with you playing at my feet, below the stove. It was stupid. I should have thought it through. But my mind was foggy, I suppose." Her words gathered pace, as if out of control.

"The next thing I knew, the pot was falling towards you, and Yorick slipped from my grasp as I went to save both of you. It all happened before I could even realise what was happening."

He broached the divide between them and took her into his arms. She let him, her shoulders heaving up and down against his chest. He held her, absorbing the sobs as he felt the tufts of her hair nuzzle against his chin.

She pulled back and continued. "We just couldn't go on like that. The idea of leaving you seemed impossible to bear, but the thought of putting the two of you in danger overshadowed it all. And for you two to see me like that, in the state of what I would become. At such a young age - it was too much to burden you with.

"There was no perfect answer. So we created the worst lie ever told. To try to protect you both. We thought you were young enough to overcome it. Children are far more resilient than adults. I was never supposed to live to tell you these things. And Pieter swore he never would."

"He didn't." Tobi reached for his shoulder, feeling the grooves where an old cardboard box had dug into his skin a few nights before. "I don't know how he lived with that lie. But it makes some sort of sense now. The toys, the relentless pursuit of fixing things, trying to create joy. To fill the hole that had been torn from his life."

"It was never supposed to be this way. I was supposed to die. That was all I wanted in those years after we made our decision. I was supposed to give him closure. But I couldn't even do that. 'A medical miracle', the doctors said. The disease would still claim me, in time, but for some unknown reason, it had stalled its progress. It still has, largely."

She cast her eyes to the wall that ran alongside the staircase. He followed her line of sight. There were two paintings on either side of the picture of Andi Osho, Gabbi's comedic heroine. They were in black and white, in stark contrast to the lively creations upstairs. Tobi hadn't noticed them before, but saw that each contained a single and obvious shape; a tulip. They were similar, but each with its own unique perspective and painted with its own energy. And nearly lost in the dark light of the basement, unless you knew what you were looking for.

"And so I had to start again. Out on my own. And all I knew, is that in whatever time I had left, I wanted to make beautiful things. To try to fill the bottomless holes left in my life."

Tobi hit away at his own tears. "Why didn't you ever come back? Later, after he died?" he said to the floor, shaking his head.

Her fingers balled up in clenched fists as she said, "I couldn't. Your father wouldn't allow it. He wanted finality. And so he created the story that he needed to tell. That was the deal. I had to give him that, at least. For everything he took on." She reached across to touch his knee, but he shifted his weight away from her advance. She withdrew her hand and carried on. "It's why I took the job here, in this pub, all those years ago. Through the whispers from across the way at the Waldorf, and in the neighbourhood, I could keep tabs on the three of you - from within the shadows. Never seen. But once Pieter died, well, those whispers went with him. And I thought I'd lost the two of you forever."

Tobi's mind wandered to Sarah. To his daughter. To the many nights he'd spent away from them. Working, consumed by paperwork, and pleasing others. He'd fooled himself into thinking that he was doing it for them. It paid for everything they had, after all. The best of everything. But wasn't he doing it for himself? Wasn't it only a selfish act, too? Pangs of guilt riddled his body as he thought of his own father; how he had lived a life that was built on an all conquering lie. And the walls he had constructed around himself to protect that untruth. Tears flowed once more at the thought of him and Rikki trying to protect their sons. But protecting no one, only closing them off to each other.

"Tobi," said Mikey from the top of the stairs. "We need you up here. We're getting closer to Yorick."

Tobi had far more questions than answers. But the one answer he needed right now was knowing where his brother was. That was a truth he still believed in.

"Please, can we try Gabbi?" he said to Rikki, watching her fingers as they twitched.

Yorick. Sunday. 18:00.

Yorick hadn't worked like this for years. Holed up in a small apartment, just him, a steady stream of strong black coffee and a laptop to hammer away at. He didn't think about the consequences of each decision. He didn't plan, answer emails or deal with people. He just executed, time after time, until the task was complete. He'd enjoyed it.

He finished copying and transmitting all the data by lunchtime and an hour later, Huang contacted him to confirm that they had everything they needed. The next phase was progressing quicker than expected. They wanted Yorick to fly out with them the following morning. Huang felt it best for Yorick to remove himself from temptation for the rest of the week. It'd be easier to lie low with him and his team. They would ensure his every need was taken care of in the east. He had agreed.

After a day spent cooped up inside, a barrage of thoughts surfaced within him. It had been a whirlwind few days. He opened a tall cupboard at the end of the kitchen counter. An assortment of cardboard boxes, tins and packets stared back at him. He moved them aside and found two cans of warm Australian lager and the dregs of a bottle of whiskey hiding in the back.

He looked at his watch. What he really wanted was a quiet drink in a place where no one knew his name. Huang didn't own his every move, yet. He pulled his phone from his pocket and looked at his recent calls list. He flicked it to life and saw Gabbi's name at the top of it. His finger hovered over it for a second and then the icon of an airplane at the top of his screen dropped him back into reality. He was disconnected from any mobile signal. He didn't know how long he'd be gone for. Huang had said a week, but Yorick felt the cloud of a London farewell hanging over him.

He moved to the door and grabbed a black bomber jacket off the coat rack, below which lay the stack of unopened envelopes. He shrugged himself into the coat, feeling it cling to his arms and shoulders, and snatched his wallet and keys off the table. He poked his head through the doorway, found the corridor empty, and moved to the end of it, away from the elevators. There he found an old brick staircase, with chipped white paint and a battered metal handrail. He skipped his way downstairs and into the fading light of the evening. He emerged outside into the deserted street that ran past the back of the apartment. It was a quiet road, and he was in luck; a black cab turned into it. He hailed it, slipped inside and said two words to the cabbie. "Plaistow Park".

The driver nodded to the road ahead of him and pulled away. Two hundred yards further back, a black sedan pulled out from the row of parked cars.

Rikki. Sunday. 18.00

Rikki left Tobi in the basement and made her way out of the back entrance of the pub. She slipped along the fence, up the rear staircase behind the chicken shop and knocked on Gabbi's door. She waited. Nothing. She tried again. In the silence, she heard the rustling of sounds from below. Charlie didn't work on Sundays. She made her way down the staircase inside the building and into the shop.

Gabbi was behind the counter. She was working away at the grill's surface with a new, damp cloth, applying pressure to it with her neat nails to work away at a tiny piece of burnt fat in the top left corner.

Rikki approached her from behind and placed her hands gently on top of her shoulders. "What are you doing, love? Charlie can see to that tomorrow," she said, knowing there was nothing that Charlie needed seeing to. Gabbi had been down here for a spell.

Her soft brown curls bounced softly as she worked harder at the corner, the pace of her fingers increasing. "Gotta make myself feel useful, somehow," she said, turning to smile at Rikki, her lips giving away a small wobble.

The matriarch nodded mournfully and moved around to the other side of the counter. She looked at her through the glass partitioning. "We've done everything we could for the Rams. And who knows what might happen before a sale goes through." They both winced at the prospect. It had been a painful morning for them, spent sifting through the final papers from the bank. They had gone through the details of what was required to list the property. The paperwork lay locked away behind the bar.

Gabbi straightened up and shrugged her shoulders. "Something on your mind, Riks? I can tell it's not just this morning weighing you down."

Rikki shifted her weight from foot to foot. She fiddled with the tray of sauces on the counter before returning them to their perfectly straight, original position. "I need to talk to you about something. But we need to do it at The Rams."

Gabbi didn't sigh often, but when she did, she told the whole room about it. Her hair folded in on itself, her nostrils flared, and her hips tilted theatrically to the right. "Can it wait until tomorrow? I just don't have the energy to deal with that place anymore today."

Rikki pursed her lips together, their flatness contrasted against the spiky tufts of red hair on her head. "It can't, love."

Yorick & Gabbi. Sunday. 19.00

The driver dropped Yorick off at the south-east corner of the park. It was empty; the light fading fast from the setting sun. He made his way past the large circular sandpit, ignoring the jungle gym and wooden huts, and cut across the grass towards the opposite corner.

He exited and made his way towards The Waldorf, and continued past it, as he knew he would. As he approached The Rams & Lion, he noticed that it looked different. It was far too dark. A flash of guilt surged through his body as he moved past the windows and saw them blocked off from the inside. He sighed to himself; he hadn't given the place a second thought after his call with Gabbi.

He peered two doors further down and saw the lights on at the chicken shop and movement inside.

"Ok, Riks. But this is it for the weekend," said Gabbi. "Let's head out the front - easier for me to lock up." She gave the flat, matte black cooking surface one last swipe, rinsed the cloth and folded it next to the sink. She grabbed her bag from the floor, rustled her keys out of it, and headed to the front entrance. Rikki fell into step behind her and immediately slammed into the back of her.

"Shit," she heard Gabbi say from under her breath.

Rikki peered around Gabbi and couldn't stop herself from barking out loud. "Thank God!" Her hands shot to her mouth.

Yorick peered down with an awkward smile over the 'closed' sign. Gabbi turned to face Rikki, her eyes wild with alarm. "What do we do?"

Rikki lowered her hands to her sides and pressed down the edges of the oversized shirt that she was wearing. "Invite him for a drink at The Rams."

"It's closed," Gabbi said through clenched teeth and worried eyes.

"We'll open it. There's no time to explain. Call it a last hurrah," she said, flaring her pupils at Gabbi.

Gabbi turned back to the door and fixed her face with a neutral expression. She fiddled with the lock, the keys jangling in her right hand as she searched for the mechanism. Eventually it slid into place and she pulled the door towards her while stepping through it, forcing Yorick back a step.

"I was just thinking about you," she gambled. It generated a broader smile from him.

"Nothing too awful, I hope. I saw the blacked-up windows," he said in response, tilting his head towards The Rams. The sheepish look she had first seen over a plate of spicy chicken darted across his face before disappearing into the street's shadows.

"All things end," said Gabbi with a forced shrug, her shoulders clenched for a beat too long at their highest point. She tried to hide the confusion she was feeling within; she didn't wear untruths well. "We're going for a last hurrah drink. Fancy joining us?"

Yorick offered a friendly glance over Gabbi's shoulder at Rikki. It lacked the defiance that she had seen the day before. She smiled back, too nervous to offer any words.

"You read my mind," he said, as his grin grew and his eyes relaxed.

Tobi & Yorick. Sunday. 19:00.

"I'll take the keys," said Rikki to Gabbi as she moved ahead of the pair on the street. She held out her hand and Gabbi handed them over. "Damn lock has been giving gyp. Typical," she said with a forced laugh.

Gabbi noticed the blacked-out windows as they approached the door and stiffened at the sight of them. Rikki fiddled with the lock, banging the key this way and that. Gabbi knew it had never been an issue in the past. She felt her fists balling up with anxiety.

At last the key found its home and Rikki gave it a sharp turn, catching the door as it opened an inch towards her. She turned to the pair and said, "You two go on in and I'll lock up behind us. Stop the stragglers." She yanked the door open with a fast jerk.

The green of Gabbi's eyes burned bright and fierce as she passed Rikki. Yorick followed closely behind. As they stepped across the threshold, Rikki placed a firm hand on Yorick's back. She pushed him harder than she had intended to, causing him to stumble into the back of Gabbi and his feet to become tangled. He faltered with his head down as he attempted to regain his balance.

He looked up and locked eyes with his brother across the room. He was hunched over a bank of computers. There were three men sitting behind the screens. He was sure he had seen the one in the middle before. The other two were the sorts of faces he had seen a thousand times in crowds. What lay before him was something out of a badly scripted 90s internet hacking movie rather than the cosy pub he remembered.

"What the fuck is this?" he said, his face contorting into a snarl.

Tobi moved across the room. His brother stood still, drawing himself to his full height as he approached. Tobi clenched his outstretched arms around Yorick, struggling to lock his arms around his younger brother's back.

"Thank God, you're ok," he murmured into Yorick's shoulder.

The intimate contact from his brother spurred Yorick's confusion. He wrestled against Tobi's grasp, freeing himself.

He turned to Gabbi with his brow furrowed. A vein on the left side of his forehead pulsed over the crest of his head. But she, too, was surveying the scene with disbelieving eyes. Rikki swept her up as they passed behind the brothers and walked over to the bar. They both took seats on high stools next to the bar and Rikki placed her hands in Gabbi's lap.

Tobi pulled away from Yorick. There was an electric air coming off his younger brother that was wild and dangerous. "Yorick, we need to talk," he said and knew that he had pitched his tone at the wrong level.

"Like hell we do," said Yorick, his eyes transfixed on the screens. "Why the fuck is he looking at a picture of me?" he bellowed towards the monitors.

Mikey turned in his chair and looked to Tobi. The refusal to meet his eyes set Yorick pacing towards the small man. Sitting down, Mikey only came to Yorick's waist.

"We know about Huang! We know everything. Guizhou, the data leaks, the government hacking, the assassination, for Christ's sake! That's why we're all here," pleaded Tobi, throwing the words at his brother's back. They travelled in slow motion, striking their target and bringing him to a halt inches from Mikey's chair.

"What are you talking about?" Yorick said, glowering over the crouched but defiant figure in front of him.

Tobi approached alongside them. "Show him, Mikey. Show him what you showed me."

Mikey's fingers worked at the keyboard and images came and went from the screen as he searched for a configuration that made sense. There were three images on the screen.

"This," he said, pointing to the one on the left. "This is the biometric scanner for an app you have on a mobile device. Correct? Well, we know it is." His pointed finger transformed into a waving hand. "The second is a mirror image of a collection of folders on one of your old work devices. They're not the actual files. We can just see all the transactions you executed on it today. Security on those dated machines hasn't kept up with the times. So, we know that this morning you transferred those files to a foreign server. Recognise them?"

Yorick leaned over his shoulder, their faces inches apart. His expression further distorted as he realised the folders were the same ones he had copied across to Huang that morning. He slapped the screen with the flat of his hand. "What are you doing?" he roared with pain.

Mikey's hand shot up to steady the wobbling screen and then to tap at the third image. It was a set of diagrams and shapes. The file names from the second image were transposed on top of the squares and circles. Some of the codes were written in a dark black font, while most of them were in a light grey. While they were watching, one flicked from light grey to black. None of it made any sense to Yorick. "This, this..." began Mikey, an urgent tone in his voice.

"I don't care about that," yelled Yorick. "You're fucking up my plans!"

Tobi's arm shot out and pulled Yorick's shoulder away from the screen. "They're setting you up, Yorick!"

Mikey resumed his tapping. "These shapes represent the MI6 database. The UK government's database of classified information. We can't see any of what that information contains, but we can see a blueprint of how it's organised. Your Chinese connections are using the packets of data you sent them to overlay onto confidential government information, giving them unprecedented knowledge of millions of citizens in the UK. And it's all being stamped with your biometric markers, Yorick. No one else."

Yorick's reaction to Tobi's arm was delayed. He threw it off of him, sending his older brother stumbling two paces backwards and into a sharp corner of a table.

Tobi bounced off it and shot straight back to his brother's side. "Your identity is all over the hack, Yorick. A MI6 hack, from China no less!"

"Bullshit. It can't be. And even if it were, it's only useless data on a bunch of nobodies. Who cares?"

Mikey flicked new images onto the screens. They were screengrabs taken from a messaging app. Yorick recognised it at once. It was the one he'd been told that only he and Huang had access to. His name was nowhere on the screen. Mikey was shaking his head as he spoke. "They've used that information to compile a retrospective image of the PM's every move from the past two weeks and to predict his movements over the next 48 hours. They're not leaving it to chance to see if the PM survives the financial scandal, Yorick. They're planning to assassinate him. And replace him with Fazir Khan."

His younger brother reached for a chair, clutching thin air as he did so. Tobi dragged one across to him, guided it to his hand, and watched him sit down. The air in the room shifted and bent around them once more.

His brother's lips moved faintly. Eventually they found their voice. "I'm due to fly out to Guizhou with Huang tomorrow morning. Let me talk to him. There must be an explanation. If what you're saying is even true."

Mikey turned to his colleagues. Their long jackets were draped over the backs of their chairs, and all three of them began fiddling with their inside pockets. From his vantage point behind Yorick, Tobi couldn't see what they were doing, but their fingers worked away at objects in their laps. Without looking up, Mikey asked, "Huang is in London, tonight?"

"Yes. I was with him last night and we're checked into a flight tomorrow morning."

"Did he travel alone?" said Mikey, looking Yorick in the eye.

"I'm not his fucking secretary. But no, he usually has a couple of colleagues who meet us at the airport before he flies," said Yorick. He dropped his head through his hands and all the way down until it hung between his knees. He cradled his forehead with his hands and rocked it from side to side.

"Tobi, I don't think we have until tomorrow morning to sort this out. We need to decide now," said Mikey. His colleagues adjusted the tops of their trousers. A metallic click rang out.

"What decision?" asked Tobi. Yorick raised his eyes from his prone position.

"Either your brother puts his trust in the people in this room, or he puts it in Huang. Either way, we're getting the hell out of here, and soon. People like Huang, with his connections, they won't just let us take down their plans and allow us to walk away."

"And what could you even do about it? Huang runs this town," said Yorick.

Mikey looked at them both, alternating glances between the brothers. He spoke carefully. "We can use your biometrics to hack back into the systems. But the only way we can clear your name is to erase it all, Yorick. If we buy enough time, we can make sure that you'll be erased from the system, gone from any involvement in this. But also removed from everything you've built in this city. Your properties, gone. Your employment history, gone. Your online presence, gone. Like a blip in the system, you'll disappear. You'll have to start over. Somewhere."

Tobi knelt before his brother, his hands on his knees. He brushed a tear from his own cheek before he spoke, his voice wavering up and down, "Yorick, we may be brothers, but we both know there's been more blood than love between us, especially since dad's death. But the one thing we've always had, is the bond of our word, Yorick. Trust mine, now. You need to let us do this for you. It's the only way for some sort of life ahead. Trust me." Tobi's eyes scanned his brother's face, looking for a sign of belonging or love.

Yorick cast his own about the room; firstly, across his brother's face, then to the ceiling, and finally along the bar. There he found the old woman, crying, and alongside her, Gabbi. His heart softened at the sight of her. His eyes found hers. He saw her hands holding onto Rikki's, gripped tightly, littered with their own tears. And fear. He shared a weak, scared smile with her. He felt the tingling in his own hands, the start of another spell of shaking. What sort of life lay ahead of him anyway?

At last he turned back to his older brother, looking down at him, sunk to his knees. Two sets of blue eyes, so similar yet distinct, met each other as he said, "I trust you."

Brothers. Sunday. Night.

Mikey and his colleagues worked feverishly throughout the early evening, combing through lines of detail. They looked for a way into a system that was designed to stop the strongest powers from gaining access. Their efforts felt like chipping away at an immovable stone, exposing tiny little blemishes for them to winkle at further, piece by piece. More in hope than expectation.

But once Yorick had given them his biometric access, it was like a great fissure had sprung open in the rock. They used his secure access to jump straight onto the trail that the Chinese hackers had set earlier in the day. Like snakes in the grass, they moved through previously unseen pathways. But unlike a reptile, they were covering their tracks, removing all evidence of the slippery trails as they went.

The tapping of their keyboards increased to a ferocious pace. Tobi sat on the seat closest to Mikey, peering over his shoulder as images, words and colours flashed onto and away from the screen before he could make sense of them. The crew was deleting the links to Yorick and Tobi. The extent of the data manipulation meant they would need most of the night to complete the job. There was nothing Tobi could do to help, but he sat and watched, transfixed by their efforts.

The hiss and fizzle of an ancient coffee machine announced its presence behind the bar. Rikki worked away in front of it, preparing a steady stream of coffee and tea, ready for whenever anyone needed it. Alongside her, a selection of bread-crumbed and pastry-wrapped bar snacks roasted in the counter-top griller. The previous run had been devoured, leaving a trail of debris over the clean tables. A clattering of coffee cups awoke Tobi from the spell he was under in front the screens. He moved over to the bar and helped Rikki lay out the cups and saucers. She had dropped one, and he bent to gather up the broken pieces.

"Rikki, there's something I have to ask. Your disease, Huntington's. Is it… hereditary?"

She took the cup's shards from him and dropped them into the bin. When she returned, she took his hands in hers, beneath the eyeline of the bar. "I did all of this to protect the two of you. But I only found out the answer much later. And, yes, it is. So no matter what I did, I'd already put you in harm's way. There's a fifty percent chance it gets passed on." She gripped his hand, squeezing his fingers, as though she were trying to squeeze the harm out of him. "You don't think you-"

"-no. I don't think it got passed on to me. But, you said a fifty percent chance-" his voice trailed off as their eyes tracked along the bar, where Yorick sat alongside Gabbi.

Gabbi had poured them each a large whiskey. Yorick held his glass, the ice cube melting from the heat of his hands. While her drink sat icily on the surface of the bar, untouched.

Yorick's thoughts were as singular as the block of ice twisting, turning and shrinking in the middle of the dark liquid. "What am I going to do?" he said into the glass.

Gabbi's hands were resting on her knees. She, too, was drawn to the unfolding mass of digital activity in front of her. It was impossible to comprehend the scene that had become her community pub on a Sunday night. She reached across with her hand and tapped Yorick on his knee. When she spoke, her voice was light, but her lips drooped heavily. "There's just about enough money in the till to pay someone to sweep up after this mess." The words fell to the ground. She, more than anyone, knew a failed attempt at humour. It hadn't stopped her before, and it wasn't about to now.

No one else in the room was talking. Rikki finished at the coffee machine and it fell quiet. She watched the small griller, willing it to cook more quickly. The clacking of computer keys was the only noise that played out across the eerie scene.

Until the sound of metal sliding on metal rang out, as if attempts were being made to dull the noise. It ended with a soft thunk. Mikey and his two colleagues stiffened. The man closest to the door reached into the pocket of his long jacket.

Tobi's eyes were drawn to his movement. He looked at the long, dark navy jacket that hung off the back of the chair. As its owner fiddled with the inside pocket, the movements were exaggerated through a long-jagged tear down the right shoulder of the material. As he looked more closely, he realised the trenchcoat was black on the top and navy on the bottom. He knew he had seen it before. His mind flashed back to a fortnight ago, on what had been a normal Monday morning.

He saw himself standing on an underground carriage; the chime of the open doors having just sounded. But in front of him was a pair of scampering feet, a woollen hat on top of a man, running as though life depended on it. It was the same jacket, the same man. Tobi had brought him here.

His mouth hung open and shock flooded his eyes. Before today, he had never given thought to what he had asked of Mikey, his men, and so many others in his life, in order for him to achieve his ambitions. He had, of course, known that the requests he had made had led to consequences. But he had allowed the distance between his worlds and theirs to sit comfortably between his desires and their realities. He remembered the feet of the man with the torn trenchcoat desperately slapping the ground that day. Had Tobi forced him to run like that? If that slit had penetrated a few millimetres deeper, would Tobi have been the reason that it carved into the flesh on the man's back? Did it matter if it was his fault that day, or only that he created the world that made those slashes inevitable? All these years he had tricked himself into thinking, believing that his success, his reputation, was built on his own sacrifices and decisions. Never had he seen the physical manifestations of the sweat, toil and blood that spilled from the machine he steered from above. But never dirtied his own hands, in its inner workings. Until today.

A soft clunk against the main door carried inside. Everyone's eyes were drawn to it. Rikki spun around from watching the griller. She felt in the pockets of her trousers. The keys to the pub jangled within them and her brain churned. Her heart raced, as she tried to remember if she had locked the door behind them.

The handle twisted.

Huang. Sunday. Night.

The door swung outward and Huang stepped through it. He strode into the pub with the walk of a man who felt at peace with any room he entered. His hands hung comfortably by his sides. His dark grey suit clung to his torso over an open-necked black shirt. There was a noticeable bulge from his inside breast pocket. Three men followed him inside, closely behind. They were shorter than Huang, but with broad chests and shoulders. They were dressed in black from head to toe. Their puffy quilted jackets made it impossible to tell what lurked beneath the folds. It mattered little; the black pistols in each of their hands drew the attention of everyone in front of them. They were pointed over the computer monitors at Mikey and his two colleagues.

"Stop typing," said their tall leader, the most relaxed of the four. "Keep your hands on the keyboard. But stop typing. I don't want to hear one click."

They did as they were told.

"You, behind the bar. Come out and sit next to them," Huang continued, motioning towards Gabbi. He then turned his gaze onto Yorick.

The crowd of four moved around the front entrance of the room in a triangle formation. Huang positioned himself at its point. One man stood nearest the front door, another to the left of Huang, both guns held steady at the men behind the bank of monitors. The third was positioned closest to the bar, his gun aimed at Yorick, Gabbi, and Rikki, now seated in a row. The one closest to the bar moved towards the basement staircase, his weapon trained down it. He disappeared into the darkness, returning a few moments later with a nod to Huang.

"You disappoint me, Yorick. I tell you to keep to yourself, yet here you are, in the middle of a family reunion."

Yorick turned his right shoulder towards Huang, straightening his chest at the gunmen. "Huang, I-?" Yorick said, levering himself up from his stool.

"Sit your pathetic self down, Yorick. And shut that lying mouth of yours for once. I won't miss it," he said, bringing his hands together in front of him. "Now, who are the three dumb monkeys before me?" Huang said, tipping his head towards the monitors. He unclasped his hands and held one up in a stopping gesture. "Wait, don't tell me." He rolled out one long finger and pointed at the man furthest from him. His hands shot up to his mouth, almost covering it as he spoke. "You look like the Iwazaru to me, he who speaks no evil." Next, his eyes flicked across Mikey and onto the man nearest the entrance, with the jagged tear on his trenchcoat. "And here is the Kikazaru, who hears no evil, yes?" He flashed his hands up to alongside his ears, mocking him with a deaf gesture. And finally, he pointed to Mikey in the middle. "And last, we must have Mizaru - blind to all this evil, yes?" he finished, lowering his hands. No one said anything in response. "This means nothing to no one?" he asked to the room.

A whisper escaped from the bar.

"What was that mother bear? You'll have to speak up," Huang said to Rikki.

"The Sanzaru," she repeated clearly.

Huang clapped his hands together. "Ah, at last I encounter a western sage. So rare in this juvenile culture. Yes, the three wise monkeys. Tasked with protecting us from evil spirits and harmful intentions - yet used as childlike pictures to send to each other on our phones." He brought his hands to his sides once more in a formal stance. "One might think of it as just silly Eastern mystique, but apt for the situation we all found ourselves in, no?" he said with a wicked smile. It curled at both corners of his mouth and hung in the air in front of them all.

"Now, we are not like two of these monkeys," he said as he drew a circle in the air around himself and his team. "We see and hear everything, Yorick. So, tell me why you are trying to erase everything that we have built over our years together. Tell me, why do you want to destroy everything that you committed to last night, before we've even begun?"

Yorick felt the weight of the glass tumbler in his hand grow heavy. He jostled it up and down in slight movements, gauging its heft.

"Maybe because I'm tired of being the little pawn in others' games, Huang. Even after all our years together, you'd sacrifice me without a second thought. For what? Fazir becomes Prime Minister. You secure better trade deals with the west for your country, but what do I get? An outpost in a foreign country playing make-believe to myself that it's what I want? That's not the path I want to choose."

Huang brought his feet together, the tips of his shoes tapping. He extended himself upwards towards the ceiling, his eyes angled across the room to Yorick. "You're right. You chose your path a long time ago. Have a sip. You know you want to. Because there's still a route out for you. We don't tolerate insubordination, but we've learnt that we need to work a bit harder with those outside of us," he smiled once more. His colleagues shifted their weight at the words in silent acknowledgement, their guns still held true and straight. "For a big man," Huang continued as he pushed his pointed hands out towards the bald figure, "you only see the small. And so, you, yourself, remain so." Huang paused before making his final statement. "Often one finds one's destiny just where one hides to avoid it. It's not too late to correct your errors and choose our path, Yorick. We'll even let your little misfit family live."

The vein across Yorick's forehead pulsed as it extended to the back of his skull. He felt the attention of the room drawn to him. Except for Mikey's men. From the corner of his eye, Yorick knew that their focus was held fast on Huang's heavies.

He stood, turning to face Huang and lifted the tumbler towards his mouth in his right hand. He paused an inch from his face. The tension in his body, felt in every sinew of his taut muscles, pulled together as though in one violent yet controlled spasm.

Gabbi reached out towards him, placing her hand on the small of his back, unsure of what he was about to do.

Yorick felt the touch in a flashing moment. And it ignited him. A bolt of coiled strength snapped through his right shoulder. His right arm exploded back and snapped forward with the speed of a striking cobra. He released the tumbler at its full extension, sending it hurtling through the air with a ferocious pace and force. Huang swerved, catching a spray of whiskey as the glass whistled past his face. It continued on its path and connected with the mouth and nose of the henchmen behind his shoulder. He had been blind to the missile and crumpled in a heap.

Two shots rapped off from the left of the room as Huang reached for his inner pocket. Another volley of shots fired. The man by the bar dropped into the stairwell. As Huang's arm emerged from his jacket, Mikey leapt from his chair, throwing himself at his midriff. He connected, sending the pistol scuttling away and towards the bar. It lost itself in and among the chair legs.

"Tobi, get them out of here!" screeched Mikey as he grappled with the longer, suppler and stronger limbs of Huang.

The world around Tobi slowed and spun. To his left, Mikey's one partner lay slumped in his chair, blood pooling at his feet, and splattered across the torn trench coat that draped limply over the back of his chair. His pistol lay at his feet next to the seeping dark red liquid. Tobi registered the henchman by the door was down, folded over and not moving. He noticed the dulled movements of the other member of Mikey's crew as he moved towards his partner. He watched him fire a shot across the stairwell as he did so. A muffled cry rolled out from down below, followed by silence.

The sound of Huang and Mikey grappling each other was earthy and muscular. The smell of sweat and blood brought Tobi back to life. He spun around to Rikki, Gabbi and Yorick in time to see the old woman's red hair as she wrenched the back door open. Gabbi and Yorick ducked and spun around the corner of the bar, Yorick frantically gesturing to his brother to follow them. Tobi slid across the floor towards them. He cast one last look behind him at the scene. From his prone position on the floor, he heard another gunshot and saw Mikey's comrade shudder backwards, the weighty force of a bullet throwing him backwards. Tobi watched as the man forced his right arm up once more and fired into the stairwell and then collapsed, crashing into the nearest table and monitor and sending himself and the equipment collapsing to the ground.

"We have to go, Tobi!" yelled Yorick, yanking him to his feet and towards the door. The last image he had inside the pub was Huang as he laid a pointed elbow into the side of Mikey's head, who collapsed - limp and still. Huang locked eyes with Tobi, pushing the body off of him. Tobi felt his weight flow into Yorick's arms as he carried them both through the back door. The next sensation he felt was his feet tearing wildly at the hard, uneven surface beneath them as they scampered into the darkness.

Sunday. Night.

The group operated on sound rather than sight as blackness settled around them. As a small cluster, they stumbled their way towards Plaistow Park. By the time they reached it, a hundred yards separated Tobi and Yorick from the two women up ahead. From somewhere behind, the sounds of advancing feet filled the otherwise quiet air. One set sounded smooth and rhythmic, the other erratic and heavy. They rounded the corner, and both brothers saw the lanky figure of Huang well ahead of one of his musclemen, who was clutching the centre of his face as he ran.

Further ahead, Rikki was struggling to keep up the pace and Tobi and Yorick soon caught up with them.

"It's me they want," Yorick said to them all, in-between quick breaths. "I'll slow them down; you need to hide and then get away." He gestured towards Gabbi and Rikki.

"Lose yourselves in the park," said Tobi, backing up his brother's words. "I'm not leaving you," he said, turning to Yorick and clutching his shoulder.

The park's bushes were thick and bulbous with trees dotted all around. Gabbi hesitated, but then took off and helped Rikki into the shadows. The older woman's strength had given way, and Gabbi searched for a spot to stash her out of sight. She found a small opening among a batch of bushes and moved off to find one for herself where she could keep an eye out.

Huang slowed as he approached the park. The entrance was narrow and flanked by trees that hung over the pathway. He raised a gun in front of him and edged across the threshold. He rotated into the park, covering his tracks with a military precision. He moved further in, nudging and prodding the foliage, strafing past the larger trees. His movements were precise and sharp. A minute later, his partner stumbled towards the entrance.

Tobi stared out across the pathway of the entrance at his brother. The shadows of the entrance were thickest beneath the small wall where they had stowed themselves. His heart was pounding at his ribcage like a drum. They waited for Huang's dazed backup to step through the entrance.

The man stepped forward on uneasy feet, his shattered and bloodied face oozing liquid. One of his hands held a gun loosely while the other pawed at his face in a useless attempt to stem the blood that was congealing and seeping from his nose and mouth.

Yorick seized his chance and stepped from the shadows. He swung his right elbow hard and down into the man's face. The softened, pulpy mass gave way as he connected, and the man fell to the floor. Tobi joined him from the shadows. He dragged the prone body back to its feet while Yorick picked up the fallen gun. Tobi wrapped his arm around the crook of the man's neck and dragged him forwards.

The path ahead broke out into a broader space that Tobi recognised. Housed in the middle of the open grass was the circular sand playpen with its small wooden huts. He had last seen the blurred shapes of Rikki and Gabbi headed in that direction and he cast his eyes about for a sign of them. His sight was adjusting to the gloom.

Yorick turned to him and manhandled the limp body from his brother, dragging it into his own clutches. "This is between me and Huang, Tobi. Find Gabbi and Rikki and get yourselves out of here. Go!" he whispered to his brother, looking down at him with a fire in his dark eyes.

"I'll stay close, brother," said Tobi as he slipped away, headed for the outskirts of the open space.

From the stillness, an anguished and primal scream erupted. "HUANG!". Yorick held the gun to his captive's head "I'm ready to face my destiny, are you?"

Tobi watched as his brother turned back and forth, the gun waving wildly as he threw the weight of the semi-conscious man from side to side. Nothing but silence greeted him in response. The sounds of approaching sirens rang out in the distance.

And then came a movement from alongside the sandpit. Huang stepped out from behind the bushes near the small wooden structures and into the sandpit. Yorick spun at the noise and raised his gun towards the sound. The muzzle shook as he saw that Huang's gun was not pointed back at him. Instead, it was pressed against a flattened tuft of red hair.

Huang pulled Rikki along with him, her feet dragging in the sand. He wrenched her up from under her shoulder, causing her to grunt in pain. She struggled in vain against his overwhelming strength.

"This why you were expendable, Yorick. Your petulance. Because you focus only on yourself," Huang said. He cracked the gun against Rikki's head sharply. "You don't think of the consequences." A trickle of blood ran down the side of her bruised face. "Your mother should have taught you better. And now, like everyone in your life, she will pay for it."

Yorick tried to steady his shaking hand. He took a step forward and wrestled the limp body in his grip into a shield. "What the hell are you talking about?" he said, hot, fierce and confused, spitting the words at Huang.

Huang barked back in an unexpected laugh, one full of bile. "Ah, the irony. The man who gave us the world in data and yet couldn't even use it to discover the truth of his own life?" he said the words aggressively into the park's surrounds. "Some family you have, Yorick."

The crack of the gunshot was violent and succinct. In the day it might have passed as a rap from the wooden slats of the playground's pathways cracking against each other as children ran and scampered across them. But in the cloak of the night, it was singular and final.

The dull and heavy thud and then pop of the bullet hitting, searing, and tearing human flesh was messy and contorted by comparison. It struck Huang from behind, just above the shoulder blade. Its powerful upward trajectory took it through the base of his skull and into his brain, where it rebounded off the front wall of the bony structure and bounced back and forth inside until it came to rest.

His right hand fell limp, the gun falling to the ground as his lifeless body toppled sideways. His long, crooked left arm remained hooked around Rikki's neck, pulling her to the ground as he fell.

Yorick dropped the body of the unknown man and sprinted forward towards Rikki. He wrenched Huang off of her and looked ahead of him. Nestled within the shadows of the small play-hut on the floor of the sandpit was the shrunken figure of Gabbi; her arms still extended, the muzzle of a gun still alive with a stream of smoke that snaked its way into the stillness of the night sky.

Monday. 01:00.

The brothers pulled and rattled assorted drawers. Tobi searched through the mismatched cutlery and extracted a couple of metal teaspoons. Yorick pulled aside jars and boxes until he found a box of old tea bags and the dregs of instant coffee that had long since darkened into a coal-like colour. Yorick shrugged at Tobi, a look Tobi hadn't seen in years, as they pooled the limited resources on the white kitchen counter.

The rolling boil of the kettle clicked off, and the steam rose, hitting the bottom of the shelves above it before spreading, leaving a faint trail of moisture in its wake. Yorick poured the hot liquid into the four cups in front of him. Two had ashen coffee granules resting at the bottom, the others held the dilapidated bags of tea. Tobi splashed milk into each of the mugs and handed a teaspoon to his brother. They stirred in silence. After a minute, they each fished out a bag from the cups in front of them and dropped them into the bin between their feet. They stood over the cups in further silence for another minute.

Tobi picked up two of the drinks and turned to the room. He hadn't been in Yorick's original apartment for close to a decade. It had changed a lot. Modern finishes were now fixed to every surface, the atmosphere radiating cleanliness and minimalism. But few signs of comfort or convenience were on display. He moved towards the black couches pressed up against the tall glass windows.

He handed the tea to Rikki and coffee to Gabbi. Neither had said a word inside the apartment. Gabbi was yet to speak since they left the playground. Yorick handed a cup of tea to Tobi as he lowered himself into a chair with his own hot drink.

The sound of Tobi's ringing smartphone broke the silence. It tinkled, like a foreign object in an unwelcome space. But Tobi had been expecting it. He watched the two small circles on the screen flash up at him, green and red. The word 'Mikey' spinning and twisting at him.

He slid the green circle to the outer edge of the phone and pulled it to his ear.

Mikey's voice, smooth and steady, spoke. "You all ok?"

Alongside him, Yorick sat heavily in his chair, slumped back, eyes closed, and hands wrapped around the mug in his lap. Gabbi was across from him, perched on the edge of her seat, staring into her mug as though it held a grim fortune. And, opposite him, Rikki. His attempts to bandage the side of her face were crudely on display, but doing the job they needed to. Her eyes were locked on his, her tea placed down on the table in front of her.

"We're ok," Tobi replied. "What about you and your men?"

Mikey sighed, breathed in, and resumed his tone. "Both took hits, but will be ok."

Tobi hung his head. He closed his eyes. "I'm sorry," was all he could muster.

"It's our work, Tobs. But they'll need to be taken care of. Financially."

"Of course. Consider it done."

Mikey changed tack and spoke a little more quickly, in a lower voice, "I need your current location. The police will have to carry out their interviews, and they need to do it tonight. I can't stall them much longer."

"We're at Yorick #1. And thanks, Mikey."

"They're prepped for self-defence, Tobs. It's what it was. As for the clean-up, leave it to me." The line clicked off and fell dead in Tobi's ear.

He didn't have the strength in him to tell the others that their night was far from over. He ran through the events of the past half hour in his mind.

Mikey had hobbled onto the scene moments after the final shot had rung out. Tobi would never be able to comprehend the calmness of thought and deed that he had shown. He had surveyed what lay before him, compartmentalised it, and made calculated decisions. He issued them instructions to leave, get away to a safe hide-out as soon as possible. Check the old woman was ok, watch her for signs of concussion. The girl is traumatised, don't let her be alone. Get yourselves away and leave the details to me. Let me do my job. Get a story together. I'll call you in thirty minutes.

The thought occurred to Tobi that he missed the sound of a landline phone disconnecting. He missed the click that signalled the end, but was followed by a tone that rolled out. Instead, his smartphone had fallen silent, a dead stop at the end of another's words.

They sipped, and they waited.

Until Rikki stood and made her way over to the door. She bent down and picked up the stack of brown envelopes that had been cast aside. Her eyes flicked across the handwriting and then shot to Tobi.

Yorick had been watching them both and shifted forward in his seat. "What's going on?"

Tobi opencd his mouth to speak, but his lips froze in the air.

It didn't matter; Rikki beat him to it. "Yorick. There's something you need to know."

Tuesday. Dead of night.

A cold and bitter wind blew straight down the runway at Luton. It was quiet and bare, except for one plane parked in the middle. A large fuelling pipe was attached to its side, the final preparations for departure being made by the limited crew inside and on the ground.

A hundred yards away, huddled in the doorway of a hangar attached to the back of the airport, were three figures. The tallest one's bare head grazed the top of the doorway. Rikki's red hair came halfway up his torso. And somewhere in-between the two stood a man with wavy brown hair and a crooked grimace on his face.

The roar of the engines warming up was loud and coarse. Yorick raised his voice to be heard above it. He avoided looking at the bandage as he said to Rikki, "Thank you. I owe you and Gabbi my life. And I'm sorry - for everything."

She stared up into his eyes and took his large hands in hers. Her rough skin scraped against the smooth texture of his. She, too, spoke loudly, but gently. "She wanted to help. She wishes you well, but..."

She couldn't be here. Those were the words that were left unsaid. The truth was that Gabbi had said very little to anyone who wasn't a policeman in the past 48 hours.

After the police had finished their enquires deep into the early hours of Monday morning, one of them had given Gabbi a lift home. She had seemed relieved to leave the three of them behind. And then they had spoken long and deep, taking them into the day. Each of them pouring over the letters and what they meant. All three struggling to make sense of what their worlds had become. And what it meant their worlds were, for all those intervening years.

"You'll get in touch as soon as you get there?" said Tobi, clapping his hand onto his younger brother's shoulder.

"I'll send a carrier pigeon at first light," he replied with a sad and toothy grin.

Mikey's damage limitation efforts had done much to erase Yorick's involvement, but their powers couldn't extend to covering every one of his tracks. The data packs that Huang's network had already acquired still had Yorick's marks all over them. They couldn't be sure what had been transferred and how sensitive it might prove to be. Only time would tell. Yorick needed to disappear, Mikey had said, for a year at least, while they waited for the dust to settle.

From there, it had been their mother who had taken the lead. Gabbi's grandmother, the same age as Rikki, lived on a farm on the outskirts of a small town called Gweru in Zimbabwe. It was lost among the wide plains that lay in the centre of the expansive country, halfway between the established cities of Harare and Bulawayo. Its streets were forgettable, lined with beige and brown brick buildings that had sprung up in the prosperity boom of the 1960s and '70s, but been allowed to fall into disrepair since. Its local population was one that had learnt to keep its head down and stay out of trouble in recent times as economic mismanagement and political corruption had spread throughout the land. The less you raised your voice about what you saw around you, the greater your chance of living a quiet, undisturbed life. Compliant silence was a virtue of good neighbours. It was the perfect hiding spot, even for a nearly seven-foot-tall bald, Dutch man.

Yorick could live on a penny and a dime out there. He would have to; there was little other choice. And he would be forced to work for it, Gabbi's grandmother had assured them.

He had delved into his significant offshore financial reserves to secure the safety of his private airborne passage at late notice. And more would be needed to grease the palms and turn the ears and eyes of customs and immigration officials when he landed on the other side.

Tobi couldn't match his brother's grin in response. He pulled him in tight and held him close. "Journey well, brother," said Tobi with one last clench of his fists against the hollow of his brother's broad back.

Yorick bent down low to wrap himself around Rikki. Somehow, their arms and angles fitted more naturally than his and Tobi's and he held her for a full minute before breaking away.

"I guess this is goodbye, mum. Again," he said.

"Hopefully not for long, Yorick. We have so much to share. When you get back," she replied, their eyes locked together as she squeezed his hands in hers.

Yorick furrowed his brow, hesitation painted on his face as he looked from Rikki to Tobi, and then nodded. He turned and headed for the metal steps in front of him in the distance.

Tobi and Rikki retreated inside to a small coffee stall. Tobi offered a soft smile and a clutch of notes to the young girl at the machine, and she fired it up. She placed two freshly brewed mugs in front of them.

They returned to the window as the fuelling truck pulled back from the plane and retreated from the lit runway. The plane reversed, turning its nose towards the darkness of the night that lay ahead of it. Its engines howled, gently at first and then more violently.

The pair sipped quietly, all other sounds inside the small departure hall now drowned out by the movements of the plane outside. It pulled off down the track, gaining momentum, speed and force until it lifted its nose to the sky and disappeared into blackness.

The sound faded as the blinking lights retreated into the distance. Tobi looked at Rikki in the reflection of the window, his voice steady and sad. "Where do we go from here?" he asked.

She brought the cup of dark, black liquid to her lips, sipping it to test the heat. She lowered it back to the cold metal surface and turned to face him, smiling as she did so. "Forward, my boy. What other option do we ever have?"

Tobi. Sunday. Morning.

The shadows were mottled and irregular and stretched out for a few hundred yards. The trees above were sprouting leaves at differing rates, some more densely than others, as their long thin branches gained weight for another season. The bench he sat on had a chill and the few remaining drops of dew yet to be sucked up by the morning sunshine. None of it bothered Tobi as he drank in the scene ahead of him.

In his hands, he played with a small puzzle square. He rotated it around his thumb, enjoying the feeling of its edges as they twisted across his skin. It was irregularly shaped, with four uneven sides, each displaying a differently cut shape, and all a little rough around their crafted edges.

"Is that the missing piece?" said Clara. She took a seat alongside him, brushing at the drops on the wooden surface with her hand and shifting her weight back and forth to get comfortable. When he failed to answer, she cut to the chase. "You don't want to take more time to think it over?" she asked, dragging her hands across the lower reaches of her coat.

Tobi slid the small shape into his pocket, bunched up his lips, and shook his head. It was a movement that had become second nature to him over the past days. "It's time. Time for someone else to make better decisions than me." He turned to her and unfurled his lips, smiling at a slanted angle. Before they settled back into place.

She offered a deflated sigh in response, "I'll draw up the papers this afternoon."

All he wanted was a fair share of what he owned of the partnership. He knew he would accept a lot less. And a clean exit. It was his name across all the accounts, no one else's. He had at least been clear in his mind about that throughout.

He cast his thoughts back over the week that had just been. He and Sarah curled up in front of a small fire he had built on the suddenly cold April night. They had sat on the floor, a blanket across their legs and their daughter sleeping underneath it, nestled in-between their entwined limbs. She was fast asleep, a simple and colourful homemade jigsaw puzzle at her feet, unfinished. He could feel the warmth of the fire on his face and hands as they lay wrapped around his wife's stomach. There was still much to discuss, but for that night, they had put it all aside. It hadn't been the time for talking. That would come. It had been the time for them.

"My only ask is what we agreed for Mikey. When the payment comes, he and his team come first," he said, watching the shadows weaving on the ground in front of him.

The hollowness of money filled Tobi with discomfort, like a heavy spoonful of cinnamon. Sweet in proportion, but with a dark ability to choke in excess. The two men were 'mending well', as Mikey had put it, while others within his network had finished the job they had started. They had scrubbed and scoured as best they could by using Yorick's access. It most likely wouldn't be enough to halt Fazir and Jennifer's relentless march to Number 10, but it had banished West & West's messy ties to the whole affair and foil any attempts on the PM's life. That was the thing with data these days; once it's gone, it's gone. Something so permanent and dangerous, erased with a keystroke. The choice of history suddenly rewritten by abstraction.

She nodded and toyed with the hem of her jacket. "And what about you?" she asked.

His eyes softened as he stared ahead of him, down the long trodden path that disappeared off into the distance. The rough, earthy track blurred into the colours of the tree trunks that surrounded them. Two butterflies rose from a bush to the left of their bench, danced and weaved together as they took to the spring sky. Tobi watched them, lost in the moment, before he said, "I've made an offer on a pub in a quiet neighbourhood. But with big dreams that are waiting to be built."

A silence fell upon them, easy and comfortable, at last, for Tobi.

She started to speak, checked herself, and tried once more, speaking into the collar of her coat, "You know... you'll always have a home in West & West, Tobi. If you change your mind."

He leaned back and placed his hand on her knee, patting it once. He pulled it back and slipped it into his pocket, running the tips of his fingers around the edges of the jigsaw piece he had cut by hand.

"This was never home," Tobi said as the sun flared brighter, causing the shadows on the ground to grow more intense and definite.

THE END.

Acknowledgements

Thank you to my family who painstakingly pored over the many iterations and shared their honest and constructive feedback along the way. And all of whom provided their support and encouragement along the way.

Thank you to the friends, colleagues and anyone who took the time to read through drafts, be bored by my ideas or just ask questions along the way; your critical eye and interest kept alive in me the desire to turn back to a draft one more time, to tweak and refine a little further, but most importantly, to realise that this project is just the start of a fulfilling life-long endeavour.

About the Author

A South African at heart but currently living in the UK, Chris James draws on his experience in the working worlds of finance and marketing, and his innate curiosity about human behaviour, to write stories about the inner machinery of what he's seen - and the underbelly of what lies below the surface in each of us.

He's always had a love of the written word and finds ideas for his novels while roaming the streets of London or traversing the trails of Table Mountain.

His mum would prefer he wrote detective stories, but is ultimately just glad he still reads before he goes to sleep at night.

Printed in Great Britain
by Amazon

79705598R00123